MURDER ON ROTTEN ROW

ELIZABETH ROSE

OLIVER-HEBER BOOKS

Cover art by Dar Albert at Wicked Smart Designs

Published by Oliver-Heber Books

0 9 8 7 6 5 4 3 2 1

A Note to My Readers:

Dear Readers,

The ***Harlowe & Fitch Historical Mystery Series*** is ongoing, with a main thread that continues to develop throughout the entire series. Mixed in with each story is a new murder mystery each time that is solved before the book is finished. While every installment can be read as a stand-alone, it is advised, and also ideal, to start from the beginning with ***Murder at Mablethorpe Castle***, Book 1, and to read them in order so as not to ruin any surprises along the way.

There will be cliffhangers. And while these are murder mysteries and not romances, there is still a romantic thread woven in as well.

See more notes at the end of this book, but for now, welcome to the world of Harlowe & Fitch, where investigation into murders in Mablethorpe and the surrounding areas is underway. A headstrong noblewoman searching for justice and a stealthy sheriff trying to make his town safe, team up to uncover that which is hidden but needs to be brought to the surface.

Elizabeth Rose

Chapter One

Mablethorpe, England, Late 1300's

"Starah come away from the window and close the shutters," Sheriff Zachariah Fitch warned his seven-year-old daughter. "It's not safe."

"Why?" asked Starah, her chin resting on her folded arms as she continued to stare out the window of their home in town. The little dark-haired girl drank in the night sky filled with glowing stars. "I like to watch the stars twinkle, Father. It makes me feel like Mother is up there watching over me."

Zachariah's heart about broke hearing his daughter speaking of her mother in such a manner. Margaret had died a year ago and Starah, as well as he, missed her deeply.

"Nightfall is amongst us," he reminded her. "That is when things get even more dangerous in the town of Mablethorpe. You know that."

"You mean, that's when all the rats come out, right?" Starah sniffled and wiped her nose on the back of her hand.

As sheriff of Mablethorpe, Zachariah knew a lot of *people* that he considered rats. However, they weren't the pesky rodents that seemed to be infiltrating the town lately.

"Yes, that's what I mean," he told his daughter. "Plus, there are a lot of people you can't trust either. Never forget that. Now come away from there, I said." Zachariah walked over and closed the shutters and latched them, wanting to keep his daughter well-protected from the evils of the town. Being a widower, he had a lot of responsibilities, especially lately. Thefts and brawls were increasing. Not to mention, he had just solved a murder at the castle, too. One could never be too cautious.

"But I thought I saw Grunt out there, Father," protested Starah, pouting at him.

"Grunt?" Zachariah headed over to stoke the fire on the hearth. It helped to keep the rats at bay if it was warm inside their small, two-story home. "That dog is at Mablethorpe Castle with Lady Vivienne, sweetheart. It's where he lives. I'm sure you're mistaken. Grunt wouldn't be here in town. Especially not at night."

Zachariah threw another log on the fire, the flames flaring up, lighting the room with an amber glow. His home had once seemed so happy and filled with life. When Margaret was alive. Life had taken a sad turn for them both, but he couldn't let it show that his wife's death still upset him. He had Starah to think about, trying his best to raise her on his own now. He also had a town to watch over and keep in order. Staying strong and pushing any emotions aside was the only way to accomplish that. Aye, there was no rest for a man like him.

"Nay, Father. I'm sure it was Grunt," his daughter insisted, crossing her arms over her chest in a huff. For such a young girl she already had quite an attitude about her. Starah surely had a mind of her own. Not unlike his friend since childhood, Lady Vivienne Harlowe.

Just then, there came a knock at his door. He proceeded with caution, since he wasn't expecting any guests this time of night. Putting down the hot poker, he walked over and talked through the bolted door. "Who is it?" His hand went to the hilt of his dagger fastened at his side. He hoped he wouldn't have to use it.

"Sheriff, it's me," came the muffled but sweet voice of a woman that he couldn't mistake. "Open up," she called to him through the door.

"Lady Vivienne?" Zachariah unbolted and yanked open the door, thinking his ears were deceiving him. After all, why would a lady from the castle ever venture to town at this time of night? Sure enough, Lady Vivienne Harlowe stood there on his doorstep acting as if she belonged there. With long, slim fingers she reached up to push back the hood of her fine linen cloak. Her bright, smiling face greeted him, her long golden tresses that she rarely wore pinned up or braided, lifting slightly in the warm June breeze. "Whatever are you doing here?" he demanded to know. "And at this late hour?"

"I was here picking up my new cloak from the local seamstress. Do you like it?" She held the dark purple cloak open, displaying it to him, turning one way and then the other. Under the cloak she wore a comely gown that seemed to be constructed of soft, burgundy velvet.

"Aye. Very nice," he said, looking at her curiously, wondering why she was really at his door. "My lady, the shops closed at half past nine with the setting of the sun, and it is nearly eleven o'clock now," he pointed out.

"I know that," she answered. "The cloak wasn't finished so I decided to stay and wait for it to be completed rather than have to return again tomorrow. Don't worry, I paid the seamstress extra to get it done tonight. Besides, I noticed that the town's gates haven't been closed at night for two days now, so I knew I was free to come and go as I pleased."

"Yes, they've been under repair. But you have done quite well in making me realize that I will have to see to the matter quickly so I can start ordering the gates closed at night once again."

Lady Vivienne was known to be unpredictable and impulsive, so he decided mayhap this truly was just a casual visit at a very odd time, after all. Even so, he didn't like the fact she'd made the seamstress work late, or that she lingered in town so long.

"Why didn't you go straight back to Mablethorpe Castle once you got the cloak?"

"I planned to, but when I left the tailor's shop, Martin suggested stopping by your home to say hello to your daughter. I wasn't tired and rather liked the idea of something to do. So, here we are," she told him, holding up her empty palms as if her presence there was naught but an offering when it was really just another worry he had to carry on his shoulders.

"Martin's here too?" Starah ran across the room, squealing with excitement. His daughter was the same age as the castle's page boy, and they played together sometimes. Lately, they had even become good friends.

"Hello, Starah." Martin poked his head out from behind Lady Vivienne as he brushed back his long blond hair from hanging in his bright blue eyes.

Zachariah glanced back up at Lady Vivienne, at a loss for words, not sure what to say. Finally, he managed to form a sentence. "Don't you have a Personal Clothier at the castle for such things?" he asked her. "It's rather silly to be traipsing around in the dark in town for something you could have attained right there where you live."

"I do, but I prefer to give my money to peasants in town who are struggling to make a living."

"I see."

"Well, are you going to invite us in or are we going to stand here on the cold threshold all night?" she asked him.

Lady Vivienne's bloodhound, Grunt, pushed his way past her, trotting into the house, his nose sniffing the ground as he moved.

"Grunt, come back here." Martin ran inside after the dog. Immediately, Starah rushed over to greet them.

"Uh ... come in?" said the sheriff, his offer being only half an invite and the other half more of a question. This was an odd situation to be in. He wasn't exactly sure what to say or do. An unescorted noblewoman arriving at the home of a male commoner late at night had the scent of trouble written all over it. But since the boy and dog were already inside, it seemed he might as well invite her into his home as well. If he didn't, she'd most likely enter anyway, so he really had no choice. "Are you here unescorted, Lady Vivienne?" He craned his neck, looking outside for her means of travel.

"Nay, of course not, silly." Vivienne glided into his home, her long gown and cloak sweeping across the floor as she walked with the grace of a queen. "My guard, Richard, is in the wagon waiting for us."

"I see." Zachariah looked outside again, finally noticing the guard in the wagon parked off to the side, out of the moonlight. It was true, just like she said. He nodded at the man, and Richard nodded back. Zachariah also noticed townsfolk peering out their windows, as well as a shop owner across the street deciding to sweep his stoop all of a sudden. "I'll leave the door open," he said aloud, already imagining how the wagging tongues would blow this out of proportion by the time the sun rose. "Are you sure you should be here?" He left the door open and turned back to talk to Vivienne.

"Why not?" She boldly took a seat at his small wooden table, making herself at home. "After all, life is too short not to stop in and say hello to an old friend when I have the chance. Don't you agree?" With two fingers, she plucked a grape from the bowl on the table, holding it up to inspect it before popping it into her mouth.

"I suppose," Zachariah muttered, nervously glancing back at the door once more before he turned and followed her trail to the center of the room. His daughter was sitting on the floor, hugging the dog. Martin sat down next to her to pet the hound. Lady Vivienne reached out and rearranged the array of fresh fruit in the bowl on his table. Zachariah cleared his throat, feeling the sweat beading on his brow. Why did he feel so nervous around her? After all, he'd known Lady Vivienne for most of his life. "So, what's been happening at the castle since I left?" he asked, trying to make small talk.

"Not much," she answered, picking up an apple and shining it on her sleeve, and then putting it back in the bowl.

He started to sit down across from her at the table, but quickly stopped himself and stayed standing instead. A flitting thought clouded his brain, reminding him that he was a commoner and shouldn't be acting so casually around her. Even though they were good friends, he knew the rules. As sheriff, he needed to keep a good reputation. And inviting a noblewoman into his home after dark, certainly wasn't the way to do it.

Grunt licked Starah's face, and the little girl squealed in delight. Lady Vivienne giggled, the tone of her cheery voice bringing more life back into the room. Laughter wasn't something that happened here often. Not anymore. Not since the death of his wife.

"Besides my uncle being grouchy as usual, everything is pretty much back to normal, I'd have to say." She lifted her chin, inspecting the grapes again, plucking another one from the bowl and reaching out to hand it to him. He shook his head, so she popped that one into her mouth as well.

"Good. Good, that things are back to normal," he said,

placing his hands on the table, drumming his fingers against the wood, hoping this wouldn't be a long visit.

"How are things here in town?" she asked in return.

"In town? Why, they're ... all right, I guess." He didn't want to tell her how bad things had become lately or dwell upon how much the townsfolk feared the rat-catcher that everyone referred to as the Pied Piper. If he mentioned this now in front of the children, he was sure Starah would be so scared she'd never be able to sleep tonight. Just seeing Martin and Grunt had relaxed the little girl, and he wanted her to stay that way. At least, for now. "Everything is the same as always."

"Oh, Father, look!" His daughter pointed at the open door. "A black cat has come to visit us. Isn't she cute?"

"What?" Zachariah's head snapped around. Sure enough, a big, fluffy black cat sat on his threshold, mewing softly. She stared at him with one eerie light green eye and the other being a shade of dark yellow. Cats often roamed freely in town and no one thought much of it. But black cats were considered by those who were superstitious to be naught but minions of witches, or perhaps even the devil. These cats were always unwelcome and considered harbingers of bad luck. A feline with two different colored eyes had to be a horrible omen indeed. Zachariah didn't like this at all. While he didn't consider himself as superstitious as most people, he still didn't want the blasted thing entering his home. "Go! Get out! Shoo." He started to walk over to the door, swishing his hands through the air, trying to chase it away.

Grunt noticed the cat and barked like crazy, running past him in such a hurry to chase it that he set Zachariah off balance, almost knocking him over. Zachariah reached out for the table to steady himself, his hands landing on Lady Vivienne's knees instead.

"Oh! I'm so sorry." He bolted upright, wiping his hands on

the back of his tunic, feeling as if he had done something wrong. "I didn't mean to ..."

"It's all right," she said, sounding calm about it, not being upset in the least. She got to her feet and shook out her gown. "No harm done."

"Lady Vivienne, we have to go after Grunt," Martin told her, looking up at her and yanking on the long tippet, or sleeve of her gown. "It's dark out there and he's run away. We have to find him." The boy started to head for the door, but Zachariah's hands shot out to grab him and stop him from leaving.

"Nay! You're not going anywhere, Martin. I'll fetch the dog," Zachariah told him. "The rest of you stay here and wait and don't leave the house before I return. Do you understand me?" He released the boy and hurried out the door, hearing the sound of running feet behind him. He stopped suddenly and turned to look. Lady Vivienne crashed into his back. He turned to catch her to keep her from falling.

"We've really got to stop doing this," she told him with a playful smile.

"Where the hell do you think you're going?"

"To find my dog before he gets lost. He's not that familiar with the streets of town." She tried to step around him, but he took a big step to the side to block her way.

"Do I need to remind you that I told you all to wait in the house?" he asked in frustration. She was only slowing him down.

"I heard you the first time, Sheriff Fitch. And must I remind you that I don't like to be told what to do?" She crossed her arms over her chest and did nothing to move. Their eyes interlocked in a showdown.

"If you heard me, then why didn't you listen to me?" he asked her.

"Sheriff, my dog is out there and there is nothing you can do right now to stop me from going after him."

"It's not safe on the streets at night, Lady Vivienne. This isn't the castle with guards watching over you at every moment to protect you. You are in my territory now. I warn you, there is danger around every corner and problems at every turn."

She gave him an odd look. "If I must remind you, there was just a murder at the castle. Or as you'd say, in my territory. So, I hardly think it's any safer there than here right now." She stepped around him and walked directly down the center of the street, calling out Grunt's name.

"Of course you'd say that," he grumbled. "Richard, can you please stay here and watch after the children? I'll stay with Lady Vivienne to protect her," he called over his shoulder, getting a nod in return from the guard. He ran to catch up to her, realizing that it didn't matter what he said, Lady Vivienne had a mind of her own and was going to do whatever she wanted. There was no way in the world she was going to listen to his warning.

"Grunt, come here, boy!" she called out, clapping her hands loudly, walking past the butcher's shop and then the bakery, which were already closed for the night. She stretched her neck, looking down the street toward the low end of town. "Oh, I think I see him down there!" She picked up her skirts and started to run. "Grunt, I'm over here."

"Nay, don't go there," he groaned, taking off after her, seeing her headed right toward the worst part of town called Rotten Row.

On Rotten Row, all the cottages constructed of wattle and daub were dilapidated, rat-infested, and full of vermin and filth. The streets were covered by rubbish mixed with the contents of chamber pots that had been dumped out of the second-story windows of the shops. This mixed and stagnated with the sticky mud on the rutted road below. Mangy dogs often scrounged through the garbage, hoping to find a bite of decomposing food to fill their bellies. During the day, the barefoot, dirty children unlucky enough to have to live there with their families, chased after a stray goat or pig that sometimes wandered down from the abbey on the hill. They made a game out of trying to catch them to give the animal to their mothers to cook for their supper, even though they'd be punished by the law if caught. Thieves hid in the shadows constantly, waiting to rob anyone who walked by. Toothless men and women dressed in nothing but rags begged for food and coin on every corner.

Aye, Rotten Row was where squalor thrived, and also where respect died quickly as disgrace was born. The Buzzard's Breath Tavern near the end of the row was the main attraction for anyone wishing to spend lots of money for a sin-filled evening. Drunkards lined the benches within, not to mention whores who strolled the spit-laden, piss-stained floor of the tavern looking to pleasure any man filled with lust. That is, as long as he sported even the smallest coin to pay for the lewd services they provided. This part of town was no place for children, respectable people of any kind, and certainly not where one would ever find a lady!

"Lady Vivienne, please go back to the house and watch the children."

"The children will be fine," she told him over her shoulder. "Richard is sitting in the wagon right outside the house. He'll protect them, if need be."

"Well, I'm trying to protect you right now, but you are not making it very easy."

LADY VIVIENNE HARLOWE stopped and turned to face the sheriff in the darkness of the night. The moon above her shed enough light down on the street to be able to see where she was going. "I appreciate your concern, Sheriff, but I assure you I know how to take care of myself."

"Really? I don't see your sword strapped to your side." His attention traveled to her waist.

"Nay, I didn't bring it with me tonight. I didn't think I'd be here past dusk." Her gaze went to his waist now. "I don't see your sword either. Or for that matter, where is your staff or mace?" She referred to the heavy, blunt weapons usually carried by the sheriff for crowd control or apprehending criminals. Or for self-defense.

"If I had known I'd be coming down to Rotten Row tonight, I would have been prepared. I had hoped to spend a quiet night with Starah. Until you arrived and everything changed in the bat of an eye."

"Sorry to have ruined your quiet night for you. I hadn't planned on chasing Grunt around town either. If you had closed the door to the house, this wouldn't be happening."

"If I had closed my door, we'd be the brunt of gossip by morning, and you know it."

Vivienne heard her dog barking, but it sounded muffled. "I think I hear Grunt, but he must be behind those buildings. I'll go this way, and you take the next passageway and we'll head him off before he gets any farther away." She took off running before the sheriff could stop her.

Heading down a small passageway that led between the tavern, she sidestepped several vagrants lying in piles of rubbish who tried to reach out for her from the darkness when they saw her pass. Vivienne followed the noise of her hound, realizing Grunt's barking seemed to become louder the further she went. Of course, it was hard to tell over the loud shouting of the sheriff from behind her, commanding her to stop. Vivienne continued heading toward Grunt, ignoring the sheriff altogether. "Grunt! I'm over here, boy." She turned a corner and stopped abruptly.

Vivienne's eyes fastened on a tall cloaked figure standing there in the night, towering over her like the messenger of death. The light of the moon was to his back so his face was shadowed. He wore a tall hat with what looked like mousetails dangling from it. The man had a leather bag flung over his shoulder. Around his waist he carried an axe, a long blade, a dagger, and something hanging from his belt that looked like a metal cage. It was difficult to tell in the darkness, but she swore she saw rat pelts hanging from his belt as well. In his hands he held two long, skinny animals that looked to her like some kind of weasels. Her heart pounded in her chest, the beating so loud that she was sure the stranger could hear it.

"Good evenin,' my lady." The man tilted his chin upward, and the moonlight hit him on the face. He smiled at her, showing blackened and broken teeth. The skin on his face reminded her of wrinkled leather. A long scar ran from one ear down to his chin. His massive arms were thick, his legs long and sturdy. He was the biggest and also scariest man she'd ever seen in her life. "Have ye seen my cat by any chance?"

"I ... I'm looking for my dog," she managed to squeak out.

"Mr. Piper, I found the cat." A boy who looked to be mayhap sixteen years of age and dressed in ragged dirty clothes approached the man. He held a black cat under one arm. Vivienne somehow knew it was the same cat that Grunt had chased from the sheriff's home. When the animal looked over at her and she saw its eyes were two different colors, she knew she wasn't mistaken. The boy then handed a long wooden staff with a cage atop it to the man he'd called Mr. Piper. She jumped back when she saw that the cage was filled with live rats! Several dead rats swung from the bottom of it, being tied by their tails with string. The stench alone, mixed with that of the waste all around her in the alley made Vivienne want to retch. Her stomach clenched, twisting and turning. Suddenly she got that same sick feeling again, like whenever trouble was about to happen.

"Vivienne!" shouted the sheriff, coming down the passageway after her. "Vivienne, where are you?" Zachariah approached and stopped behind her, yanking his dagger from his waistbelt. "Get away from her, rat-catcher," he warned the man, stepping in front of Vivienne to protect her. "If you even try to touch her, you'll be sorry."

The rat-catcher chuckled lowly. "You think that little blade is going to stop me?"

"I'm the Sheriff of Mablethorpe and can have you arrested for threatening me."

"Hrmph," grunted the man, putting the animals he held down on the ground. "Go find some rats for me, my precious pets." The weasel-like animals slunk away into the dark crevices of the alley. The rat-catcher then yanked the cat out of the boy's arms. The black cat hissed and clawed at him, scratching him on the hand. "Damn it! Get back to work you no-good thing," he yelled at the cat, throwing it to the ground. The cat screeched and ran off, disappearing into the night. Then the man collected the staff with the cage atop it with rats inside, taking it from his helper. "Sheriff, what I said to you was an observation, not a threat," he ground out in anger. "If I had wanted to kill you or this pretty little lady, you'd both already be dead. Now, excuse me. I have rats to catch. Get goin', boy!" he spat, pushing his companion. "We're way behind on our rat quota for the night."

"Lady Vivienne. Are you all right? Did he hurt you?" Zachariah quickly turned back to her once the rat-catcher and his helper had disappeared down the alley toward Rotten Row. The sheriff still held his dagger gripped tightly in his hand.

"Yes, I'm fine, Zachariah," she said in a mere whisper. She

was so shaken that she'd even forgotten to call him sheriff, even though they'd agreed to use each other's titles.

"Dammit, he could have killed you. Don't you understand how dangerous it is to be in this part of town? Especially this late at night?" Zachariah wasn't happy with her, and wasn't shy about letting her know it.

"That was the ... the Pied Piper, wasn't it?" She'd heard of the rat-catcher that all the townsfolk feared. Now she could see their reason for being so frightened of the man. He was grotesque, repugnant, and downright scary.

"Yes," he answered, slowly lowering his blade. "Come on, I'm getting you back to my home and then you and Martin are returning to the castle immediately." He took her arm and turned to go.

"Wait," she protested, pulling out of his grip. "I won't leave without Grunt. Don't you hear him? He is still barking and it sounds like he is just up ahead. I've got to go to him."

The sheriff blew out a puff of air from his mouth. "Since I can see there is no way in hell I am going to stop you, I'll go with you." Together they hurried toward the sound of barking. When they got to the end of the alley, Vivienne saw Grunt barking at something behind a large wooden vat outside the back of the tavern.

"Grunt? What's the matter?" asked Vivienne, feeling that horrible twisting in her stomach again. It was the same feeling she had seven years ago when her parents had both been murdered. A shiver ran through her, making her realize that whatever her hound was barking at, it wasn't just a stray cat or a cornered rat. Nay, it was surely something even worse.

"Stand back, I'll get him." The sheriff rushed forward, reaching down for the dog, but stopped. With his gaze fixed on something on the ground, his body stiffened. "Good God, it can't be."

"Can't be what?" Vivienne rushed over to him before he could object. Her gaze drifted downward, settling on something ... or someone lying on the ground behind the barrel. A cloud covering the moon made it impossible to see exactly what it was.

"Don't look, Vivienne," warned Zachariah, trying to block her view with his hand.

"Nay! I want to see." She grabbed his hand and lowered it, straining her eyes to discover what it was that took her dog's interest. The clouds parted, and the moonlight shone down brightly just then. Immediately, she wished she had listened to the sheriff, after all. There on the ground was the dead body of a woman with her head covered in blood. On top of her were at least two dozen rats, gnawing at her flesh, mainly her face. "Nay!" she cried, covering her mouth. Vivienne's eyes closed and her body swayed. She felt lightheaded and ill. It brought back memories of that awful night she'd seen her father killed on the road. And then her mother was murdered right after. So much blood. Such lifeless eyes. She turned away, gripping on to the sheriff's arm, hiding her face against his shoulder. "Who–who is it?" she asked, having to know.

"I'm not sure yet," he answered. "I need to get closer look to try to identify the woman. You're going to have to let go of my arm to let me do it, sweetheart."

Of all the times for him to call her sweetheart, why now? She released his arm and instead reached down to pet Grunt behind the ears.

"Good boy, Grunt. You did it again. You found a dead person. Thank you, for letting us know." Grunt licked her hand and whimpered, sitting down at her feet.

"Open up! Open the door," yelled Zachariah, banging on the back door to the tavern.

"Use the front door," came the muffled voice of a man from

within. Then the door opened a little and a man poked his nose out.

"I'm Sheriff Fitch, now open this door at once. I have a dead body and need to call my constables for assistance."

"Oh, why didn't ye say so, Sheriff?" The man opened the door, holding a lantern high, giving off more light.

Vivienne held on to Grunt's collar, turning to see the tavern owner glaring out the door at her. From the corner of her eye she saw people starting to wander down the alleyway toward them, curious as to what all the shouting was about. They were frightening, and looked to her like thieves and whores and perhaps even murderers. Surely not anyone she'd want to meet up with in a dark alley alone. Then again, they weren't as horrifying right now as the dead woman on the ground. Vivienne grabbed Grunt by the collar and moved closer to the sheriff, taking the dog with her.

"Get inside," Zachariah commanded with a nod of his head. "I'll call for my constables and one of them will escort you back to Richard. Then I want you and Martin to get back in the wagon and return to the castle where you belong."

"What about Starah?" asked Vivienne. "You can't leave her alone at a time like this."

With one hand on the door, the sheriff's gaze traveled back to the corpse. He pressed his lips together, shaking his head. "You're right. I hate to ask this of you, but since I'll be working tonight, after all, is there any way you can take my daughter back to the castle with you? Just for tonight? It's too late to ask Mrs. Dorson to watch her, and, of course, I can't leave her alone."

"Of course, you can't. And yes, I will. I'd be happy to do so," Vivienne answered, thinking of nothing but the safety of the poor child.

"Good. Now, come on." He motioned with his head once more for her to enter the tavern.

Vivienne looked back to the dead body, her heart going out to the poor woman who lost her life and also her family. No one deserved such a horrible way to die, in an alley, being eaten by rats.

"Sheriff, what do you think happened to her?" she asked, having to know.

"I'm not sure yet. It's too early to tell. Now, get inside."

"Was it ... murder?" She could see a gaping wound on the side of the woman's head. She figured even if she fell, she wouldn't have hit her head that hard to do so much damage. And because of all the blood, the rats were drawn to her in a feeding frenzy, having already devoured her eyes. It was a most horrendous sight.

"Don't be mentioning murder to anyone," he said in a low voice.

"Then it truly is, isn't it?" Her attention was back on the sheriff. "If not, you would have said as much."

Zachariah spoke softly so only she could hear. "I believe that is the mayor's wife and that means all hell is about to break loose."

"The mayor's wife?" she repeated in surprise. So it seemed it wasn't just a beggar or a whore. "She wouldn't have been drinking in the tavern, would she? And on Rotten Row?"

"Nay, she wouldn't," he agreed, releasing a deep breath. "It's also most unlikely that she'd even be out at night alone at all. I'm almost afraid to say this to you, but I believe it could have been murder, after all."

"And I'm almost afraid to say this to you, Sheriff, but you know that now I will have to help you investigate this death because I won't stop until justice is served."

"Yes. I was afraid you'd say that." The sheriff groaned and ushered her into the tavern, with Grunt leading the way.

Chapter Two

Vivienne barely slept a wink, tossing and turning all night long. She'd been so disturbed by what happened on Rotten Row that it must have triggered that same nightmare that had been haunting her for the last seven years of her life.

Lying in the back of a wagon filled with trunks and hay, sixteen-year-old Vivienne held her newborn baby boy close to her chest. Her nine-year-old brother, Adrian was asleep in the hay next to her. Her parents drove the team of horses pulling the wagon down the bumpy road.

Vivienne lay in the hay of the wagon too exhausted from giving birth earlier that day to even sleep at all. She smiled down at the newborn who had a tuft of blond hair, the same color as hers and clear, bright blue eyes. He was a cute little baby. Everything was perfect about him. Well, almost everything. Opening the blanket, she ran her fingers over the brown heart-shaped birthmark on the bottom of her son's left foot. Her mother said he'd been kissed by an angel. Vivienne smiled, wrapping him back up, knowing that indeed he was an angelic child. She had been blessed to be given a son, and she just wished her late husband could have seen him before his untimely death.

Suddenly, Vivienne felt her stomach twist into a knot. She couldn't help feeling that something was horribly wrong, or perhaps about to happen. The twisting feeling inside her gut felt like the sharp blade of a dagger, such as the one she had strapped to her side. The last time she felt this way was six months ago when she'd lost her husband, George, after he was kicked by a horse and died. She reached down to touch the hilt of her blade, feeling odd. The thought flashed through her mind that she'd need her dagger tonight for protection, although she had no idea where this thought came from. The feel of the cold, sharp metal in her hand was so opposite the warmth of new life from her baby pressed up against her.

After her mother took the baby from her, Vivienne had finally dozed off, but was abruptly woken after too long. What roused her was the sound of neighing horses and the jerk of the wagon as it halted, coming to a complete and sudden stop. She heard voices, and they sounded menacing if she wasn't mistaken.

"Off the wagon," commanded a gruff male voice.

"Nay. Leave us alone. We just want to pass," her father replied, doing all he could to protect his family, she was sure. Vivienne's heart sped up. She realized these roads were filled with bandits and perhaps they were about to be robbed. Her fingers closed over the hilt of her dagger strapped to her side. She would fight to help protect her family if need be.

The next thing she heard sounded like a sword being drawn from a scabbard, followed by the sounds of a struggle. Slowly, she pulled her blade from its sheath and rolled over in the hay, trying to see what was happening.

"Abiathar!" shouted her mother. "Nay!" she screamed and started crying.

Before Vivienne could get to her knees to look over the back of the bench seat, she heard the sickening sound of a body hitting the ground.

"Kill her, too!" commanded another man.

"Nay," Vivienne mumbled to herself, pushing up to a half-sitting position to see what was happening. She saw her mother struggling with a man as he pulled her off the wagon and to the ground. The basket with her baby in it was still on the bench seat. Vivienne started to panic. She needed to get to her baby as well as to help her poor mother. Since her father was so quiet and not protecting them, she was sure he'd been killed.

"Sister, what's happening?" Her brother rubbed a sleepy eye, looking up at her from under the hay.

"Adrian, stay down," she warned her brother in a hushed voice. "We're being attacked by bandits. Keep quiet, so they don't know you are here."

"Who won't know?" he asked and she silenced him with her finger to his lips.

"Mother is in trouble. I have to help her as well as to protect my baby." Not wanting to be seen, Vivienne quietly flipped over the far side of the wagon, letting her feet silently drop to the ground. She hoped to be able to sneak up to the front of the wagon and grab the basket with her baby, without the ruffians noticing her. It was night and very dark, so that would give her cover. Only a partial moon lit the sky, but was mainly hidden by clouds.

Gripping her dagger tightly, she crept around to the front of the wagon, scared because she knew she was still weak from giving birth. How would she fight off a full-grown man? Especially in her condition? Her toe hit something on the ground. When she looked down she saw the bloody, lifeless body of her father lying in a crumpled heap. Biting her tongue so as not to cry out, she quickly hunkered down to check for signs of life. His throat had been slit and there was no hope he could survive such a heinous act. He was no longer moving. It was too late for her father, but mayhap she could still save her mother and her son. She was their only hope now. Slipping her dagger back into her *waistbelt, she reached down and took her father's sword from his hand. Since he was only a foot soldier, he didn't own one of the longer, heavier swords mainly used by knights. His was a shorter, lighter blade, devised for closer, hand-to-hand combat. Therefore, Vivienne was able to lift it, having even learned from her father how to use it, at her insistence. Holding it in two hands, she stepped around the front of the wagon, ready to strike down whoever had killed him.*

"My lady, I see my father arriving in the courtyard."

Vivienne's eyes shot open, her heart about beating out of her chest from the bad dream. It took her a moment to realize she was safe at her aunt and uncle's castle, and the voice she was hearing was from Starah, the sheriff's daughter.

"Starah?" Vivienne shot up to a sitting position in bed. She glanced over to the open window to see that the little girl had pushed a chair up to the opening and was leaning out, waving. Grunt had spent the night in the chamber with them and was now barking furiously at the little girl, in his own way warning her of her dangerous position. His front two paws were up on the chair.

"Father! I'm up here. Do you see me, Father?" Starah shouted. "Grunt is here too."

"Stop that at once!" Vivienne shot out of bed and ran across the room, grabbing Starah and holding her close to her chest in a protective hug. "You could have fallen out the window and broken your neck," she scolded. "Nobles don't shout at the top of their lungs from windows. Especially not so early in the morning. What were you thinking?"

"But I'm not a noble," the little girl reminded her, looking up at her with big, sad, brown eyes that were the same color as Zachariah's. "I miss my father and wanted him to see me. And Grunt too." She reached out and pet Grunt on the head. The dog reached up and licked her face, causing her to giggle.

Vivienne glanced out the window to see Zachariah riding his horse into the courtyard. He was staring up at her window, waving and smiling at her.

"He saw you," she assured Starah. "Now down from there and don't do that again." Vivienne didn't acknowledge the sheriff, but instead pulled the little girl off the chair and put her on the floor. Then she quickly closed the shutters, feeling embarrassed since she'd been standing there in only a thin nightrail and was sure Zachariah had noticed.

"I want to greet my father in the courtyard!" Starah ran across the floor in bare feet, headed for the door.

"You might want to get dressed first," Vivienne called out, reaching for her own gown.

"Why? Father has seen me in my nightclothes before."

"I'm sure he has. However, I don't think Martin has seen you in nightclothes, has he?"

"Oooooh. Nay." Starah had been reaching for the door latch, but slowly lowered her hand when she heard Martin's name mentioned. "Mayhap I should get dressed first after all, like you said."

"It would be a good idea." Vivienne pulled her purple velvet gown over her head. In the past, she'd saved her more expensive gowns for fancy gatherings and dances, but not anymore. Instead, she lived each day as if it were her last, since no one knew how long they had on this earth. She learned that with the deaths of her parents. Sometimes, she even wore overly-large tunics and breeches and boots like a man. But that usually only happened when she was sparring with her late father's sword in the practice yard with the knights or squires.

"What's that?"

"What do you mean, honey?" Vivienne looked over to see Starah pointing at her necklace. Vivienne's hand slapped her chest and she quickly covered the ornate ring she wore from a chain hanging around her neck. She always wore it under her clothing to conceal it since her mother's dying words were to keep it a secret. It was King Edward III's ring. Her mother told her with her last breath that Vivienne was the bastard child of the king. It seemed that Vivienne's mother had been mistress to the king before she married Abiathar and had a child with him.

"That's a pretty ring. It has a shiny stone like Midnight's eyes."

"Midnight?" Vivienne hid the necklace under her clothing.

"The kitty cat that came to my house last night. I decided to name her Midnight."

"Ooooh, that cat." Vivienne grabbed the little girl's clothes and helped her to quickly dress.

"I hope my father will let me keep Midnight. I've been feeding her scraps of food and she likes it."

"That cat has come to your door before?" she asked in surprise.

"Yes. But I didn't tell Father. He never saw Midnight until last night. Do you think he'll let me keep her? She likes me and I like her."

"I don't think so," she told the girl. "That cat belongs to someone else."

"Really? Who?"

Vivienne couldn't tell the little girl about the rat-catcher ... the Pied Piper. Just seeing that awful man was more disgusting than the smell of the stench of the dead rats he carried around on display. His image was embedded in Vivienne's mind now and she couldn't shake it. Aye, it was more than frightening. The last thing she wanted was for Starah to be scared. Vivienne walked over and picked up her boar's bristle brush, coming back and running it through Starah's hair.

"It doesn't matter who the cat belongs to, it just matters that you don't feed her anymore. Do you understand?" The last thing Vivienne wanted was for the Pied Piper to go looking for his cat and turn up at the sheriff's door.

"But she's hungry," whined the little girl.

"Believe me, that cat has more than enough food to eat on the streets without you feeding her too." She thought about how the Pied Piper had thrown down his cat and ordered it to go out and kill and collect rats for him. Ugh, the thought made her feel ill.

The sound of rapping on her door took Vivienne's attention. She called out since she didn't have a handmaid. "Who is it?"

"It's me, Martin, Lady Vivienne."

"Come on in, Martin. The door is unlocked."

Starah jumped up and ran across the room to meet him. Martin opened the door and the little boy walked in to be greeted by Grunt, jumping up and putting his front paws on Martin's shoulders and licking the boy's face. From the force of the big dog, Martin fell to the ground laughing. Starah laughed along with him.

"Grunt, stop that." Vivienne put down the brush and pushed her feet into her shoes. Then she headed to the door.

"He just wants someone to play with him," Martin told her, teasing the dog by petting him and then quickly pulling his hand away, making the dog jump for it.

"If Midnight was here, she could play with Grunt too," said Starah.

"Enough with all the talk about the cat. Now get up. Both of you." Vivienne reached out and helped put both the children back on their feet. "Did you have a message for me, Martin?" Vivienne was sure the sheriff must have sent for her, but the boy probably forgot to tell her since he'd been so busy playing with the dog.

"Oh, yes. Sheriff Fitch wants you to bring his daughter and meet him in the great hall."

"Then, that is what we'll do, and we will not keep him waiting. The sheriff is a busy man. Grunt, lead the way. There is much work to do, for me as well."

"Father!" Zachariah was in the great hall talking to Lord and Lady Mablethorpe when he heard his daughter's shout. He turned around to see Starah running to him with her arms outstretched. He scooped her up, giving her a kiss on the cheek and a big hug. After being up most of the night investigating the murder, it felt more than good to hold his daughter again, knowing she was safe and alive.

"Hello, darling. Did you sleep well last night?" he asked her.

"Not really."

"Why not?"

"Well, I shared the bed with Lady Vivienne." The little girl made a face and rolled her eyes.

Zachariah chuckled. "What's the matter? Does she hog the covers?"

"Nay, but she tosses and turns all night long. I finally had to sleep on the floor with Grunt since she was keeping me awake."

"Oh really?" His gaze darted over to Vivienne. "I'm sorry to hear that."

"Good morning, Sheriff." Vivienne stifled a yawn, causing him to smile. So, it seemed his daughter was telling the truth.

"Lady Vivienne, I need to talk to you."

"Did you find out more about the—"

Zachariah cut her off with a scowl and shake of his head. "Starah, I need to speak with Lady Vivienne in private," he told his daughter.

"I will take her to get something to eat if you'd like," offered Vivienne's aunt, Lady Mablethorpe.

"That would be wonderful. Thank you." He put Starah down.

"Mayhap after we eat, we can take Grunt over to the kennels," Martin told the little girl. Excitement filled his words. "After all, he's a hound and I'm sure he'll want to see how the construction of the kennels is going."

"Martin?" came Lord Mablethorpe's deep voice. "You are a page of my castle now and need to continue your training with Sir Guy, yet I hardly ever see you with him."

"He's busy on the practice field, my lord," Martin answered.

"Then until he is finished, you are to be supervised by his squire, Milo. You know that. Do I need to report to your father that you are not proving to be a good page?"

The boy's eyes opened wide in fright. "Nay, my lord. Please don't tell my father. I'll be better from now on, I promise." Martin frowned and looked down to the floor, kicking at the rushes.

"Uncle, I'm sure Martin is only trying to see to the needs of our visitors," Vivienne interrupted. "I will personally make sure he is being guided by either Milo or Sir Guy as soon as he returns from the kennels."

"Vivienne, you are once again going to cause trouble by getting involved, putting your nose where it does not belong," complained Lord Mablethorpe. "Let me handle the boy. Just keep out of this."

"Gilbert, he's just a child," said the man's wife softly, gently touching him on the arm. "Let them go to the kennels. Children need to play."

"Ellen, you will be the death of me yet, the way you are always siding with Vivienne." Lord Mablethorpe threw his hands in the air and stormed off. "Go! Do whatever you want, I don't care. Just don't come crying to me when something goes wrong."

"Lady Vivienne?" Martin looked up to her in question. "What does that mean?"

She smiled at him sweetly, her look one of encouragement. "It means, you can take Starah and Grunt to the kennels, but don't be too long." Lady Vivienne used her friendly, calm tone, and both the children smiled back.

"Yay!" said Martin, taking Starah's hand and running through the great hall with Grunt following right on their heels.

"Just be back soon so you can to continue your training to be a page," she called out after the boy.

"I will, Lady Vivienne. Thank you." Martin exited the great hall with Starah and Grunt.

"So adorable, don't you agree?" Vivienne glanced over at Zachariah. Her blue eyes lit up with admiration before she turned her head again and watched the children go.

"I am fond of hounds but wouldn't go as far as saying Grunt is adorable." Zachariah chuckled lowly when he saw the look on Vivienne's face.

"You know what I mean."

"I do. And yes, you are right, I suppose. But do you think it is wise to get so attached to the page boy? After all, he'll be leaving again someday after he completes his training, remember."

"I know that, Sheriff, thank you for pointing out the fact. However, it will be quite some time before Martin is old enough to become a knight, so I am not worrying about his departure at this time." Her tone became cold and clipped. "However, I don't think it is up to you who I get attached to, so please keep your opinions to yourself from now on."

Zachariah realized he'd crossed a line with Vivienne and shouldn't have been so vocal with his thoughts about her actions. Vivienne had probably formed this attachment to the boy since she'd lost her son as a newborn and she felt as if she needed to fill that void. He supposed there was nothing wrong with her acting like the boy's mother. For now. But he hated the thought of seeing her sad again when it came time for Martin to leave Mablethorpe Castle after his training to head back home. How empty Vivienne's heart was going to feel then, and he wasn't going to be sure how to help her.

"Sheriff, will you and your daughter be staying long at Mablethorpe Castle?" asked Vivienne's aunt, pulling him from his thoughts. "If so, you know there is a room waiting for you."

Lady Mablethorpe was a kind woman, and the sister of Vivienne's late mother, Flanie. He remembered Vivienne's mother as being tall and thin. And also very pretty, just like Vivienne. But Lady Ellen Irvine was just the opposite, being much shorter and rounder altogether. Lord and Lady Mablethorpe had taken Vivienne in after the night her parents were murdered when she lost both her brother and her baby as well. They didn't have any living children of their own, and he supposed, in a way, they now thought of Vivienne as their daughter because she was their ward.

"Thank you, Lady Mablethorpe, but nay. This time, I will be staying in town since the crime happened on Rotten Row."

"Crime? What crime?" asked the woman.

"It's too soon to be talking about it," he told her, not wanting gossip to spread before he even had suspects in line.

"He means the murder," Vivienne blurted out.

"Murder? Oh, heavens, not again!" Lady Mablethorpe's hand went to her mouth, and she gasped in surprise.

"Lady Vivienne? Can you please hold your tongue until after we've discussed things first?" Zachariah ground out.

"Oh, so sorry." Vivienne tapped a finger against her lips.

"Vivienne, please don't tell me you are getting involved with helping the sheriff with another murder investigation," said her aunt. Worry creased her brow. "Your uncle is going to be furious when he finds out about it. I am not happy about it either."

"Aunt Ellen, you know why I have to do this. And yes, thankfully, the sheriff has agreed to let me help him again."

"Well, I wouldn't exactly put it that way." Zachariah scratched the back of his neck, thinking of how Vivienne had come out and told him she'd be helping, without bothering to even ask him if it was all right.

"Please promise me that you won't go anywhere near Rotten Row. It's too dangerous," warned Lady Mablethorpe.

"I agree," mumbled Zachariah.

"I am constantly hearing about brawls and thefts there, not to mention it is where the whores congregate," Lady Mablethorpe continued. "I also heard that the rats are so bad down there that they even had to hire a rat-catcher."

"Yes, that's true," said Vivienne, her eyes flashing over to Zachariah. He slowly shook his head, hoping to hell she wasn't going to tell her aunt about already having met the Pied Piper.

"Don't worry, Aunt Ellen, I'm not afraid." Vivienne stood tall and spoke boldly. Her voice didn't even quaver. Zachariah was impressed by her bravado. "After all, even the Pied Piper doesn't scare me anymore."

Zachariah groaned. "Did you have to mention the Pied Piper?" he asked softly, even though it was already too late for her to stay quiet about the man. Why hadn't she heeded his warning to stay silent?

"What?" gasped her aunt. "Are you talking about that rat-catcher who has the entire town terrorized? I've heard him called the Pied Piper."

"He's the one," mumbled Zachariah, feeling hopeless about Vivienne keeping silent about anything now.

"Vivienne, please don't tell me you met him." Her aunt looked absolutely aghast by the thought.

"I did," answered Vivienne. "The man is just there doing his job, trying to rid the town of rats," she explained with a shrug. "Anyone who goes to Rotten Row, especially at night, is bound to see him sooner or later. I'm sure he can't help it if his appearance frightens people and he smells so ... disgusting." She crossed her arms over herself in a protective hug. Zachariah couldn't help notice the slight shudder of her body when she said it. So mayhap the rat-catcher still bothered her after all.

"Well, I'd better go check on the children and make sure they have something to eat," said Lady Mablethorpe. She started to leave and then stopped and looked back at them. "By the way, who was murdered?"

Vivienne started to open her mouth but Zachariah had to hush her. "That information is not public yet, but you'll know soon," he answered for her.

"I understand. Just promise me you won't go down to Rotten Row anymore, Vivienne," said her aunt, wringing her hands together. "I don't want yours to be the next death."

As soon as Lady Mablethorpe walked away, Vivienne turned to the sheriff. "All right, tell me everything you learned last night in the tavern. Also, when will I have a chance to view the victim's body?"

"Let's talk out in the courtyard where there are not so many eyes watching and ears listening." He took her by the arm and escorted her to the door.

"Good Morning, Lady Vivienne and Sheriff Fitch." Leif, the jongleur nodded to them, walking by with his lute.

"How are you feeling, Leif?" asked Vivienne.

"Much better. And my lute is in perfect working order now thanks to you," answered the boy.

"Don't forget you are to assist the steward in inventory of

the undercroft as well as help the woodward repair fences as soon as you are able."

"I didn't forget, my lady. I am headed to the undercroft now."

"Excuse me my lady," interrupted Maria, the kitchen maid, walking up with a tray that contained apple hand pies. "Would you and the sheriff care to have something to eat? Cook is also preparing a beef and vegetable soup and I am sure he'd give you a taste. You can even have your meal in the kitchen if you'd prefer." The girl smiled, seeming tired but also relaxed.

"We'll just take a few of these," said Vivienne, handing Zachariah a hand pie and taking one for herself as well. "Did you and Cook muck out the stables yet?"

"Aye, my lady. We did so first thing this morning. We'll be helping out in the stable later today as well."

"Fine. Keep up the good work," she told the girl, taking a bite of the pie as they walked.

"I think you are what holds this castle together," commented Zachariah, devouring the pie in three bites. "Damn that was good." He licked his lips.

"I like to think of myself as everyone's friend at the castle," she admitted as they headed out to the courtyard.

"But you are a noble and they are peasants and servants."

"That is why it is even more important. I want them to feel at ease with me."

"I'm not sure that'll earn you respect."

"It'll earn me more than respect, Sheriff. It'll earn me their trust as well. I feel that is what's really important."

"Mmmph," he grunted and she could tell that he wasn't in agreement with that.

Before they could even discuss the murder case, Martin and Starah ran up with Grunt leading the way.

"Back so soon?" asked Vivienne.

Grunt sniffed the air, looking up at her with sad eyes.

"I think Grunt is hungry," said Martin. "We're taking him to the kitchen for a treat."

"Yes, I believe this is what he wants." Vivienne handed Grunt the rest of her pie and the dog snarfed it down in one bite.

"Father, can we go home now?" asked Starah.

"Why are you in a hurry to go home?" Zachariah wanted to know. "Aren't you having a good time here at the castle?"

"Yes, but I'm worried about Midnight."

"Who?"

"I'm sure everything's fine," said Vivienne, not wanting the girl's father to be angry with her if he found out she'd been feeding the rat-catcher's cat.

"You children move too fast for me." Lady Mablethorpe waddled across the courtyard, holding up the hem of her gown so it wouldn't brush over the cobbled stones. "Starah, I want you and Martin to get something to eat."

"Go with Lady Mablethorpe," said Zachariah. "I'll be back later for you, Starah."

"I'll be gone for a while as well," Vivienne told her aunt.

Her aunt sighed and took Starah by the hand. "Just remember what I said about staying away from Rotten Row."

As soon as they left, Vivienne spun around on her heel. "Let's go," she told Zachariah. "I just need to saddle my horse and we'll be on our way. I suppose you left your horse in the stable?"

"Yes, but where do you think you're going?"

She looked at him and grinned. "Why, Sheriff, I'd think you'd know better than anyone by now that when trying to solve a murder you must start at the scene of the crime. We are going directly to Rotten Row."

Chapter Three

Grunt accompanied them to town, eagerly leading the way as if the dog knew where they were headed. Vivienne hadn't objected since Grunt had been the one to find these last two corpses. The dog was helpful so she didn't want to push him away.

"I don't think it's a good idea for you to accompany me to Rotten Row," said Zachariah in concern from atop his horse, just like Vivienne knew he would.

"I don't think it's a good idea for you to try to stop me, Sheriff. You know I will just get involved in helping solve this murder one way or another."

"I know," he answered, followed by a deep sigh.

"Are you going to tell me what you've learned? And by the way, don't think I didn't realize you were trying to get rid of me last night when you asked me to take your daughter with me back to the castle. Very clever, Sheriff. If I hadn't been so worried about the children's safety, you know I wouldn't have allowed you to send me away so easily."

"Lady Vivienne, I did it for your own good. You seemed to

be very upset after having met the rat-catcher, not to mention viewing the corpse."

"Yes," she said, repositioning herself in the saddle, riding astride as she always did even though she wore a gown and it was more than improper for a lady to ride this way. Still, she didn't care. "I will admit it took me by surprise. I might have been a little stunned, I suppose. But this morning, I am well-rested and ready to delve right into the investigation."

"Well-rested?" He looked at her from the corner of his eye and grinned. "Not according to my daughter you're not. I mean, how could you be with all that tossing and turning all night long?" He chuckled softly.

"Sheriff Fitch, I find it hard to believe you find humor in the fact I was once again having that nightmare about my parents being murdered and my brother and son going missing."

"I'm sorry. I didn't realize—"

"And if I must point out, you were the one who couldn't help me find answers of any kind, regarding that situation." She continued talking, not letting him get a word in.

"I know that, Vivienne," he said, not bothering to use her title. He seemed to do this when he became distracted or upset.

She looked at him and raised a brow. "What did you call me?"

"I mean, Lady Vivienne," he quickly corrected himself. "If I must point out, I told you I never gave up looking. I promised you someday I will find all the answers you seek, and I still stand by those words."

Vivienne could see how upset her accusation had made Zachariah and she felt bad about even mentioning it now. "I'm sorry," she told him. "I know how hard it is and that you are doing your best to help me. But in the meantime, I will go mad if I cannot help others find answers who are in the same situation as me."

"I understand," he told her. "That is the reason I am not turning you away. I just worry for your safety, that's all. Especially since we're talking about the worst part of town and, as such, somewhere a lady should never even be seen."

"I appreciate your concern. However, it is daytime now. Also, although Rotten Row is not a good place to be, you will be there with me, so I feel safe. Plus, we are there for a purpose and it cannot be ignored. Next time we go there at night, however, I assure you I will be bringing my father's sword along with me."

"Then let's hope we won't need to be on Rotten Row at night again."

She smiled at him, knowing that is exactly the time they'd need to be there since that is when the murder most likely took place. It is also the time when the Pied Piper comes to town to catch rats. Something deep in her gut told her that he was a man they needed to investigate thoroughly, because even if he wasn't the murderer, he might have seen the killer.

"Was it the mayor's wife who was murdered then, after all?"

"Yes, it was Florence," Zachariah answered with a nod. "Her husband, Randolf, identified her body last night. He was at the tavern with his council members at the time."

"How did she die?" Vivienne was curious as to the details.

"It seems she was hit over the head by a rock."

"Seems? What does that mean? Did a physician look at the body or not?"

"Yes, the physician was there at my request. So was the coroner. They both said she was hit in the head but they didn't think it was enough force to kill her. However, it did cause enough blood to attract rats to her body, whether it was done purposely or not."

"A hit on the head? This sounds familiar," she said, thinking about the last murder. "I'd like to take a look at the body, please."

He grimaced and shook his head. "Nay, Lady Vivienne. I can't let you do that." His expression was a sour one, as if he didn't even want to picture it happening in his mind.

"Why not?" she demanded to know. "If I am assisting you in this investigation, then I'll need to see things for myself. In case you miss something."

"I understand that. But you also need to realize that Florence's body is a bloody mess and quite chewed up since the rats got to her before we did. You don't want to see that again, trust me."

"Oh," she said, swallowing hard, remembering how the corpse looked last night in the alleyway with all the rats gnawing on it in the dark and the woman's eyes eaten, leaving gaping holes on her face. It was frightening enough then. In the daylight it was bound to look even worse. "I can do it," she assured him, sitting straighter in the saddle and lifting her chin high with bravado, trying to impress him. The warm June breeze blew the ends of her long, loose hair that was only partially tied back with one thin braid trailing down the center of her back. Vivienne felt determined to do this rather than confident that she really could. Still, she had to try. For the sake of the mayor and his family. She wouldn't abandon those in dire need of her help. "I want to view the corpse again to try to find out what really happened. Please, let me do this. I need it. To help the mayor and his family find the answers they seek."

"You're not going to like it, and everything tells me to deny your request. However, if you are that adamant about it, then so be it."

"Where is the body being held?" Since this was the town and not her castle, she didn't know where they kept corpses that needed to be buried.

"The victim's body is at the coroner's office right now. It is customary for the coroner to examine it closely if he feels the death was possibly brought on by foul play," Zachariah explained. "However, because of the rat problem the town is having at the moment, it is crucial that Florence's body be buried soon. If not, the rats will be infesting the coroner's office next."

"Then we'll have to investigate quickly, I suppose. Please, lead me to his home."

ZACHARIAH DISMOUNTED his horse outside of the coroner's house at the edge of town, reaching up to help Vivienne dismount. She didn't need or want his help. In one motion, she swung her legs over to one side of the horse, flipping then to her belly and sliding down until her feet hit the ground. Grunt ran over panting, and sat down at her feet.

"Good boy, Grunt," she said, petting the dog on the head. "I think I see another soup bone in your future." Vivienne stood up straight, looking out over the town of Mablethorpe in the daylight. She'd been here before, but only at the sheriff's home or on High Street with the shops and church. A few times she'd even visited the marketplace square.

Off in the far distance she could see Mablethorpe Castle rising majestically high, looking out over both the town and the seaside. Farmland and the peasants' cottages made of wattle and daub dotted the land around it. To the east of her, the main road led all the way to the coast with its large, sandy beaches. She could see ships docked in the harbor. Fishing boats bobbed up and down on the North Sea while gulls cried out and circled around them, hoping to snatch away some food. To the west of her was the rest of the town.

They were in the high part of town now where the officials like the coroner, the bailiff, and the sheriff lived in homes constructed of wood planks that were joined together. The second floors of the buildings stretched out farther than the first, casting shadows down on the narrow streets. The entire town was surrounded by high stone walls with a gate leading into the town that could close out unwanted intruders if need be. The roads in front of the more respected establishments were paved with cobblestones, like here. They wound around, leading off to other streets, close to buildings since there wasn't a lot of room and the passageways were quite narrow.

St. Peter's church could be seen off in the distance with its tall bell tower which rang out, echoing through the air at the top of each hour. It was loud and the clanging could be heard all the way over to Mablethorpe Castle. In front of the church was a large empty area known as the town square. By decree of the king many years ago, Mablethorpe was granted a market town charter and allowed to have a marketplace open for selling and buying on certain days and times. Trade was common at the market as well. Sometimes even merchants from overseas docked in the harbor and came to town with their goods in tow. But if one didn't belong to the town of Mablethorpe, they had to be granted permission to sell their wares and were charged a tax. This only usually happened when a trade fair was in progress, which was only a few times a year. These trade fairs seemed to be big and impressive, sometimes even lasting as long as two weeks at a time. The guild masters regulated what could be sold at the market and they also maintained the pricing.

Mablethorpe Abbey was atop a hill off in the distance. It was a double monastery like the one in the nearby village of Maltby le Marsh. That meant that it housed both monks and nuns, but of course in segregated living quarters. The monastery raised sheep for wool trade as well as farmed bees to make candles from the beeswax and mead from the honey itself. This was the monks and nuns way of bringing in money for the church.

Merchants in town had their shops lining the streets with large wooden signs with painted pictures hanging above the doors. Since not many commoners could read or write, this served as a way to let them know what went on inside each establishment. The blacksmith's shop had a hammer and anvil on its sign, while above the cordwainer's shop was a boot and a shoe. The tavern had a barrel above it, and the chandler had a big candle on his sign, while the tailor showed a needle and thread. There were also artisans and craftsmen in town who weren't shy about selling their wares right on the street or at the marketplace.

It was a busy little town with people hurrying back and forth. Merchants walked the streets with their wares, calling out what they sold. The butcher always had a line of stray dogs following him. Old women sold flowers and the alewives walked through the streets with mugs of ale and wine. Everyone's favorite had to the baker when the scent of freshly baked bread filled the air, masking all the rancid stench. Children with torn clothes and dirt on their faces and no shoes on their feet watched with big eyes from the shadows of the shops. Down the hill at the low part of town but not far off from the marketplace were the rundown cottages where the very poor and question-able types of people lived. That was also where the tavern was found, as well as the smelly tannery, which had to be one of the worst professions to hold.

"In here, Lady Vivienne," said Zachariah, taking her atten-tion. She followed the sheriff. He knocked on the door and ducked as he entered through the door that wasn't even as tall as he. Zachariah was taller than the average man, and Vivienne was tall for a lady, but on average the people were much shorter than they. "Gandalf? Are you here?" Zachariah called out, getting an answer in reply.

"Hello, Sheriff Fitch." A short man holding a scroll and quill walked out from an adjoining room. He was nearly bald, but wore what little stringy hair he had swept over the top of his head, fooling no one.

"Lady Vivienne, this is the coroner's scribe, Torsten," Zachariah introduced them. "He helps by keeping records of all the deaths in town, and especially the ones that are not ordinary."

"Like a murder." Vivienne nodded.

"That's right. Nice to meet you, my lady." Torsten bowed, his hair falling from the bald part he tried to hide. In one motion, the man swept it back where it belonged. "Might I be bold enough to ask what brings you to the coroner's office, Lady Vivienne?"

"Lady Vivienne is here assisting me in investigating the murder of the mayor's wife," Zachariah explained.

"Ah, yes," said the small man. "It was indeed an odd death, I'll have to agree. But I can't say the coroner has yet ruled it as an actual murder."

"May we see Gandalf now?" asked Vivienne, anxious to move forward with the investigation.

"Gandalf is in with the corpse now. Please follow me." Torsten led the way up to a second floor and through a narrow corridor. He opened the door and immediately the stench of the rotting corpse filled the air as he entered the room.

Vivienne coughed and covered her nose with her hand, stopping in the doorway.

"You don't have to do this," Zachariah reminded her under his breath.

"Yes, I do," she reminded him in turn, pushing past him,

taking a direct path to the table holding the body. The coroner turned around in surprise.

"Sheriff? Who is this?" Gandalf was a frail-looking older man with white hair and a mustache that melded with his long beard that trailed halfway down his chest. He stood slumped over and looked like a strong wind could knock him down if he wasn't careful.

"I am Lady Vivienne from Mablethorpe Castle," she announced before the sheriff had a chance to open his mouth. "I am helping Sheriff Fitch to investigate the death of the mayor's wife. We would like to see the body now."

She looked over at Zachariah who in turn nodded to the coroner. "That's right," he agreed.

"This is not common to have a female here, let alone a noblewoman," warned Gandalf, being cautious about letting Vivienne near the deceased woman's body.

"It's all right," Zachariah assured him. "She has my permission to be here."

"If you say so." Gandalf shrugged and held out his arm in open invitation. Vivienne walked forward to the body which was naked with only a sheet covering it. The sheet was pulled back to expose the top half of the woman's partially-eaten flesh.

Vivienne stopped in her tracks and almost gagged when she realized the woman's eyeballs were totally gone, having been eaten by the rats. She'd seen it in the dark, but in the light it was even more horrifying. Still holding her hand cloth over her nose, she bent closer, inspecting the corpse. There was dried blood on the side of the woman's head, but Vivienne didn't notice any other marks except for scratches and bite marks that were most likely from the rats. She quickly diverted her gaze away from the woman's face.

"Is it normal to view the body naked?" she asked, feeling a little embarrassed since she was standing there with three men.

"It is," Gandalf told her in his crackly voice. "There is no other way for me to determine if there was foul play involved in a death."

"Are there any marks below her waist or on her legs?"

"Nay," said Gandalf with a shrug. "Take a look for yourself." He yanked back the sheet, exposing the entire body of the corpse, flipping it to one side, letting her see that what he said was true.

Vivienne noticed the dead woman's skin on the back of her arms and even her legs looked grayish underneath if she wasn't mistaken.

Grunt quietly stayed at Vivienne's side sniffing around the floor.

"How could you think it was anything *but* murder?" she asked the coroner. "I mean, the woman was found lying in the alley behind a tavern in the dead of the night. I hardly think that is normal that she'd purposely go there at night and by herself. Especially since Florence didn't partake of the drink or go out alone at night and occupy taverns. There was obviously foul play involved here, anyone can see that."

"She liked her honeyed mead," stated the scribe. "Everyone knows that. It is just about all she ever drank."

"That's right," said the coroner. "All the nuns and monks at the abbey liked her since she was their best customer."

"I didn't know that," said Vivienne, thinking this could be an important fact.

"Lady Vivienne," said Zachariah, gently touching her elbow. "I don't believe the coroner has ruled out murder, it is just that we have yet to actually discover the cause of death to find proof of how she died. Until we do, there is no way of telling anything for sure."

"So it really wasn't the hit to her head that killed her," said Vivienne.

"Nay," answered Torsten. "We don't believe so."

"I think she was either already dead or close to it when someone hit her over the head," added Gandalf, still inspecting the body.

"Why do you say that?"

"There were no signs of a struggle," said the sheriff. "If she had been fighting for her life, she would have tried to hit or scratch or even run away."

"Could someone have hit her after she was dead, for some reason?" Vivienne was trying to consider every angle.

"Mayhap," said the sheriff. "But I believe she was still alive when it happened. There is too much blood for that, but then again, with the rats gnawing at her body, it makes it hard to tell for sure."

"I found vomit as well as diarrhea on the deceased one's clothes," said Gandalf. "She could have been ill for some time and it finally consumed her."

"Oh. I see." Slowly, Vivienne opened her eyes once more looking at the body. All of a sudden, the answer came to her. "I think she was poisoned and then someone dumped her body behind the tavern. For some reason they also hit her over the head. Mayhap to make it look like something different."

"Really. Why would you say that?" asked Gandalf. "Poisoning usually shows a burst of blood vessels in the eyes, but since the rats got to her eyes first, we cannot know that for sure."

"Her arms and legs have a bluish tint to them," surveyed Vivienne. "And you confirmed there were signs of vomit as well as diarrhea at the crime scene."

"Yes, that's true," answered Zachariah.

"Her face also seems contorted as if she might have had a seizure," said Gandalf. "That is usually a sign of strychnine poisoning, but once again, because of the rats we can't be sure of anything."

"Was her tongue white and fuzzy?" asked Vivienne, not having the stomach to check for herself.

"I don't know. But there seems to be enough of her mouth left to take a look." Gandalf leaned over the corpse to inspect it while Vivienne turned around and busied herself petting Grunt, not wanting to see.

"It is hard to tell for sure, but I believe Lady Vivienne is correct," Gandalf answered. "I do see something in her mouth that looks white and fuzzy."

"It's arsenic poisoning." Vivienne stopped petting Grunt and stood upright. "I'm sure of it," she blurted out.

"Lady Vivienne, how can you possibly be certain of anything when the coroner can't even tell?" asked Zachariah. "That is naught but speculation."

"Nay, it's not a guess it is from experience, I tell you. I am sorry to have to say that when I was young, I saw the effects of arsenic on a child who had eaten rat poison. It looked a lot like this. Minus the rats, of course," she added under her breath.

"Rat poison," repeated Torsten, sitting down at a table and unrolling the scroll to record what she just said. "So mayhap the Pied Piper killed her."

"That would be naught but speculation as well," Zachariah informed him. "Please don't write that down yet because I still need to interview people to come up with suspects. I think we're finished here, thank you." He took Vivienne's arm to escort her to the door.

"Wait a minute, Sheriff." Vivienne turned back to the coroner. "May I see the deceased's woman's clothes, please?"

Gandalf looked up at the sheriff, receiving a nod from him. He shuffled over to a box and opened it up. Taking out a bundle of clothes, he headed back over to her and placed them on the floor. Then he handed a long wooden pole that was the length of her forearm to Vivienne.

"What's this for?" she asked, taking the tool from him.

"You don't want to touch the clothes," Zachariah warned her. "Since we don't know yet what killed her, it is best to be careful."

"Believe me, I have no desire to actually touch them." She used the stick to poke at the clothes, opening them up to inspect them.

"The woman's gown was ripped and bloodied from the rats," she said aloud. "I also notice something spilled on the sleeve. It seems to be a little sticky and have a gray tinge to it." She used the tip of the stick to poke at the sticky part. Then, leaning over the gown, she bravely sniffed the area, hoping she wouldn't pass out.

"Lady Vivienne, what are you doing?" asked the sheriff.

"Shhh," she shushed him, as if that would help her pick up a scent, which it wouldn't. Still, a faint sweet scent seemed to be mixed in with the stench of everything else filling the room right now. "Honey," she said aloud.

"What?" asked the scribe.

"You smelled honey?" asked Gandalf.

"Yes. That sticky spot is honey. That leads me to believe this woman drank honeyed mead laced with poison," she said aloud.

"She did like her mead," mumbled the coroner. "And everyone knew it."

Vivienne continued. "My guess is that the murderer laced the mead with arsenic which has no scent or taste to it, but sometimes leaves a slight gray stain as seen here." She thumped the area with the stick. "I noticed this same gray tint on the backside of Florence's arms and even a little on her legs."

"Yes, I see that now," said the coroner, looking back at the body. "I didn't even notice that. Thank you."

"Yes, I do believe arsenic is what killed her." Satisfied, she got up and put the stick down on a table.

Grunt sniffed the area with the honeyed mead, but Vivienne made sure her dog didn't get close enough to lick it so he wouldn't be poisoned as well.

"She might be right," said Zachariah, looking over her shoulder at the spot on the clothing. "It makes sense. So, if the murderer was familiar with arsenic, he'd know it couldn't be traced in Florence's death."

"We'll need to question that rat killer," said the coroner. "I'm sure he uses arsenic all the time as a rat poison."

"Yes, that's true," said Vivienne, wiping her hands on her skirt. "I'd also like to hear what the mayor has to say about all this."

"I've already questioned the mayor, as well as everyone in the tavern last night, including the town's councilmen," Zachariah told her.

"You did, but I did not." She stared at him until he shrugged his shoulders and looked in the opposite direction.

"I'm sure questioning everyone again wouldn't hurt," he finally agreed.

"Glad you see it my way. Let's go, Grunt," she said to her hound, heading out the door. "We have a lot of work to do, so we'd better get started."

Chapter Four

"So tell me, Mr. Mayor, what was your wife doing out alone at night? Especially on Rotten Row?" Vivienne asked, pacing back and forth at the mayor's home, making Zachariah uncomfortable with the situation. Grunt sniffed around the room quietly.

"Sheriff, I answered all your questions last night," said the mayor, pouring himself a drink from across the room. "What is this all about?"

"Sorry, Randolf, but Lady Vivienne is assisting me in this investigation to find out exactly what happened to your wife. If you don't mind answering her questions, I'd appreciate it." He sank down atop a chair, wanting to leave.

"Would either of you care for a drink?" The mayor held up his cup.

Zachariah felt like he could use a drink about now since Vivienne wasn't the easiest person to work with. He was about to accept when he saw Vivienne shaking her head and mouthing the word, 'no.'

"We're good," he answered.

"Is that honeyed mead by any chance?" asked Vivienne.

"Nay. It's whisky," said the mayor. "But if you'd like mead, I'm sure there is some around here somewhere since that was my wife's favorite drink."

"Who knew that?" asked Vivienne, crossing her arms over her chest.

"Who knew what?" The mayor took a drink.

"I am talking about your wife's favorite drink being honeyed mead," she continued.

"Well, everyone knew that, I suppose. Florence even used to go to the monastery and watch the monks make it at times. She got a bottle of mead every few days. On market days, she bought it from a vendor."

"I see." Vivienne's hand went to her chin in thought. "Where exactly did Florence get her mead when it was from a vendor?"

"Usually from the market in the town square."

"Sheriff, was there a market in the town square lately?" asked Vivienne.

"Yes," he answered. "Actually, there was one yesterday."

"Did your wife buy any mead from the market yesterday?" Vivienne continued to fire her questions at the mayor.

"No. Yes. Oh, I don't know." The mayor ran a hand over his hair and sat down in a chair. "Sheriff, why is she asking me about my wife's favorite drink? What does any of this have to do with her death? And why aren't you out there trying to find out who killed her?"

"That is exactly what we are trying to do, Randolf," Zachariah told him. "There has been some new evidence in the case, so these questions are crucial."

"Evidence? What kind of evidence?" asked the mayor.

Zachariah's eyes met with Vivienne's. He wasn't sure if it was too early to say anything, but he figured the mayor had a right to know. "We believe your wife was poisoned."

"Poisoned?" The mayor dropped his cup to the floor and sprang to his feet. "God's eyes, how could this be?"

"Signs point to the idea that the murderer might have put arsenic in your wife's favorite honeyed mead," Vivienne told him. "Do you know who might have wanted her dead?"

The mayor slowly shook his head, seeming to be in shock. Once again, he sank down upon his chair. "Nay. I have no idea. Everyone liked Florence. Who would have done such a thing? Sheriff, I demand you find my wife's murderer and kill him for what he's done."

"Mr. Mayor it is our intention to make sure justice is served," Vivienne told him. "Now, can you tell me where you were last night when your wife was murdered?"

"I was attending a council meeting at the town hall."

"With whom?" asked Vivienne.

"I already told the sheriff all this," snapped the mayor.

"Please, Randolf. Just answer the question," said Zachariah softly.

"It was a meeting between me, the bailiff, the town clerk, and the market inspector."

"And their names, please," continued Vivienne.

"I have them all," said Zachariah, standing up.

"Well, were you with these men the entire night?" asked Vivienne.

"Nay. Just until the meeting ended about nine o'clock."

"Then, did you come home to your wife?"

"Nay," said Randolf, running a hand through his hair again. "I went to the tavern for a drink with the men, just like I always do."

"A drink?" Vivienne's eyes flashed over to Zachariah.

Zachariah cleared his throat. "The mayor has also told me that he was visiting ... a female friend at the tavern that night as well."

51

"A whore? You were cheating on your wife, weren't you?" asked Vivienne.

"Every man needs to have a little fun once in a while. There's no law against that." The mayor jumped up. "What the hell difference does it make?"

"Can this prostitute confirm you were with her?" asked Vivienne.

"Well ... she could, but she won't."

"Why not?"

"I didn't want word getting out about me visiting her. You know. I couldn't have my wife finding out."

"Nay, we couldn't have that, could we?" Vivienne asked in a snide tone.

"So I made the wench promise not to tell anyone about our frequent visits."

"Frequent? How frequent?" asked Vivienne, looking thoroughly disgusted with the mayor.

The front door slammed and a girl called out. "Father? Father, where are you?"

Grunt ran over to investigate as the mayor's daughter walked in and stopped when she saw them.

"Hello, Maleine," Zachariah greeted her. "I'd like you to meet Lady Vivienne from Mablethorpe Castle."

"Hello, Sheriff. Lady Vivienne," she said with a slight curtsy. Then she reached out and pet Grunt on the head. "Why is everyone here? And where is Mother?"

VIVIENNE SUDDENLY REALIZED that the mayor's daughter had no idea her mother was dead.

"Maleine, have you been out of town, perhaps?" asked Vivienne.

"Why yes, my lady. I often travel with the blacksmith and

his wife to watch over their children when they journey back and forth to Theddlethorpe to deliver nails and other items he makes in the forge. They also have family there and sometimes stay for weeks at a time. With six children, they need my help. We just returned today."

"When did you leave?" asked Vivienne.

"Early yesterday morning."

"Then she doesn't know yet," said Vivienne under her breath. Her gaze shot over to the sheriff.

"Know what?" asked Maleine. "Is something wrong? And where is my mother? She is always here to greet me. I brought her a hand cloth with her initials stitched on it that I bought from a seamstress in Theddlethorpe. I used the money I earned watching the children to do it. I think Mother will love it." Maleine pulled it out from her bag and held it with two hands, smiling down at it.

"Maleine, I'm afraid there is some bad news," said Zachariah.

"Bad news?" She looked up in question. Her father remained silent, which Vivienne thought was odd. He didn't even come to hug the girl, but just stayed in his chair, staring at the floor.

"Sweetheart, I'm afraid last night your mother ... died," Vivienne told her.

"What?" Maleine's head snapped up and her eyes became glassy. "Nay, this can't be true."

"It is," said her father, slowly standing.

"I never should have left her when she was feeling ill."

"Daughter, your mother was brutally murdered, and I think I know exactly who did it."

"Nay!" cried the girl, dropping the hand cloth and rushing over to her father, burying her face against his chest and clinging to him as she cried.

"Excuse me, Mr. Mayor, but I thought you said you had no idea who would want to kill your wife," Vivienne interrupted.

"Yes, that's what you said," agreed Zachariah, walking over to stand next to her.

Grunt headed to the other side of the room to sniff around.

"I don't know why he would want to kill my wife, but since you told me Florence was poisoned, I think it had to be that wretched rat killer," snapped the mayor. "When I hired him to help with the rat infestation, he told me he uses arsenic to poison the rats. Since that is what killed my dear Florence, then he certainly is guilty."

Grunt barked like crazy from the other side of the room, chasing a rat that poked its head out from a hole in the wall. The dog ran in circles, knocking into the table that held the mayor's bottles with drinks in them. There was a loud crash and one of the bottles toppled and broke on the floor. A stain of liquid quickly spread out, pooling in a large puddle and the rat disappeared.

"Nay, Grunt! Bad boy," Vivienne shouted, pulling her dog by the collar back to the center of the room. The rat poked his nose out again and bravely hurried over and started licking the puddle.

"We're sorry about that, Mayor," apologized the sheriff.

"I'll clean it up, Father," said Maleine.

"Nay, Maleine. I'll do it later. Sit down," he said, putting his arm around his daughter and having a seat as he pulled her closer. "We have guests now and need to give them our undivided attention. It is important that your mother's killer is found."

"Yes, Father," sniffled Maleine, wiping her eyes with her sleeve.

"Did you want to use this?" Zachariah picked up the hand cloth that Maleine dropped and gave it to her.

"Thank you," said Maleine, gripping the hand cloth with her mother's embroidered initials on it as if it were a lifeline. "But I could never use this. Not now. I had it made for Mother." She played with the cloth, her sad eyes focused upon it. "I never should have left her when she was ill."

"Maleine, that is the second time you said your mother was ill," said Vivienne.

"Yes, and the first we are hearing about it," added the sheriff.

"Florence was always feeling sickly," said the mayor. "It was probably from all the mead she drank."

"Nay, Father. When I left she was so ill that she sent me to the market to buy her mead. The blacksmith's family was waiting for me, so after I purchased it, I had to ask the vendor to leave the bottle on the doorstep for Mother."

"Did you know about this, Mr. Mayor?" asked Vivienne.

"Nay," he answered. "I left for work early yesterday morning. I came home midday for something to eat before I had to leave again."

"And your wife was fine at that time?" asked Zachariah.

"She said her stomach was upset, but I honestly didn't think much of it. You see, sometimes when she didn't want to be with me, she used that excuse."

"Father, how can you say that about Mother? She always wanted to be with you."

"Nay, Daughter. Not always. Lately, she seemed secretive and almost as if she was trying to avoid me."

"Why didn't you tell us that before?" asked the sheriff.

"Especially since we questioned you twice," added Vivienne.

"I'm sorry," said the mayor. "I just thought Florence was angry with me because ..." He looked at his daughter and then back to them. "You know," he added, making it quite clear he didn't want to talk about bedding the whore in front of his daughter.

"Well, I suppose that'll be all for now," said the sheriff. He was about to leave when he noticed something across the room. "What's this?" He walked over to the puddle of liquid and hunkered down. "This rat is dead."

"I just saw it drinking from that puddle," said Vivienne.

"Mayor, what was in that bottle?" asked Zachariah.

"That is the bottle I bought at the market for mother," said Maleine, running over to look. "It was the one that contained her honeyed mead."

"God's eyes, it must have had arsenic in it," said the mayor, following them across the room. "Someone must have tainted it while it was on the doorstep."

"I think he's right," agreed Vivienne. "If the rat died that quickly, there had to be a good amount of arsenic in the mead."

"Thank God Maleine or I didn't drink from it," said the mayor, shaking his head. "Sheriff, this is proof that the rat-catcher did it. He might be trying to kill me as well."

"Why would he want to kill any of you?" asked the sheriff. "It makes no sense."

"Yes, it does," said the mayor. "He wanted me to pay him twice what I offered him to hunt the rats and I refused. We just don't have the funds for what he asked. It seemed to make him angry, but he ended up taking the job anyway."

"Well, I think we found the tainted mead that killed Florence," said Vivienne. "But now, my only question is, how and why did her body end up being found in an alley behind the tavern?"

Chapter Five

Vivienne walked out of the mayor's house with Grunt leading the way. The sheriff and the mayor were right behind her.

"Make sure you wear gloves to clean up that mess," Zachariah instructed. "And don't let your daughter near it. Also, don't let her leave the house until we find out if it truly was the rat-catcher who poisoned your wife's drink. He might be trying to kill your entire family for some reason."

"Aye, Sheriff," said the mayor. "I want that rat-catcher caught and put behind bars at once. I won't have my daughter's life or even my own endangered by that madman."

"We're doing what we can, just be patient," said Zachariah. "We don't really know anything for sure, yet."

"Well, one thing I know is that I loved my wife and she loved me."

"Really," scoffed Vivienne. "If so, I'd hardly think you'd be occupying an upstairs room at the tavern so often."

"Lady Vivienne, please," said the sheriff. "That happens more than you think. To both married and unmarried men. It doesn't mean anything, really."

Vivienne rolled her eyes and looked the other way.

"Maleine is taking the death of her mother pretty hard," said the mayor. "I'd better get back inside to comfort her. I don't know what we're going to do without Florence. I feel bad now for cheating on her. Mayhap I should have worked harder at paying her more attention."

"One last thing, Mayor," Vivienne stopped him. "Do you think someone poisoned the mead on your doorstep or broke into your house to do so?"

"Oh. I hadn't thought of that," he answered. "Mayhap that damned rat-catcher broke in when I was gone, killed Florence and then dumped her body behind the tavern that night. I mean, I was gone a long time. I suppose anything could have happened."

"There was no signs of forced entry, was there?"

"Nay," said the sheriff. "But that doesn't mean the man didn't sneak in through an open window."

"The whole thing just seems odd," said Vivienne.

"Lady Vivienne, you almost sound as if you suspect me of killing my own wife," said the mayor. "I don't like that at all."

"The evidence is stacking up against you," she answered.

"Did it ever occur to you that mayhap that damned rat-catcher is trying to blame me? I am innocent, I tell you. I never could have harmed Florence. She was my wife."

"I'm sorry, but you don't seem that devoted to her," said Vivienne, getting a dirty look from the sheriff.

"Sheriff, I told you everywhere I went and what I did yesterday. I have people who can confirm my whereabouts every minute of the day."

"Yes, I know," he answered. "And no one is accusing you of anything, I assure you. Right now, all we are doing is collecting the facts."

"Thank you, Sheriff. I would like to get back to my daughter now, if you don't mind."

"Go right ahead," Zachariah answered. "If we have any more questions, we'll let you know."

"Sheriff, please catch that Pied Piper and hang him for what he did." Anger showed in the mayor's eyes. His face became red. "I know it was him, and he needs to pay for his crime. My daughter is devastated and so am I. Neither of us deserve this. Florence didn't deserve to die. You are in charge in this town, so please find the rat-catcher and make him pay for what he did."

"I cannot arrest anyone yet. I need stronger evidence before I can accuse him or anyone for Florence's death."

"If you won't do something about that menace, then I will take matters into my own hands."

"Nay!" shouted the sheriff. "If you do that, you'll be the one I'm arresting instead. Now, please, Randolf, let me do my job. Leave the investigation to me and Lady Vivienne. Right now, all I want you to do is to watch over your daughter and don't let her out of your sight. The coroner is eager to get your wife buried since her body is so mutilated from the rats. The funeral will be planned for tomorrow."

"Thank you, Sheriff," said the mayor, not bothering to thank Vivienne, although she knew men like him would never give proper acknowledgment to any woman. Not even his own wife. She despised the man already, knowing he was visiting whores so often. She didn't know his wife and only just met his daughter, but she felt sorry for both the women. No one deserved to have a husband or father who thought nothing about occupying the bed of a whore.

The mayor disappeared back into his house while Vivienne and Zachariah headed back to their horses. Grunt sniffed around, waiting for them to leave.

"Why so quiet?" asked Zachariah, helping her to mount her

steed. Since she was so distracted by her thoughts, she let him do so.

"I don't like the mayor and neither do I trust him."

"I figured as much." The sheriff mounted his horse as well. "I know things look suspicious, but like he said, someone could be trying to put the blame on him. What we really need to discover is the murderer's motive. Once we know that, all the pieces will fall into place, I'm sure."

"We need to question the council next, and then those in the tavern," she told him. "I know you already did, but I want to do it again. We also need to find that whore to confirm the mayor's story. I think it's odd that he won't tell us her name."

"You need to understand that it's all part of protecting his reputation," Zachariah told her. "Don't worry, I know the whores and I'll find out which one he was with last night."

"You do?" That was the last thing she thought he'd say. "Please don't tell me you think men should ignore their wives and have a little fun too, as the mayor says."

"Nay, Vivienne. I know them because I am the sheriff. I keep a close eye on those who inhabit Rotten Row."

"Hrmmph," she said with a sniff, turning her horse. "We need to find the Pied Piper and question him as well."

"He won't show up until after dark," said Zachariah.

"Well, where are we off to next?" she asked.

"To my home."

"Why?" She didn't understand this in the least. They had so much work to do and he wanted to go home to relax? What kind of a sheriff was he?

"I had Constable Dorson's wife, Agatha set up some interviews for me. I need to get home before the women arrive."

"Interviews? Women? I don't understand. Does this have to do with the murder?"

"Nay," he told her, turning his horse and starting back to his home. "I need to hire someone to watch Starah for me while I'm working. I don't want to leave her with Constable Dorson's wife anymore, since I think her own three children are too much for her to handle."

"So, we're going to your home to interview nursemaids at a time like this? Really?"

"Yes, we are. I cannot watch over my daughter properly while I'm working. I need help doing so. It's for her own safety."

"I understand that. But why don't you just leave Starah at the castle? There are plenty of people to look after her there while you work. Plus, she adores Martin and Grunt."

"Nay, I can't do that," he said softly.

"Why not?" she asked as they rode back toward his home. "I am offering you an answer to your problem."

"Starah and I are not nobles. We don't belong at the castle like you do."

"At least let Starah stay at the castle until we find Florence's murderer."

"And then what?" He turned and looked at her with eyes that had a longing she couldn't explain. "I want things to get back to normal for Starah. It's been hard for her this past year without her mother."

"Yes, I understand. Just like it'll be hard for that dear child, Maleine, now, too, without her mother."

"Maleine is sixteen and hardly a child. Starah is seven and needs a mother to guide her."

That took Vivienne by surprise that he'd said it in that way. "So ... are you implying that you will soon be looking to get married again?" She could see his need, but for some reason this bothered her to think of Zachariah with a new bride.

"Mayhap someday, yes," he told her. "But as of right now I am in need of someone to care for and watch over my daughter. Actually, I was hoping that you could help me out."

"Me?" Vivienne's heart stood still. "What was he saying? Surely, he didn't mean that he wanted her to act as Starah's mother, did he? Or was he implying even more? Such as possibly wanting to marry her someday? The thought pleased her and horrified her at the same time. "Sheriff Fitch, if I must remind you, we agreed that our relationship would be nothing but platonic and professional now that we are working together."

"Aye, of course," he said, looking over his shoulder as he spoke. "That is why I am counting on you. For your professional opinion of which woman I should hire as a live-in nursemaid for my daughter."

"Live-in?" A sharp twinge of jealousy raked through her.

"Of course. I never know when I'll be called away for my job just like we saw last night. I can't very well be leaving my young daughter alone at any moment, and neither can I be knocking on someone's door at midnight asking them to watch over my child. I have two bedrooms, so there will be plenty of room for a nursemaid to share one with Starah."

"Yes. Plenty of room," she choked out, knowing already that she was going to hate this task. Even though they were only friends, a small part of her didn't want any woman living in the same house as Zachariah.

≈

"And what was wrong with that one?" Zachariah asked Vivienne, throwing his hands in the air. Lady Vivienne had sent away the fourth woman he'd interviewed and it was becoming tiresome. Each woman so far had been young and pretty and also sounded experienced enough with caring for children that she would have made a good nursemaid for Starah. But with each woman who came to his door, Vivienne seemed to find something new wrong with her. She'd said they were either too lazy, too disciplined, or not nearly disciplined enough. None of this made any sense. It was starting to be a big waste of his time. He honestly wished now that he hadn't asked Vivienne to help him interview the potential nursemaids because he was starting to think somehow she was jealous.

"That one just didn't seem like the type of woman that Starah would want. Replacing her mother, I mean."

"Really." He sat back on his chair with his arms folded over his chest, plunking his booted feet atop the table. Grunt laid under the table, looking as bored as he felt right now. "And tell me, how do you know that? Have you discussed with my daughter the types of people she likes to be around?"

"Nay, not really." Vivienne sat at the table looking ever so proper with her back straight and every hair in place. She reached out and picked up the wooden cup he'd given her with wine in it. "However, I know how little girls think and feel since I was a little girl at one time too." She took a dainty sip of the wine.

"You haven't been a little girl for quite some time now, Vivienne. Remember, I knew you back then. You didn't like anyone telling you what to do and still don't, I see."

He realized his mistake of calling her Vivienne without the title of lady attached as soon as he saw her eyes open wide. She pretended not to be looking at him, but she watched him closely from the side of her eye.

"What is that supposed to mean?" She focused her interest inside her cup.

"Oh, I don't know." He leaned back in his chair, balancing on two of its legs only. "Mayhap you're feeling a little ... jealous, shall we say?"

She was taking another proper sip of wine and almost

started choking when she heard that. He was about to pat her on the back when he heard a voice from his open door.

"Hello? Is anyone home?" came a woman's voice from the door. "Is this yer cat? It was sittin' outside yer door lookin' like it wanted to come in."

Zachariah looked up to see an old, plump woman standing on his threshold with that damned rat-catcher's black cat cradled in one arm. She had a big canvas bag with a long strap pushed over her shoulder.

"God's teeth, please don't bring that thing in here," growled Zachariah, seeing the cat's one yellow eye and the other green one staring at him, looking positively as evil as the cat's owner.

Grunt spied the cat as well and darted out from under the table barking, knocking into his chair, setting Zachariah off balance. Back he went, his arms flaying in the air as he ended up prone on the floor looking up at the damned ceiling. He heard the cat hiss. When he glanced back at the door he saw the cat jump from the old woman's arms. Grunt ran out the door, chasing it down the street.

"Not again," he moaned.

"Grunt, get back here!" Vivienne sprang to her feet and hurried to the door, but since the old woman was blocking the exit, Vivienne stopped in her tracks. "Are you here to interview for the nursemaid job?" she asked. "Because if so, the job is yours." She stepped around the old woman and ran out the door after her dog.

Zachariah hurriedly pushed up from his position on the floor, getting to his knees. "I'm Sheriff Zachariah Fitch," he introduced himself, standing and brushing his hands together to remove the dirt. "Who are you?"

"I'm Nairnie," said the woman, looking over her shoulder out the door. "Was that a noblewoman who just ran out of here like her undergarments were on fire?"

"Aye." He chuckled at the analogy. "Lady Vivienne Harlowe from Mablethorpe Castle often takes off in a flash, leaving a puff of dust in her wake."

"Ah, I see." She entered the house without being invited in, waddling over to Vivienne's vacated chair. "My feet are killin' me." With a plop, she dropped her large bag on his table and proceeded to sit down, pulling off one shoe and rubbing her foot. God's teeth was this really happening?

"So ... Nairnie, was it? What brings you to my door?" he asked, picking up his overturned chair, hoping to hell she wasn't really here for the job of nursemaid.

"Are ye blind and deaf?" she spat, still rubbing her foot. "I was bringin' yer cat back to ye."

"Oh, nay. You don't understand. That wasn't my cat. I don't have a cat at all."

"Good boy, Grunt," said Vivienne, holding the dog's collar, coming back into the house. She closed the door behind her. Grunt ran right over to Nairnie and started licking her foot. "Oh, Grunt likes you," said Vivienne, her eyes meeting his. "That's always a good sign when an animal likes a person. It shows that person can be trusted. Don't you agree, Sheriff?"

"Huh?" Zachariah wasn't sure what was going on here, but this was all taking a very odd turn.

"I do love animals, especially hounds," said Nairnie with a chuckle, reaching out to pet Grunt. "My son has over a dozen dogs," she told them.

"A dozen? That's crazy," mumbled Zachariah, brushing the dirt from the floor off his clothes.

"Ye're no' a very tidy one, Sheriff Fitch, are ye?" She looked him up and down with one eye squinted. "I think this place could use a good cleanin' and airin' out." She put her shoe back on and got up and walked over to the stairs leading to the second floor. "What's up there?" She stretched her neck, trying to see.

"There are two bedrooms up there," Vivienne so gracefully supplied the information. "You'll be sharing one of them with the sheriff's seven-year-old daughter, Starah."

"Now, wait a minute," he said, wanting to tell Vivienne that he'd never agreed to this.

"Starah, huh? That's an odd name. Almost as odd as Summer, Spring, Autumn, and Winter."

"What?" asked Zachariah, thinking this woman was addled, talking about the seasons.

"Those are the names of the ladies that were under my care at one time," Nairnie explained.

"Oh, so you were a handmaid to noblewomen," said Vivienne with a nod, sounding very impressed. He couldn't say he felt the same way. "Sheriff, that says a lot about her," Vivienne continued. "That means she can definitely be trusted."

"Does it now?" he asked, giving her a sarcastic glance. Lady Vivienne should know better than anyone that it wasn't necessarily always true.

"Of course, I can be trusted," said the old woman, her hands going to her hips. "Dinna let the fact that my grandsons were once pirates and that I'm married to an ex-pirate, as well, make ye think otherwise, lassie."

"Pirates?" he asked. God's teeth could this get any worse? While Zachariah figured Nairnie was making some sort of ill jest, it only made him wonder about her state of mind.

"Aye, pirates," she answered. "Of course, I didna ken they were pirates at first, but thanks to Lord Rowen the Restless, I found them and straightened those boys out. They're no' pirates anymore, I promise."

"Rowen the Restless?" asked Zachariah, having heard of him. "Are you saying you know one of the Legendary Bastards of the Crown?" He saw Vivienne's head snap up when he said that.

"Of course, I do," said Nairnie, running her finger along the wooden railing leading to the upstairs. "Hrmph," she said with a sniff. "This place hasna had a lassie livin' here for quite a while, has it?"

"Nay, not besides the sheriff's young daughter," said Vivienne, giving this stranger more information about him than he wanted her to know. "You see, his wife died a year ago. Being sheriff, he's always getting called away at any hour of the day or night. He is in dire need of a nursemaid to watch over the little girl since he can't leave her alone."

"I see. And you're lookin' to hire someone, are ye?"

"Well, I ..." He couldn't even finish his sentence before Vivienne broke in again and interrupted.

"Are you Scottish?" she asked. "I notice the way you speak."

"I am, lassie. But I live here in England now."

"What do you know about the Legendary Bastards of the Crown?"

"I know all about the king's triplets, Rowen, Rook and Reed. They are my friends. I thought everyone kent about them, but obviously, ye dinna."

"I don't know anything about them but would like to know more."

"Well, that's a story for a different day."

Vivienne rushed over to Nairnie. "Will you take the job as nursemaid, Nairnie? I know you said you're married, but the sheriff and I are investigating a murder right now and we are in dire need of hiring someone right away."

"*We?*" asked Zachariah, but both the women ignored him and just kept on talking.

"Ye are investigatin' a murder?" Nairnie sounded surprised and also very interested.

"Yes. I know it is odd since I'm a woman, but it's true."

"Ye're a noblewoman."

"I am. However, I'm not your average noblewoman, I'm afraid."

"I can see that, lassie. No' many noblewomen I've met would be alone in town with the sheriff and runnin' around the streets chasin' after a dog."

"Oh, you don't understand. You see, Sheriff Fitch and I have been friends since we were children."

"Excuse me," said Zachariah, meaning to dismiss Nairnie so he could get back to interviewing proper nursemaids. "Have you any experience with young children at all?"

"Of course, Sheriff. I have many grandchildren."

"That sounds divine," said Vivienne, standing right in front of Nairnie. "I'd love to know how many and what all their names are."

"If I can say something, here." Zachariah tried once again, but couldn't seem to get either of their attention.

"Och, I could go on for days talkin' about the little tykes." Nairnie swiped her hand through the air.

"Where do you live, Nairnie? And where is your husband right now?" asked Vivienne.

"I've lived in many places through the years from the Highlands of Scotland, to the coast of Cornwall, to Ravenscar, and even on a ship on the North Sea. I move around a lot ye see. I was just visitin' Lady Autumn and Lord Ravenscar. Lady Autumn is a healer and used to work at Mablethorpe Manor, givin' aid to those men who were injured fightin' for the king. Even though she lives in Ravenscar now, we came back to visit the place. My husband, Bear, works as a sea captain, huntin' down those who are deceivin' the king."

"Bear? What kind of name is that?" asked Zachariah.

"Well, his real name is Bacchus and I used to call him Buzzard on the ship, but he prefers to be called Bear."

"Sorry I asked. What ship are you talking about?" asked Zachariah.

"The Falcon. The pirate ship I was on with my grandsons. Dinna ye listen when I talk?"

"Not that anyone listens when I talk," he mumbled under his breath.

"Will you take the job, Nairnie? Please?" begged Vivienne.

"Lady Vivienne, we need to discuss this in private," Zachariah told her.

"Hmmm." Nairnie put her hands on her hips, cocked her head and squinted one eye again as she studied him. "Bear is goin' to be gone for a while at sea, so he willna miss me. I'll tell ye what I'll do. I'll give ye one week as a trial period. I'll ken after that if it's goin' to work or no'. Now, where's the little girl I'll be watchin' over?" She looked one way and then the other.

"Oh, thank you!" Vivienne looked so happy about this that he wouldn't be surprised if she hugged and kiss Nairnie next. Grunt was once again at Nairnie's feet, wagging his tail and licking her hand. Damn, this was going to make it hard to turn the old woman away now. But he couldn't have someone he didn't know, and who was also related to pirates, watching over his daughter. It wasn't safe nor was it right.

"I didn't agree to this," he finally pointed out. "Nairnie, I don't even know you. I cannot hire just anyone off the street. I need confirmation from someone reliable that you are a person I can trust with my daughter."

"Oh, ye're one of those, are ye? All right, then. Would the word of two nobles put yer mind at ease?"

"Well, it would certainly help. However, I don't have time to wait for you to contact anyone and have them send back a missive. I need to hire someone immediately as Lady Vivienne told you."

"Then ye're in luck, because I have two nobles right outside who will vouch for me." She waddled over to the door and stuck her head outside. "Lord and Lady Ravenscar, can ye please come in here and tell this doited sheriff that I am someone he can trust?"

"What? You have nobles outside waiting for you?" asked Zachariah in surprise.

"I told ye I was here with them. I swear, ye dinna listen, Sheriff. I hope ye'll change that bad habit right away. After all, I'm goin' to have my hands full cookin' and cleanin' for ye no' to mention tendin' to yer daughter. I canna have a man in my home that doesna listen to a word I say."

"*My* home," he said softly, correcting her, starting to wonder if it was so.

Vivienne and Nairnie greeted the nobles who were now standing on his doorstep.

"Hello, Lord and Lady Ravenscar," said Vivienne. "The sheriff just wants verification of Nairnie's character before we hire her to watch over the sheriff's young daughter."

"I trust Nairnie with my life," said Lord Ravenscar. "She is like a mother to me."

"She watched over me and my sisters as well before we were married," added the red-headed Lady Autumn. "You can't go wrong with someone like her."

"Nairnie, I think you'll be perfect for the job and will find things to your liking here," said Vivienne.

"Och, I get the feelin' I'll like it too," Nairnie answered.

"Lord and Lady Ravenscar, would you care to come in for a visit and have a cup of ale?" asked Vivienne, totally taking over the sheriff's abode.

"We'd love to," said Lady Autumn. "I think it would be a welcome respite before we head home."

"Please. Come in," said Zachariah, not even believing this was happening. "Welcome to my home. *Our* home," he corrected himself, knowing that because of Vivienne there was no way of getting out of hiring the old woman now.

Chapter Six

Vivienne got up from the table later that day after Lord and Lady Ravenscar had left. She had just finished eating dinner at the sheriff's home at the insistence of Zachariah's new nursemaid, Nairnie. Earlier, she and the sheriff had returned to the castle to collect Starah and brought her back home.

"Nairnie, that was delicious soup," she told her, looking over to Grunt who had his chin on the sheriff's lap. Little Starah never seemed to smile more and even ate something called hardtack which Nairnie told them was what pirates ate on the ship. The flat, hard bread was made from flour, water, and salt and had to be soaked in the broth in order to make it soft enough to chew. She also made very tasty, soft buns with butter and garlic on top.

"How'd ye like the buns, Sheriff?" asked the old woman. "Those were my grandson Aaron's favorite when I cooked for the crew on the pirate ship."

"Besides almost breaking my tooth on them, I'd have to admit I've never had anything quite like it before," mumbled the sheriff.

"Nay, not the hardtack," said Nairnie with a chuckle. "I only made that because Starah wanted to know how it tasted. I was talking about the soft, garlic butter buns."

"Oh. Yes, those were very good." Zachariah had been quiet during the meal, barely having said a word. Vivienne figured it was because he was still trying to accept what was happening now in his home.

"Were you really on a pirate ship, Nairnie?" Starah's eyes grew wide.

"Of course, not Sarah. She's just trying to entertain us with her stories," the sheriff told his daughter.

"Aye, I certainly was, lassie," Nairnie answered, scowling at Zachariah for saying that as she cleared away the empty plates, stacking them atop each other. "They were real pirates as sure as the day is long."

"Did you find treasure, too?" continued Starah.

"Don't answer that." Zachariah raised his hand in the air. "And please refrain yourself from speaking of such things around my daughter again."

"Why?" asked Nairnie. "It's true. Plus, my grandsons are all married now and livin' respectable lives, so there's nothin' to worry about."

"Isn't there?" he asked.

"Father, will Nairnie really be living here with us now? I like her," said his daughter, reaching out and placing her hand on Nairnie's arm. "She's funny."

"For now," was all he said, heading to the door. "Make sure she's in bed early, and no bedtime stories that have to do with pirates," he warned.

"Aye, Sheriff, whatever ye say." Nairnie shrugged. "I suppose I can tell her about Lord Ravenscar's dogs or mayhap how Baron Mowbry was murdered as he slept."

"Nay! No talk about murders," Zachariah exploded. The

room became silent. He shook his head, looking like he wanted to get away from them. "Dogs would be fine though. Just no talk of cats, please."

He held the door open for Vivienne and they exited, closing the door behind him. She decided not to anger him more so didn't say another word about Nairnie. It was already dark outside and the spring air took on a clammy chill. Vivienne shivered and wrapped her cloak tighter around her.

"Cold?" he asked, helping her to mount her horse. Grunt sniffed the air, looked around and then proceeded to bay at the moon. His howl echoed in the near-empty streets of town. This was the time of night when the people in the high part of town went to bed and stayed inside their houses. However, the low part of town would just be starting to come to life.

"Nay, I'm fine. I'm just anticipating meeting up with the Pied Piper again, I guess."

"Lady Vivienne, I'd like to take you back to the castle and confront the Pied Piper on my own. For your own safety."

"Sheriff Fitch, do not even suggest that again. I thought I made it clear to you that I wanted to talk with this rat-catcher to question him about the murder."

"And I thought I made it clear to you that I don't want you anywhere near him."

She looked over at him in the moonlight and raised a brow. "If you take me home, I'll just turn right around and come back to Rotten Row by myself. Is that what you want?"

"Arrrgh," he ground out. "You are so damned stubborn!"

"Did you expect anything different?"

"I suppose not. Come on, let's go. I hear the Pied Piper usually shows up on Rotten Row just after dark."

"Where does he stay while he's in Mablethorpe rat-catching?"

"I'd have to guess in a hole under a bridge somewhere like a troll, or mayhap in a swamp in the woods like an ogre, I don't know."

The sheriff was in such a foul mood that Vivienne thought she'd try to lighten things up with a little small talk instead of talking about the murder. However, the only thing she could think to talk about only riled him more.

"That Nairnie is a godsend, isn't she? And such a good cook, too."

That only got her another grumble under his breath.

"What's the matter? Don't you like her?"

"Does it really matter if I do or not?"

"What does that mean?"

"Nothing."

"If you have something bothering you, then please, tell me what it is."

"All right, I will. I think it is interesting how you found fault in every one of the young or good-looking women who applied for the position of nursemaid today, yet when the old crone showed up at my door you hired her before even knowing anything about her."

"What?" That took her by surprise. She wasn't expecting him to even notice, but it was the truth. She hadn't wanted any of the young, good-looking women living with the sheriff because for some reason it bothered her. True, an old, ugly hag was a better choice in her opinion, but Nairnie had things about her that were admirable too. "Lord and Lady Ravenscar confirmed that she was to be trusted and even raved about her. That should make you feel at ease."

"True. But you hired her before they even said a word or before we even knew they were there."

"Well, she seemed nice. And both Grunt and that cat liked her."

"Grunt likes anyone who will give him food. He probably smelled sausage on her. And as for that damned cat, if I see it at my door again, I'll skin it alive, I swear."

"Is that any way to talk? Starah liked that cat."

"It's the rat-catcher's pet and I don't want it near my home or my daughter."

"Nairnie is experienced, being older and all."

"Yes, that's true."

Vivienne smiled.

"Probably most experienced in thieving and pillaging. I'll be lucky to go home to find my belongings still there."

"If you don't like her, then why didn't you say something earlier?"

"I tried to, but no one would listen to me!"

"Just give her a chance. I'm sure she's exactly what you're looking for, but you just don't know it yet."

"How can I not know it when you've so graciously already told me what to think?"

Grunt saw something and took off at a run.

"Come on. I think Grunt might have spotted the Pied Piper." Vivienne kicked her heels into her horse and took off following her hound. Zachariah was right behind her. She tried to stay calm, but could see exactly where Grunt was headed and wasn't sure she liked it. The dog chased something or someone down a narrow passageway between two buildings, and there was no mistaking where it led. Behind the tavern, where they'd found Florence's dead body.

She stopped her horse, looking back at Zachariah. "We'll have to continue on foot since the horses won't fit down the narrow passageway."

"Nay. I don't want to leave our horses here unattended again. We were lucky last time not to have them stolen."

"Then stay here with them. I'll go." She started to dismount, but he stopped her.

"No, you won't. We'll both stick together. It's safer that way. We'll stay out here on the road."

"But what about Grunt? We can't just leave him."

"He'll return when he gets hungry enough."

"Nay. I want to go find him." She slid off her horse, her body freezing in place when she heard a man's deep voice from behind her.

"Looking for me, my lady?"

She spun around on her heel to come face-to-face with none other than the Pied Piper. The scary-looking man stood there holding his staff with the rat cage at the top of it. It was filled with live rats, and several dead rats hung by their tails from the cage, swinging back and forth in the foul-smelling breeze. This time, the rat-catcher had a lit torch in his other hand. The fire-light illuminated every crease and wrinkle on his leather-worn face. A small, black beard and mustache covered the lower part of his face. And atop the hat on his head was a live rat climbing around. She gasped when she saw two more rats on him, one peeking out from behind his neck and the other sitting on his shoulder eating something. It was enough to make anyone want to retch or run for their life.

"Rat-catcher, I'm Sheriff Fitch and I have a few questions for you regarding the murder of the mayor's wife." Zachariah jumped off his horse, coming up right next to her, stepping in front of her in a subtle act of protection.

"I didn't kill that woman and leave her body behind the tavern, if that's what you want to know."

"How did you know where her body was found?" Vivienne stepped to the side so she could have a full view of the rat-catcher.

"I own these streets at night." His dark eyes penetrated her, making her feel scared. "I know everything that goes on out here on Rotten Row."

"Good. Then mayhap you could be a help to us. Did you see any suspicious activity last night?" asked the sheriff.

"That depends what you and the little lady here consider suspicious." He continued to peruse Vivienne making her question her choice to want to talk to him. She only hoped he wasn't plotting in his head how to kill her next.

"Did you see anyone dumping the body behind the tavern?" asked Zachariah.

"What's it worth to you?" the rat-catcher sneered, showing his rotten teeth.

"Look, Rat-catcher," snapped Zachariah. "You are under suspicion of murder unless you can prove your whereabouts and that you had nothing to do with it."

"It's Mr. Piper, not Rat-catcher," he corrected the sheriff. "Or as most people call me ... the Pied Piper." He chuckled, his deep voice rattling in his chest. The mouse on his head squeaked and jumped off, almost hitting Vivienne. She cried out and jumped back. "A little squeamish, aren't you, wench? After all, I thought you'd be more used to the rats by now since you didn't even scream when you saw them gnawing away on that dead woman."

"How did you know that?" she asked, feeling the mad thumping of her heart in her chest. "You were there. Watching us, weren't you?"

"Like I said ... I own the streets of Rotten Row at night. It's my job. My lady," he added and laughed loudly this time. "However, I don't think a frail thing like you is supposed to be anywhere near this end of town." He took a step closer to her, and she took one back.

Zachariah unsheathed his sword and held it up to the Pied Piper in warning. "Get any closer to Lady Vivienne, and I will be forced to use my blade on you. Now, tell me where you were at the time of the murder."

"I can't answer that since I don't know when the wench was killed. However, I can tell you I was right here on Rotten Row all night, collecting rats as usual."

"Then you are a suspect, since you were in the area."

"Nay. I had nothing to do with that murder, like I told ye."

"Can anyone confirm that for you?"

"I can," came a voice from the inky night. Then the young man that Vivienne had seen with the rat-catcher last night, stepped into the light of the torch.

"Who are you?" asked the sheriff, holding his blade toward them both now.

"He's my assistant. I'm training him to do what I do," the Pied Piper interrupted.

"My name is Wymond," said the boy. He was tall and lanky, dressed in dirty, torn clothes and had long scraggly brown hair. He wore a small hat but no cloak like the rat-catcher. It made Vivienne wonder if the boy was perhaps cold. Especially since she could see his bare toes sticking out of the holes in his worn boots.

"Wymond, you were with Piper last night. I saw you," said Zachariah.

"That's right. I was," said the boy with a sharp nod.

"The entire night?" asked Vivienne.

"Yes, my lady." Wymond seemed eager to answer their questions. "He didn't kill the woman and neither did I."

"Did you see who did?" asked Vivienne.

The boy's gaze slowly moved over to the Pied Piper, but he didn't answer.

"We didn't see nothin' I told ye," growled the rat-catcher. "Now be on your way. We have work to do." He handed the torch to Wymond and picked up some kind of horn hanging from his belt. He blew a few notes on it, and instantly something came scurrying out of the narrow passageway where Grunt had disappeared. It didn't sound like Grunt, but mayhap a much smaller animal or perhaps several rats.

"What's that?" she asked, moving closer to the sheriff, her eyes darting one way and then the other, now noticing rats on each side of her. They were probably being drawn to the firelight of the torch.

"No need to be frightened, my little lady." The Piper dropped his horn to his side, letting it swing from his belt. Then he hunkered down and held out one arm. The rats that were on him seemed to become frightened and jumped to the ground and disappeared into the night. Then she saw two long, skinny animals with short legs that kept them close to the ground shoot out of the darkness. They were those weasel-like animals she'd seen previously. Each of them held a dead rat in its mouth. They jumped up on the Piper's arm, climbing up and settling themselves on his shoulders. Wymond hurriedly collected the dead rats, shoving them into a box hanging at his side.

"These are just my pets. Ferrets, they're called," said Wymond, taking something from his pouch. He held up what looked like food in each hand, feeding the ferrets. "They are trained to help us hunt rats. When they do, they are rewarded."

"I see," said Vivienne, wanting more than anything to be away from here. She didn't like the darkness, the foul stench, the bad part of town, and certainly not this scary man called the Pied Piper and his assistant with rat-killing weasels.

"Wymond, find that damned cat," ordered the Pied Piper. "We have work to do and we're falling behind schedule."

"Yes, Mr. Piper," said Wymond, handing the torch back to the rat-catcher and hurrying away into the night, following the trail the rats had taken.

"Is there anything else you'd like to know, Sheriff?" asked

the Pied Piper. "If not, I have work to do. You and the pretty little lady are welcome to accompany me if you'd like." He laughed heartily once again. "Although, my job is not for the squeamish, I'll warn you."

"Nay," said Zachariah, lowering his sword. "Just keep me informed if you see or hear anything suspicious. That is, information that can help us solve this murder."

"Of course, Sheriff. Why wouldn't I?" He started to turn away, when Vivienne called out.

"You use arsenic to kill the rats, don't you?"

He slowly turned back around. His dark eyes drilled into her. "Sometimes. And other times, I stab them to death with my dagger, or hack them to pieces with my axe. Or if I'm feeling lazy, I'll just break their necks with my bare hands. Why do you ask?"

After hearing that, Vivienne couldn't bring herself to speak. She kept picturing all the horrible things the man could do and they all included killing.

"The victim drank mead laced with arsenic," Zachariah told him.

"And so you think I did it?"

"Well, you do use arsenic," she said, her confidence suddenly fading under the rat-catcher's constant perusal.

"So do many others. For instance, the tanner uses arsenic in pigments in dyes, the healer for medicinal purposes, or even the executioner. Mayhap you two should be looking elsewhere for your killer. As I already told you, I am innocent."

"Where can one get arsenic?" asked Vivienne.

"They can steal it or buy it from an apothecary," he said. "I actually had some of my arsenic stolen two nights ago." He reached down and touched some leather ties hanging from his belt. "I kept it right here, but as you can see it's gone now. You'd better start looking for a thief as well as a murderer, if you ask me."

"Why didn't you say that sooner?" asked Zachariah.

"Why didn't you ask me sooner? Now excuse me, but I have rats to catch." He turned and walked away just as Grunt shot out from between the buildings, running to Vivienne's side.

"Let's get the hell out of here." The sheriff sheathed his blade. Then without asking permission, he lifted Vivienne atop her horse.

"Do you believe his story?" she asked as the sheriff mounted his steed.

"Not in the least. Do you?"

"I'd like to, but I'm not sure. It seems to me that Wymond was afraid of the Pied Piper. It was almost as if he wanted to say something more, but instead kept quiet."

"We'll talk about this on the morrow," he told her. "Right now, I'm taking you back to the castle where you belong."

"But what about the others? Shouldn't we be questioning the mayor's council members, or the people who were in the tavern the night of the murder? I think we should try to find out which whore the mayor was with that night and question her as well."

"I told you, I've already spoken to them. Now, I think you should start listening to me, Lady Vivienne, and do as I say. After all, I am the sheriff of this town and I make the decisions, not you."

"All right," she answered, knowing he was still upset that she'd gone over his head by hiring Nairnie. Mayhap she had been a little forceful where that was concerned. But once she heard that the old woman knew the Legendary Bastards of the Crown, she was determined to keep her there. After all, Vivienne was a bastard of King Edward too, even if no one really knew it. She reached out and touched the king's ring she wore hidden under her clothes. Mayhap Nairnie could help her somehow to meet the king and get some answers. Part of her was curious and wanted to someday meet her true father. Vivienne had lots of questions and mayhap by meeting King Edward and understanding her mother's secret, she could finally find those answers she sought. Mayhap not tonight or anytime soon, but hopefully someday her quest would be fulfilled.

Chapter Seven

Zachariah awoke the next morning and dressed for the funeral of the mayor's wife. Even though this case was far from being solved, the corpse needed to be buried. He didn't like attending funerals. It only reminded him of his wife's death a year ago. He'd been avoiding going to the graveyard or taking his daughter there because it was too hard to face the truth.

Making his way downstairs, the scent of something cooking took his interest. To his surprise, Nairnie was already awake and had something bubbling on the hearth. It made his stomach grumble. Starah was sitting at the table, already dressed and eating.

"Sweetheart? You're up early," he said, surprised since Starah had always been a late sleeper.

"Well, what do ye expect?" came Nairnie's voice from the hearth. Her back was toward him and she stirred something in a big pot hanging over the fire. "There is so much to do around here that I can't be sleepin' away the day."

"Good morning to you, too, Nairnie. Something smells delicious. What is it?" He went over to the hearth and tried peeking into the top of the pot, but there was a lid on it. He reached out for it and Nairnie's ladle came down hard atop his hand. "Ow! What did you do that for?" He rubbed his hand.

"It's hot, Sheriff. Ye would have burned yer hand."

"Oh. Thank you." He wiped his palm on his tunic. "I'm not thinking straight yet. I didn't get much sleep last night."

"I'm makin' vegetable pottage for supper but it willna be done for hours yet." She put down her ladle and held out an open hand.

"What?" he asked, eyeing up her palm.

"I'll need money for food. Ye dinna have much to eat in this house and yer daughter needs to stay healthy."

"There's enough food," he assured her. "We don't eat much. Wait until tomorrow when the market opens again in the square, and you can shop then."

She grunted. "Well at least give me money so the poor lass can get a new pair of shoes. She's outgrown the ones she is wearin' and it is goin' to make her toes crooked." Once again, her open palm shot out right under his nose.

Zachariah realized Nairnie was a stubborn wench, much like Vivienne. She also wasn't going to leave him alone until he gave her what she wanted. "Here," he said, pulling a coin from his pouch and handing it to her.

She looked at the lone coin and frowned. "That might get her a pair of wooden pattens if she's lucky, but I doubt it." She sighed loudly. "I guess I'll have to see if I can make a deal with the cordwainer. How about an advance on my pay?"

"An advance? I never said anything about that."

"Ye never said anythin' about what I'll be paid either," she so blatantly reminded him.

"That's right. I guess I didn't."

"Two shillin's a week should be fine, startin' with half of that right now."

"What? Nay. That is too much. I was only paying Mrs. Dorson half that amount to watch her."

"I canna even live in poverty at that rate."

"I'm not a noble, so how much do you think I can really pay you?"

"Two shillin's a week." Still, her open palm stayed under his nose.

"You are getting your meals, as well as a roof over your head, and a place to sleep. One shilling is quite sufficient."

"Hrmph! Then mayhap this arrangement isna goin' to work after all. Perhaps ye should get the constable's wife to watch the child instead. I dinna work for less than two shillin's a week."

He couldn't ask the constable's wife to watch Starah again since Mrs. Dorson was already too busy with her own three children. Plus, Starah didn't like being there and proved it by running away from the woman. He released a deep breath and reluctantly handed over a shilling. "All right, but half now and the other half at the end of the week."

"Thank ye!" Nairnie snapped her hand closed. "What are yer plans for the day, Sheriff Fitch?" She walked over to another pot sitting by the hearth and scooped out some porridge and handed him the bowl and then a spoon. The scent of cinnamon wafted up through the air. Plus, he saw bilberries half-hidden in the porridge. This was the way his wife used to make it. Pleased, he sat down with the bowl of food and started eating.

"I'm not used to having to report my plans for the day to anyone." He scooped up a big spoonful of porridge and devoured it, licking his lips afterward.

"If I'm goin' to be watchin' the lass and also tendin' to yer needs, then I'll require a schedule."

A schedule? Really? He couldn't believe this woman, but decided not to stir the pot of trouble any more. He had a big day ahead of him and just wanted to eat right now in peace.

"For starters, I'm going to the funeral for the murdered woman." He continued to eat, noticing Starah looking at something under the table. "I'll collect Lady Vivienne and we'll go, then stop by to question some of the council members, I suppose. Starah, what are you doing?"

"Nothing." His daughter's head snapped up and she looked as guilty as all hell.

"You're lying to me and I don't like that."

"Why would ye think the lass is lyin'?" asked Nairnie from the other side of the room.

"Because, I'm a sheriff and I know when someone is lying to me. Just like my daughter is doing right now." He leaned over and looked under the table to find the rat-catcher's cat sitting there licking her lips. The animal blinked her two-toned eyes and meowed softly. "What's this?"

"Her name is Midnight, Father," said Starah. "She's my new pet."

"Nay, she's not." He grabbed the cat by the scruff of the neck and hurried over and threw her out the door. The cat screeched and ran away.

"Why did you do that to Midnight?" Starah shouted at him.

"Because that is not your cat and she cannot stay here. I don't want to see her in our house again. Do you understand?" He sat down and continued eating.

"But Midnight likes me. We're friends." Tears formed in Starah's eyes, tugging at his heartstrings. Still, he couldn't have that cat in his house. It would only bring bad luck and lots of trouble.

"She only likes you because you feed her. Besides, black cats are cursed and usually belong to witches. We don't want her here, believe me."

"Ah, so ye're superstitious and afraid of a harmless cat, I

see," said Nairnie with a soft chuckle. This woman was starting to irritate him.

"Nay, I'm not superstitious. Not really." He supposed he was, but didn't want to admit it. "And I'm surely not afraid of anything." He finished off his porridge and threw the spoon down into the empty bowl.

"Then prove it. Let yer daughter keep the cat. Midnight seems to be a stray, so what does it matter since the cat makes her happy?" Nairnie continued.

"She's not a stray! She belongs to the rat-catcher and I don't want trouble when he comes looking for her." He pushed up from the table, already aggravated for the day, heading for the door.

"Ah, so she's a workin' cat then, I see."

"Nay, she's not. The dang thing doesn't seem to be any good at catching rats," he added under his breath, remembering how angry the Pied Piper was with the cat but pleased with his ferrets doing their job.

"Father, can I come with you to the funeral?" asked Starah, making him stop in his tracks.

"Why would you want to do that?" he asked without even turning around.

"Because I want to visit Mother. We never visit her in the graveyard."

Zachariah squeezed his eyes closed, not wanting to disappoint his daughter, but still not ready to accept the fact that neither of them would ever see Margaret again. He dealt with death a lot as sheriff, but this was different. The death of his wife was harder for him to accept. Taking his daughter to the gravesite was even more difficult for him. The day of his wife's funeral, trying to comfort his child as she cried for her mother was the hardest thing he'd ever had to do. Dammit, he had enough stress right now and didn't need this in his life too.

"Not today," he said softly.

"Then when?" his daughter pressed him for an answer.

"Aye, when?" echoed Nairnie. "It is important for the lass to visit her late mother's grave."

"Soon," was all he said, hurrying out the door. God's eyes, would this ever get any easier?

LADY VIVIENNE STOOD at Zachariah's side as the gravediggers lowered the coffin of Florence into the ground at the graveyard of St. Peter's Church at the far end of town. The priest said a quick prayer and gave a blessing. It was drizzling out, and there weren't many people attending the funeral today, probably not wanting to get wet in the approaching storm. Grunt was sitting under a tree, not liking the rain either.

Vivienne noticed Maleine clinging to her father. The girl wept bitterly. Her father looked more upset than usual, probably finally coming to terms that his wife had been murdered. His face remained stoic with his mouth turned down into a frown. Constable Dorson was there as well as a small group of men whom she guessed to be the mayor's council members.

The service ended abruptly as lightning flashed through the sky, followed by a low rumble in the distance. The gravediggers quickly shoveled dirt over the coffin as the rain started to fall even faster. Everyone began to walk away.

"Sheriff, we need to question those men," Vivienne told him, not wanting the council members to leave.

"Aye," he answered, his eyes focused on the coffin. Zachariah seemed irritable this morning. He didn't talk much and neither did he discuss the murder case at all. That truly concerned her. The sheriff usually could think of nothing else when he was investigating a case. Then she noticed his eyes flash over to a nearby tombstone. When she looked in that direction, she realized it was the grave of his wife, Margaret. Now things made sense to her. He was still in mourning and having a hard time with Margaret's death. She felt his pain. Vivienne knew better than anyone, the void left by the death of a loved one.

"Mayhap you'd like to visit Margaret's gravesite? I'll detain the council members and let them know we need to question them." She hurried off before he could object. Vivienne paused only for a quick stop to pay her regards to the mayor and his daughter. "I am so sorry for your loss," she told them, laying her hand on Maleine's shoulder. The poor girl was so upset that her entire body shook.

"Lady Vivienne, please find my mother's murderer," begged Maleine. "I want the person who did this to her to be punished."

"That's exactly what we're going to do," said Zachariah, brushing past them, flagging down the men on the mayor's council.

"What is the sheriff doing?" The mayor stretched his neck in the direction that Zachariah had taken.

"Those are your council members, are they not?" she asked him.

"Aye. So?"

"We need to question them about the night of your wife's murder."

"I see." His gaze stayed focused on the men. "I suppose I'd better be present for this. After all, they are my council." He started to step away, but Vivienne stopped him.

"Nay, Mayor. We'll talk with your council. It is more important that you stay with Maleine right now. After all, her mother just died and she needs you. This is a hard time for her."

"Of course. I understand that," he told her. "But Florence wasn't even her mother."

"What do you mean?" she asked.

"It's true, my lady. My mother died when I was a baby," answered Maleine, wiping her tears with a small hand cloth but not the one she'd had embroidered with her mother's initials. That one she wore looped through her belt. "Florence was my stepmother. However, she is still the only mother I ever really knew since my own mother died when I was very young."

"Oh, I'm sorry," said Vivienne, bothered by the fact that the mayor would even bring that up at a time like this. He didn't seem to be a very considerate man.

"We need to get out of the rain," the mayor told them.

"Yes, Father. Let's go home." Maleine held tightly to her father's arm, keeping him from following Zachariah and the council members as the sheriff and the men headed toward the church.

"Lady Vivienne, you'll let me know what my council members say, won't you?"

"Of course, Mayor," she answered, not wanting to point out right now that it was private information since the men were suspects and she and the sheriff were in the middle of an investigation. If she told him this, she was afraid that the mayor would never leave. She didn't want Maleine to have to be alone right now.

"I'm pretty sure that none of the council would have murdered my wife," the mayor insisted. "They work for me. We are friends. However, I'm more than sure it was done by that rat-catcher. He needs to be caught and put behind bars before he goes after someone else."

"Why would he do that? I mean, if he was the murderer?" she asked.

"He's a damned rat-catcher from Rotten Row and cannot be trusted, that's why."

"Has he given you any reason not to trust him?" she asked.

"He murdered my wife! Isn't that reason enough?"

Maleine started crying harder. Vivienne wanted to comfort her as much as she could. "Everything will be all right," she told her, brushing a wet strand of hair from Maleine's eyes. "I promise you, the sheriff and I will find your mother's murderer and justice will be served. I won't stop searching until we have our answers."

"Thank you," said Maleine with a sniffle. "That's all we want. Right, Father?" She looked up at her father who actually reached out to give her a hug.

"Yes, of course, Maleine. We want justice to be served, and that rat-catcher punished for killing Florence."

It wasn't an ideal place to question the suspects, but since it was raining, Zachariah called the councilmen into the sacristy of the church. The town's priest, Father Francis didn't like the idea, so Zachariah decided to talk to all the councilmen at the same time in order to make the questioning go faster.

"Councilmen, this is Lady Vivienne Harlowe who is helping me to investigate the murder of the mayor's wife, Florence," Zachariah introduced her. Vivienne's dog scurried under a table and lay down.

"It was murder then? Really?" asked one of the men.

"Yes," he answered.

"Are we suspects?" asked another man.

"We just want to ask some questions about your where-abouts the night of the murder. I know you've already been through this but it is for Lady Vivienne's sake. Can each of you state your name and position on the town council."

"Sheriff, is this really necessary?" complained one of the men whom Vivienne recognized. "You know us all."

"Like I said, it is for the sake of Lady Vivienne. Why don't you start, Burchard?"

"I am Burchard the bailiff, and Lady Vivienne already knows me since I work for her uncle." Burchard was a married man with several children.

Vivienne knew the bailiff well. While he lived in the town, he collected rents for her uncle. The man was good at his job but he did have an explosive nature about him.

"Yes, I know you, Burchard, thank you," she said with a nod. "What about you?" she asked a handsome, younger man sitting next to Burchard.

"I am Elias, my lady. I will tell you anything you want to know." He answered with respect. She liked that. His smile put her at ease.

"What exactly is your job, on the council, Elias?" she asked with curiosity.

"I am the market inspector, my lady."

"Market inspector," she repeated. "Tell me what your job entails. I am not familiar with this position."

"It is my job to maintain order within the market," he explained. "I oversee everything and ensure the quality of the goods being sold. I settle disputes between buyers and sellers, check weights and measurements, and ensure fair trade and price controls."

"My, that sounds like a very important job. You have many responsibilities."

"I do my best, my lady. Thank you."

"I'm Hammond, the town's chamberlain," said the ruddy-looking man next to him. He had oily hair and his clothes weren't as clean or unwrinkled as the market inspector's.

"And your responsibility is what?" she asked.

Hammond made a sour face and looked over at Zachariah. "Sheriff, this is nonsense. Everyone knows what a chamberlain does."

"Just answer the question please, Hammond."

Shaking his head, Hammond told her. "I manage the town's finances, including collecting and disbursing funds. Are you satisfied now?"

"Hammond, please just cooperate. It'll be over with soon," said the sheriff.

"What about you?" Vivienne asked a small man with thinning hair who had remained quiet this entire time. "Who are you and what position do you hold on the town council?"

"I am the town clerk. I keep official records and documents for the town," he answered softly.

"Your name?" she prompted him since he didn't seem to be in much of a sharing mood.

His eyebrows raised and his gaze flashed over to the sheriff and then back to her. He seemed shifty. She didn't like that. "Maurice?" he said.

"Are you asking me or telling me?" She thought the man reminded her a lot of a mouse. Or mayhap one of the rats being hunted down by the Pied Piper.

"Maurice. My name's Maurice, my lady," he said, not able to meet her gaze.

"All four of you were at the town council meeting with the mayor the night of the murder, is this correct?" Zachariah paced back and forth in the small room. It was Vivienne's opinion that he was still disturbed about something. That is, something that had nothing to do with the murder.

"Aye," three of the men answered. Maurice just nodded but remained silent.

"What time did the meeting end?" asked Vivienne.

The men looked at each other and finally Burchard answered. "It was about nine o'clock, my lady."

"Where did each of you go after the meeting?" she continued.

Once again they looked at each other. This time, Hammond answered.

"We went to the tavern for a drink. Like we usually do after the town meetings."

"They were all inside the tavern when we found Florence's body," Zachariah told her softly. "You remember. We saw them when we walked through."

"What about the mayor? I don't remember seeing him there that night." She knew that the mayor was up in the whore's bed, but wanted to see if the men would mention this.

"He wasn't there," said Elias, touching his nose, which was a sure sign that the man was lying.

"I see," she answered. "The mayor went up to the rooms above the tavern to spend time with one of the working women. Didn't he?"

The men all mumbled and shrugged but didn't answer.

"The mayor already told us this, so none of you need to be afraid to mention it," said Zachariah.

"Aye, he did," said Burchard. "He left us and went up to the second floor like he does often."

"Yes," said Elias. "That's what happened."

"That's right," Hammond added.

Maurice said nothing, just nodded silently.

"Does he normally spend a good amount of time up there?" she asked.

"Aye," said Hammond. "Sometimes an hour, and other times it seems like half the night."

"He does like the working girls," added Burchard.

"What was the name of the whore who the mayor spent

time with that night?" asked Vivienne, but none of the men would tell her. She glanced over to Zachariah for help.

"If any of you know, you need to speak up. If not, you are withholding information and that could be punishable by law."

"Joy," said the mouse, Maurice.

"Pardon me?" asked Vivienne.

"His favorite, as well as most men's favorite is Joy."

The room became so quiet that she could hear Grunt breathing from his spot on the floor. Vivienne felt as if mayhap the church wasn't a good place to be talking about prostitutes. Especially if Father Francis was listening, which she was sure he was. She'd seen him from the corner of her eye lurking just outside the open door. She decided she'd better move on to a different question.

"Did any of you see that rat-catcher called the Pied Piper that night?"

"Aye, of course we did," said Burchard.

"He's been walking the streets with his assistant every night," added Elias.

"It's his job to catch rats," Hammond explained. "Where else would he be?"

"Was he near the tavern the night of the murder?"

"Aye. He and that odd boy who works with him were outside the entrance when we arrived," Elias told her.

"The Pied Piper is trouble, I tell you," Burchard ground out. "He looked like he wanted to kill someone that night, I swear he did. I wouldn't be surprised if he was the one who did away with poor Florence."

"Would the Pied Piper have had a reason to kill the mayor's wife?"

"How in the name of the devil would we know?" asked Hammond.

"The man's a killer," spat Burchard. "Once he gets going

swinging his dagger and axe, there is no telling if he'll be able to stop."

"I agree," said Elias. "It seems suspicious that he was right near where the body was found. He did it!"

"No one needs to point fingers at anyone, and I'll thank you all to leave the accusations to me and Lady Vivienne," said the sheriff.

"I do appreciate your thoughts. From all of you," said Vivienne, thinking that Maurice was the only one who didn't seem to be much help at all. Other than telling her the name of the whore, which none of the others seemed to want to do.

"Thank you, men. I think that'll be all for now," said the sheriff as thunder boomed overhead and the rain pelted down outside.

The men all got up to leave, but Vivienne wasn't quite finished asking questions.

"Did any of you know Florence personally?"

They looked at each other again and finally Burchard spoke up. "We all did, Lady Vivienne. After all, she was the mayor's wife so why wouldn't we?"

"That's right," said Hammond. "Everyone in town knows each other."

"Did Florence seem like the type of woman who would go out at night by herself? Especially to Rotten Row?" Vivienne tried her best to get some kind of new information before the men left.

"Why do you ask that?" Hammond sniffed and looked at the ground. "Are you insinuating she was doing something illicit?"

"Nay. Not at all," gasped Vivienne. "Of course not. I only wondered why she was at the tavern in the first place."

"She means that no woman would go out at night alone to Rotten Row unless she was a whore." This came from Burchard.

"Nay! She wasn't," Maurice finally spoke up. "Florence was

a kind woman and you are all insulting her character," he defended her.

"Aye, he's right," said Elias. "May she rest in peace."

"Lady Vivienne is only asking since that is where the body was found. No one is calling Florence a whore," said Zachariah, trying to maintain peace. "We are only striving to justify the reason why Florence was even at the tavern in the alley that night, that's all."

Lightning flashed and thunder crashed in the sky again, so loud and near that it caused Vivienne to jump. Grunt whined and ran across the room, hiding behind some of the priest's hanging vestments.

"All right, that's enough for today," said Zachariah, his eyes focused out the door. "If we have more questions for any of you, you'll be notified. Thank you all for your time and cooperation. You are free to leave now."

The councilmen wasted no time in rushing out the door, even though it was pouring rain outside.

"Are you finished, Sheriff?" Father Francis stuck his head into the room, having been standing nearby listening as Vivienne knew he'd been. "I'd like to close up the sacristy now. Plus, I need to go write my sermon for Sunday."

"Aye, thank you, Father," said the sheriff, his attention once more on the storm. "We were just leaving. You have been very accommodating." He headed to the door and Vivienne started to follow.

"Yes, thank you, Father Francis," she called back over her shoulder, lifting the hood of her cloak to cover her head from the rain. "Grunt," she called out. "Come on, Grunt. Where are you?"

The sheriff stepped out into the pouring rain, but she didn't follow.

"Sheriff, don't you think it would be better if we waited inside the church until the rain let up?"

"Nay, I need to get home. If you want to stay here, feel free to do so. Starah doesn't like storms. I should be there for her."

"I understand," she said, watching his gaze roam over to the graveyard once more. She thought he might like time alone with his daughter since he seemed so distressed today. "I'm going to stay dry inside the church for a little while until the rain lets up. Besides, Grunt is afraid of storms too and he's not listening to me. I will meet up with you at your home in a little while."

"Whatever you want," he said, quickly mounting his horse and taking off at a gallop, not even bothering to say goodbye to her.

"My lady?" Father Francis approached her. "Would you like to wait inside the church until the rain stops?"

"Yes, Father, that would be nice. Besides, I don't think I can even drag my dog outside in the storm right now."

"Your hound is right here," he said, nodding to Grunt who sat right behind her, not doing a thing to leave the church. "I've closed up the sacristy, but ask you to please make sure the door to the church is closed securely when you leave."

"Of course, I will. Thank you so much." Vivienne stood there for a few minutes enjoying watching the rain fall as Father Francis left the church and headed home. The thunder and lightning had subsided a little, but the storm was far from over. Something about watching the rain come down seemed peaceful to her. It was nice since she usually felt unsettled to her very core after the horrible trauma she had been through with her family. Seeing the graveyard also brought thoughts of her parents' deaths rising to the surface once again.

The sky remained dark and the rain continued to fall. Vivienne sat down on the stoop in the open doorway of the church to wait it out. She was able to watch the rain and yet stay protected from getting wet this way. Grunt came slinking out of the shadows and lay down next to her, putting his nose between his paws. He looked up at her with big, sad eyes.

"Don't worry, Grunt, the rain will stop soon. Then you'll be able to go out and play." She ran her hand through his fur and then leaned over and kissed her dog on the head. Grunt made a grunting sound, causing her to laugh aloud. This is why she'd named the dog this to begin with.

Vivienne suddenly felt a chill run up her spine and her body stiffened. She had the odd feeling that someone or something was watching her. When she turned to look outside, she looked past her horse to the graveyard where a slight movement caught her eye. She blinked, thinking she was going mad, but she thought she saw a white, ghostly-looking figure floating among the tombstones. The spirit seemed to be wearing a long cloak. At the top of his head his hair seemed to be shaped into a tonsure, like a monk. She couldn't see a face but the ghost lifted his arm and seemed to be calling her over to him. Almost as if he wanted her to follow. Even Grunt picked up his head and, with focused attention, watched in silence.

"Do you see him too, Grunt? I'm not imagining him, am I?"

The dog whined and stood up as the ghostly figure dissipated and faded away. The rain was letting up now and all she wanted was to get out of here. She left the building with her dog, closing the door of the church behind her. Once again, chills ran up her spine. Something wasn't right here. She needed to leave at once.

"Come on, Grunt. Let's go to the sheriff's house. I'm getting a bad feeling staying here." She was about to mount her steed when Grunt took off at a run after something. She thought at first he was chasing down the ghost they'd seen, but then she saw a black blur dart behind a standing tombstone. Something told her it must be the rat-catcher's cat again. "Grunt, get back here," she shouted, but the dog disappeared, taking off into the graveyard. Not wanting to bring the horse into the graveyard for fear the animal might step on something the wrong way and go lame, she decided to head after her hound on foot. "Grunt, let's go!" she called out, noticing the clouds overhead turning black now. Before she knew it, the sky opened up and even more rain came barreling down upon her. A light steam or perhaps a fog started to rise up from the ground, making her feel even more uneasy. It was getting hard to see anything now. She started regretting not leaving with the sheriff earlier after all. "Grunt, where are you? Please. I want to go."

She thought she heard her hound barking and headed slowly in that direction, no longer able to even see much through the thick fog. This was crazy! The graveyard was the last place she wanted to be right now, but she wouldn't leave without her dog. Lightning flashed through the sky, illuminating the fog and enabling her to see the silhouette of someone standing near a tombstone up ahead. She stopped in her tracks and her heart jumped into her throat. As the fog parted a little, she could see the silhouette of a man in a long cloak. And he was carrying a staff. There was no doubt in her mind now that it was the Pied Piper. Then he turned and quickly disappeared in the fog.

Grunt came running over from the opposite side of the graveyard to chase the man, barking furiously. She ran up to intervene.

"Come here, Grunt! Right now. Get over here." She tried to head off her hound. The dog stopped and turned around and looked at her in question. Then, to her relief, he ran to her and sat down at her feet. "Good boy." Vivienne dropped to her knees, hugging Grunt, thankful that the Pied Piper hadn't hurt him. Rain continued to fall, soaking her to the skin. Then Grunt whined and with his tail between his legs walked around one of the gravestones just up ahead where she'd seen the figure of the man.

She got up to follow him. "Oh, no, you don't! We are leaving right now." She walked over to her dog, realizing he'd led her right to the fresh grave of the mayor's wife. Looking down to the ground, she opened her mouth and let out a blood-curling scream.

Chapter Eight

Vivienne turned to run and bumped right into someone. She glanced up to see a man covered head to toe in a long cloak. Once again, she screamed. "Nay! Leave me alone!" she cried, banging her fists against the man's chest, thinking it was the Pied Piper coming to kill her. "Don't hurt me!" she cried.

"Vivienne, for heaven's sake it's just me. What is wrong with you?"

Zachariah. At once, she stopped pounding her fists against his chest and looked up at him. He pushed back his hood to reveal his identity. Thanks be he was here.

"Oh, Zachariah!" She fell into his arms, her body trembling.

"I came back to get you," he told her. "I wasn't thinking straight this morning and never should have left you here alone."

"I saw a ghostly figure in the graveyard," she blurted out. "He looked like a monk and he was summoning me. Grunt saw him too," she told him.

"Shhhh," he said, pulling her against his chest, wrapping his arms around her in a protective manner. Normally she wouldn't allow him to do this. But right now, it was exactly what she wanted and needed.

"Grunt ran after the ghost and I followed. That's when I saw the Pied Piper."

"Vivienne, first of all, there is no such thing as a ghost. Second, the Pied Piper doesn't even come to town until the sun sets. You must have been imagining things."

"Nay, I wasn't. Grunt saw them too."

"Sometimes our minds play tricks on us. Especially during a storm."

She pushed out of his embrace, frustrated that he was making light of this serious situation. "If you don't believe me, than how do you explain that?" She pointed to the ground atop Florence's grave. There was a huge pile of dead and bloodied rats on the ground. There was even a conglomeration of them with their tails all tied together. Those were still alive and gnawing on each other, trying to get free.

"God's teeth, what the hell is that?"

"It's the work of the Pied Piper, that's what it is," she told him. "See? I told you he was here. I am lucky to be alive right now."

Zachariah hunkered down to inspect the grotesque mess of rats. There had to be at least fifty or more. Vivienne had never seen so many rats, dead or alive, in one place before. Grunt sniffed at the rats and she reached down to grab his collar and pull him away.

"This isn't good," mumbled the sheriff.

"Nay, it isn't," she agreed. "What does it mean?"

"I think someone is trying to leave the mayor a message."

"I think there is no doubt it is the Pied Piper. What are you going to do about it?"

"Nothing for now." He stood up and brushed off his hands.

"Nothing? A killer drops fifty rats atop the grave of the

woman he murdered and you are telling me that you are going to do absolutely nothing about it?"

"Calm down. I will look into it, but later. Right now, it's pouring rain, you're wet and upset. I am going to take you home." He put his arm around her and escorted her back to her horse.

"Come on, Grunt," she called to her dog and he hurried after them.

Zachariah helped her mount her horse and then he took the reins of his horse and tied it to hers. Then he did something she didn't expect at all. He climbed atop her horse with her, wrapping a protective arm around her.

"What are you doing?" she asked.

"Shhhh," came his hot whisper in her ear as he held her tightly. "You are shaking from fear as well as the cold. I cannot let you ride alone. I'm taking you back to my home where you'll sit by the fire and dry off and have some of Nairnie's hot pottage until you feel better."

"How is Starah?" she asked, knowing how frightened his daughter was of storms.

"It's the oddest thing, but I arrived home to discover that Starah was fine. She didn't even seem to mind the storm. Nairnie was telling her stories about falling off a ship into the water and almost drowning before her pirate grandsons pulled her out."

"What?" That made Vivienne laugh. "She was making up stories again, wasn't she?"

"It seems so, but it did wonders so I didn't say a thing. It took Starah's interest so intently that my daughter didn't even hear me walk in."

"Mayhap it is good having Nairnie there after all. No?"

"Perhaps you're right. I suppose I judged the old woman too

quickly," he said, as they traveled slowly atop the horse back to his home with Grunt happily leading the way.

"You go inside and get dry. I'll take the horses to the stable to have the stable hand care for them." Zachariah jumped down from the horse and when he did, his warmth went with him. He helped her to the ground and then headed for the stable across the street while she entered his house with Grunt.

"Hello," she said, opening the door, seeing Nairnie sitting on a chair with her arms around Starah. The little girl was smiling.

"Grunt!" shouted Starah, jumping off the chair and running over to hug Vivienne's dog.

"My lady, ye are soakin' wet," said Nairnie, getting up and grabbing a blanket and heading toward her. "Come to the fire and get warm."

"I'll dry off Grunt," offered Starah.

"Thank you," said Vivienne, her teeth chattering since she was so wet and cold. Her gown felt extremely heavy from all the rain and her shoes squished with every step she took.

"Och, nay, this is no good," said Nairnie. "Come upstairs and I'll find ye somethin' dry to wear."

Vivienne laughed. "Thank you, Nairnie, but I really don't think I'd fit into any of your clothes."

"Stop all the clishmaclaver and listen to me, lass. If ye dinna get dry fast, ye're goin' to become sick and I'll have a hell of a time tryin' to cure ye."

"All right," said Vivienne, not wanting to argue with her. "I'll do as you say."

It took Zachariah longer at the stable than he would have liked, but the only stable hand there had several horses to wipe down and tend to already, so with Vivienne's horse as well, he decided he'd better help out. Finally, he made his way back across the street, sloshing through the puddles, being careful not to slip on the wet cobblestones.

He pushed open the door to find Starah on the floor drying the dog with a hand cloth.

"Where is Lady Vivienne?" he asked, taking off his cloak and shaking off the water and then closing the door and hanging the cloak on a hook.

"Nairnie took her upstairs so she wouldn't get sick," said his daughter.

"What does that mean?" He hurried over to the cook fire on the hearth and leaned over and rubbed his hands together to get warm.

"It means she needed dry clothes and I saw to it," came Nairnie's voice as she came down the stairs with Vivienne right behind her. His jaw dropped when he saw Vivienne wearing one of his late wife's gowns. His stomach clenched and he wasn't sure if he should be pleased, be angry, or ignore it all together. He stood up, his eyes fastened to Vivienne.

"I'm sorry about this, but Nairnie insisted I get out of my wet clothes," Vivienne told him, looking a lot like Margaret in that simple brown dress. But she wasn't Margaret, Vivienne was a lady. She was a noblewoman who shouldn't be wearing the coarse clothes of a mere commoner. He also wasn't sure he wanted to see her in clothes that were once his wife's. Vivienne stopped at the bottom of the stairs and looked up at him with those big blue eyes. He couldn't help noticing her concern as well as her unease. He felt uncomfortable, too. "I shouldn't stay," she told him. "I'm sure my aunt and uncle will be worried about me so I should head home. I'll just get my clothes and leave." She turned to go back upstairs.

Nairnie cleared her throat. When he looked at the old

woman she was giving him that disapproving glare with one of her eyes squinted. Damn, why did she have to do that?

"Nay, it's all right. Please, stay," he told Vivienne.

She turned around, seeming unsure of what to do.

"Come sit by the fire, lass. Have some pottage to warm up," instructed Nairnie. "Both of ye." She pushed a chair up to the edge of the hearth.

"I don't know," said Vivienne. "I really should get back to the castle."

"There's no sense in goin' anywhere until this godawful rain let's up." Nairnie dished out a bowl of pottage and nodded at the chair. "Come, lassie. I dinna have all day to wait."

Zachariah extended his arm to the chair. "Please. I'd like you stay and be my guest."

"Are you sure?" she asked. He couldn't deny noticing the tremble in her voice.

"The horses need a break from the rain too," he told her, walking over and gently guiding her to the chair with his hand resting on her elbow. "Besides, you are pretty shaken by what happened and we should discuss it."

"What happened?" asked Nairnie, handing the bowl of food and a spoon to Vivienne as soon as she was seated.

"Grunt and I saw something in the graveyard that looked like a ... a ghost."

"You saw a ghost? Really?" Starah's eyes opened wide and she hugged the dog closer.

"Nay, it wasn't a ghost, Starah," Zachariah tried to calm his daughter before she started crying. "There are no such things as ghosts."

"Blethers, I wouldna say that's true," said Nairnie, handing a bowl of food to him next. "I mean, I could tell ye stories —"

"Please don't. No more stories for now. He pulled up a wooden stool and seated himself next to Vivienne near the fire.

"Hrmph," sniffed Nairnie. "Whatever ye say, Sheriff."

"Starah, leave the dog alone now and get something to eat please," Zachariah instructed his daughter.

"The lass and I already ate." Nairnie picked up a soup bone from a side table where it seemed to have been placed to cool. "However, I think Grunt might like this."

"Oh, I believe you are right," said Vivienne, blowing on her food and taking a bite.

"Can I give it to him?" Starah jumped up excitedly, and so did the dog.

"Yes, you can," Zachariah told her. "But take it upstairs so I can talk with Lady Vivienne in private about ... about work."

"Yes, Father. Come on, Grunt, this is for you." Starah took the bone from Nairnie and headed toward the stairs.

The dog whined and looked at Vivienne with longing in his eyes.

"Go on, Grunt. It's all right. You deserve it," said Vivienne with a giggle, making Zachariah's heart hurt just a little.

Nairnie busied herself cleaning everything, pretending not to listen, even though he knew she wasn't about to miss a word spoken.

"Why do you think the Pied Piper left those rats on Florence's grave?" asked Vivienne, hunkered under the blanket eating, wearing her dry clothes. Still, her hair was wet and matted down. Blonde strands clung to her neck and chest.

"Ye found dead rats upon a woman's grave?" Nairnie stood up and looked across the room at them.

"Yes, Nairnie, that's right," said Zachariah. "Now, if you don't mind, this is something I need to discuss with Lady Vivienne. Alone. We need to talk about the murder."

"Just pretend I am no' here," she said, throwing her nose in the air and putting her hands on her wide hips. "However, I am good at figurin' things out. Mayhap ye should tell me what ye ken and I'll be able to help too."

"Thank you, but no." Zachariah finished off his pottage and got up and walked across the room handing Nairnie his empty bowl. "Would you like some ale, Lady Vivienne?"

"Aye, that would be nice," she answered.

"Nay, give her some honeyed mead. It's in that leather flask on the table." Nairnie pointed across the room.

His eyes met with Vivienne's and he was sure she was thinking the same thing as he.

"Where did that mead come from, Nairnie?" he asked her.

"I got it from Lady Ravenscar as a present. I was takin' it back home, but since I'm here now, I thought I'd share it with ye two."

"I don't think so," he said. "Lady Vivienne and I will have ale instead."

"What? Why? It is some of the best mead ye'll ever taste. Lady Vivienne, dinna ye want to try it? Ye're a noble and should have somethin' better to drink than just ale."

"Nairnie, thank you, but I think the sheriff and I are both a little hesitant to do so, but it's only because Florence died from drinking honeyed mead laced with arsenic."

"What?" Nairnie never sounded so insulted as right now. "Ye two dinna trust me? Ye think I'm goin' to try to kill ye?"

"Nay, of course not. We didn't say that," Zachariah spoke up.

"Ye didna have to say it. I can read people just like a book." She stormed over to the flask and pulled off the stopper. "If it was poisoned, do ye think I'd do this?" She held up the flask and downed a good amount of mead. Then she smacked her lips together. "Ah, that is good. And since ye two dinna want any, there will be more for me." She replaced the cork on the large leather flask.

"That doesn't prove anything," said Zachariah. "Arsenic poisoning could sometimes take up to several days to kill a person."

"Well, if I'm no' dead in a few days ye'll ken I was tellin' the truth. However, dinna think there will be any mead left by then because there willna be."

"Nairnie, I changed my mind. I think I'd like some of your honeyed mead after all," said Vivienne, making Zachariah wonder if she had lost her mind.

"Lady Vivienne, do you think that's a wise thing to do?" he asked.

"I trust Nairnie, and I want her to know it." Vivienne was going to drink it!

"Yes, but I'm sure there is another way to get your point across." He tried to discourage her reckless action, but to no avail.

"Bring me the flask, Nairnie." Vivienne held out her hand. "After the day I had, I think a good drink of honeyed mead is exactly what I need."

"Gladly, lassie." Nairnie handed the flask to Vivienne, smiling smugly at Zachariah. God's tongue, he prayed the old woman wasn't some kind of crazy killer. He basically knew nothing about her or what she was capable of doing. If anything happened to Vivienne he'd never forgive himself. He wanted to end this, but if he tried to stop Vivienne from drinking the mead again, she'd never forgive him and only want to do it even more to spite him. Nairnie would hate him too. Mayhap it was best to let Vivienne make her own decisions. He decided to trust her judgment regarding Nairnie, mainly because he had no choice. Instead, he would just change the subject. He turned away from Vivienne since he couldn't bear to watch her drinking the mead.

"We don't know that the Pied Piper was the one to leave the

rats on the grave," he said, taking off his wet shoes and placing them close to the fire.

"Who else would do a thing like that?" asked Vivienne. "Unless it was that boy named Wymond."

"Wymond? Who is he?" asked Nairnie, cleaning up as she continued to listen to their conversation.

"Wymond works with the rat-catcher," Vivienne explained. "Mmmm, this really is good mead, Nairnie. Thank you for sharing."

"Of course," she said with a sniff, throwing Zachariah a dirty look. Lately, he felt like an outsider in his own home, and it was all because of women.

"I saw the silhouette of the rat-catcher in the graveyard," said Vivienne. "I think the mayor is right that he's a killer. For some reason the Pied Piper murdered Florence. The rats placed atop her grave prove it."

"I'm not sure," he told her. "It doesn't make any sense. I mean, it sounds as if everyone liked Florence. Why would anyone want to kill her?"

"Mayhap it was done as a message to the mayor," said Nairnie.

"What do you mean?" asked Vivienne, finishing off her pottage.

"I mean, mayhap this rat-catcher has a bone to pick with the mayor about somethin' or another. It could be his way of sendin' a silent message."

"Yes." Zachariah put his hand to his chin in thought. "It could be a warning or a threat. I think we need to find out more about this Pied Piper."

"Another meeting with him?" Vivienne looked terrified.

"I will take Constable Dorson with me to question him tonight. I want you back safe at the castle."

He was sure Vivienne would object. But when she slowly nodded and agreed, he almost fell over.

"Yes, that might be the best for now," she told him. "I've been away from the castle for quite a while and have things to tend to there."

"Then put your shoes on and I'll escort you back to the castle now. I don't hear the rain coming down anymore so it might be a good time to leave," he told her.

"I suppose that would be best." She stood up, still looking quite shaken. If Vivienne was agreeing to go home instead of continuing to help with this investigation, that told him that whatever happened in the graveyard earlier really had her shaken. "Let me get Grunt and then we'll go."

"Aye," he said, glad she wasn't fighting him as usual. Mayhap he could step up this investigation while she was gone because he didn't like seeing Vivienne like this. She shouldn't be inhabiting places like Rotten Row or chasing ghosts in grave-yards and being terrorized by big piles of dead rats. Lady Vivienne was a lady and deserved so much better. Aye, she warranted a much better lifestyle than what she was living lately. She was a noblewoman in a whole different class than he, and should have everything that someone of her status needed or wanted. And definitely much more than he could ever offer.

Chapter Nine

Vivienne tossed and turned all night long and wasn't able to avoid her continuing nightmare ...,

Gripping the hilt of her father's sword with two hands, Vivienne slowly stepped around the front of the wagon, just in time to see a shadowy figure stab her mother with his sword and then throw her body to the ground. Too scared to even speak, she froze. Standing in the dark, fear consumed her, making her feel as if she were in hell.

"Someone's coming. Hurry, let's get out of here," came the voice of another shadowy form atop a horse. The man who stabbed her mother withdrew his sword and headed toward his waiting horse.

"Mother! Nay!" screamed her little brother. Vivienne's head snapped around to see Adrian standing in the hay in the back of the wagon, looking over the edge, terror on his face.

"Dammit. There's someone else," shouted the first bandit to the second.

"Kill him, too," commanded the ruffian's companion. "Leave no witnesses."

The first man rushed over, but Vivienne wasn't about to let

him kill her brother too. Guilt already ate away at her that she wasn't able to save her parents. She stepped out in front of the attacker, wildly swinging her father's sword in the air. Mayhap it was her anger controlling her actions, but somehow she managed to stab the man in his right shoulder with her blade. The tip stuck into his flesh and she was sure she felt the metal meet his bone. Quickly, she pulled the blade back, seeing the blood oozing from the man's wound.

"Aaaaah!" the attacker screamed, one hand gripping at his bleeding shoulder from where Vivienne had struck him.

"Dammit, there's a girl here too," shouted the other man from his horse.

The fighting frightened the horses, causing them to rear up and paw at the air, whinnying loudly. The wagon jerked and her brother fell back in the hay with his feet in the air. Then the horses took off down the road at a run, pulling the wagon along with them. The sound of Vivienne's crying baby from the bench seat inside the basket caused her to panic and become furious all at the same time.

Her baby, her newborn child was gone! She'd only held him briefly and had never even had the chance to give him a name. Grief filled her completely. Her head swarmed with confusion. How could any of this be happening? Who would do such a thing? Why? The deep longing for her baby was so strong that she thought she could hear the little boy crying, but it was only in her mind. Her days of being a mother were suddenly cut short. Her newborn never had the chance to know her. He never even had the chance to live! The cries echoed in her mind, making her think she was going mad.

Vivienne's eyes sprang open to reveal she was at Mablethorpe Castle and in her own bed. Yet, the crying of a baby continued. It was her baby! Her son was frightened and needed her. It wasn't a dream, after all. Hearing the sound coming from outside, she jumped out of bed and ran over to the partially open window. Pulling back the shutters, she frantically searched the courtyard below. Grunt had been sleeping atop her bed and ran to the window and put his front paws up on the edge, peering out into the courtyard with her.

"You hear the crying baby too, don't you, Grunt?" Vivienne's heart beat rapidly with anxiety coursing through her entire body. She wanted her baby! She needed to feel him in her arms again. He was here, and she had to find him and protect him. Then she pinpointed the whereabouts of the crying baby and all hope was dashed in a mere instant. The wet nurse hurried through the courtyard carrying a newborn in her arms. One of the noblewomen who had recently given birth was at her side.

Vivienne's spirits were dashed. She held on to the window, feeling her legs wobbling and also the need to steady herself. Grunt turned and looked at her with concern. Coming to her senses, she realized how silly she'd been. So involved in her nightmare, and so desperate to find her baby and be the mother she should have been to the boy, she let her imagination fool her.

"It's not my baby," she said, reaching out and petting Grunt on the head. "Of course, you wouldn't know him since you haven't been around long enough, but he was the perfect baby, Grunt. He had beautiful blue eyes and a tuft of blond hair. He was also kissed by an angel on the bottom of his foot."

Grunt whined and wagged his tail. "You would have liked my son, Grunt. I think you two would have been good friends. I miss him so much that I'm not sure I will ever be able to stop my heart from hurting."

Someone rapped on her door, sending Grunt running across the room.

"Who is it?" she called out, hurrying over to the door but not opening it.

"It's me, Lady Vivienne," came a small voice from the other side.

"Martin?" She yanked open the door to see the young page boy standing there with a wooden sword in his hand and a big smile on his face. Grunt leaped forward and licked him on the face, causing him to laugh.

"Grunt! I missed you." Martin reached out to pet the dog with his free hand.

"Good morning, Martin. How are you today?" She liked Martin a lot. Ever since he'd come to the castle to be fostered, she had cared for him the way she would have if he had been her own son. She didn't know much about his parents, but from what her aunt told her, Martin's father was mean and often beat him. No child should have to bear that kind of abuse. Neither should any child ever be afraid of their own parent, the way Martin often seemed to be when she mentioned his father.

"I have my own sword now, and Sir Guy is teaching me how to use it." Martin held up the wooden blade proudly.

"Well, that is wonderful news. I'm happy for you," she told him.

"I practiced a lot yesterday when you and Grunt were gone. And I helped Adam take care of the hunting hounds in the new kennels too."

"Just as you should. Thank you, Martin. You are doing an excellent job."

"I missed Grunt," he said again, putting down the sword to hug the dog with both arms. Grunt's tail went crazy with his excitement of seeing Martin. "Were you off hunting the rat king yesterday, Grunt?"

"I think you mean the Pied Piper, Martin."

"Aye, the man who kills rats." He picked up his wooden sword and started swiping it back and forth, making rat noises with his mouth.

"Was there a message for me by any chance?" She figured someone sent him to her door, but he'd been so distracted with his new sword and from seeing the dog that he probably already forgot why he'd come.

"Oh, yes. Lord Mablethorpe wants you to join them down in the great hall for the meal to break the fast."

"Please tell him I am not hungry." She yawned, wishing for more sleep, although she knew she would never get it. "Let him know that I am not done sleeping yet."

"Should I tell Sheriff Fitch that same thing, my lady?"

That woke her up. "The sheriff is here? Now?" She started looking up and down the corridor.

"Aye. He's waiting in the great hall and seems in a hurry to leave."

"What did he say? Did he ask for me?"

"Aye, he wondered where you were," said Martin, using both hands on the sword now, waving it through the air making a figure eight. "Look what I learned to do. Sir Guy said when I get good enough with the wooden sword he'll see to it that I get a real one someday. I can't wait!"

"Yes, that nice, Martin. Now please run down to the great hall and tell the sheriff not to leave without me. I will be there as soon as I dress."

"All right." He looked down at the dog. "Come on, Grunt. You can have some of my food if you want it."

Closing the door, Vivienne ran to the wardrobe to find something to wear. She stopped in her tracks when she spotted the gown hanging over the back of the chair that she'd worn yesterday. The gown of Zachariah's late wife. Damn, she wished she'd never let Nairnie talk her into putting it on. She'd seen the look on Zachariah's face when she'd strolled down the stairs wearing it as if she'd had the right to. She knew the horrible feeling of losing a loved one. He obviously never got over

Margaret's death since he still had her clothes in the house after an entire year. She also didn't miss the fact that he'd kept looking over toward his wife's grave when they were at the funeral for the mayor's wife.

"I'll give it back to him, that's what I'll do," she said to herself. "That should help matters." She quickly folded up the plain brown gown and then headed over to the wardrobe to try to find something to wear that wouldn't remind the sheriff of his wife. Neither did she want to wave the fact under his nose that she was a noble and Margaret was not. "Nay, nay, nay," she said, looking through the gowns hanging in her wardrobe. "Too fancy. Looks too much like his late wife's gown. Too ugly. Too pretty." She discarded each piece of clothing hanging there because this morning nothing seemed to be right. Vivienne looked at one more gown and it happened to be one of her mother's that they'd kept here for when they visited with Aunt Ellen. Reverently touching the soft velvet, she ran her fingers over it, thinking of how much she missed her mother. She wished her mother was there right now since she felt as if she needed a female to talk to about how much she missed her baby, and also how she missed the chance of ever being a mother.

"None of these will do," she said with a sigh, realizing that everything was filled with memories and things that hurt her and made her want to forget. Then she spied exactly what she'd wear today. It was something that would make her feel like no other.

～

Zachariah had graciously accepted the meal in the great hall while he waited for Vivienne, not wanting to insult Lord and Lady Mablethorpe even though Nairnie had already fed him this morning, insisting he needed to eat. If he kept this up, he wouldn't fit in his breeches much longer. His eyes roamed over to the corridor again, wishing Vivienne would hurry. He had a lot of work to do and she was only slowing him down. He saw Martin and Grunt enter the great hall but still no Vivienne.

"Hello, Sheriff. How are you this fine morning?"

Zachariah looked up from his trencher to see Leif, the travelling musician, standing there with his lute.

"Good morning, Leif. I'm fine. The question is, how are you feeling?"

"I'm feeling much better. The healer says I'll be back to normal soon." Leif touched his side where he'd been stabbed recently during the sheriff's last murder investigation. "Would you like to hear a new song I wrote?" Before Zachariah could answer, the boy started plucking the strings on his lute and singing.

"More ale, Sheriff?"

He looked up to see the kitchen maid, Maria, refilling his drink. "Yes. Thank you," he told her, holding out his cup to be refilled.

"Cook says you should come back to the castle later tonight. He's making his famous lamb in mint gravy. Lady Vivienne told us that is one of your favorite meals."

"Tell Cook I appreciate the thought, but I am very busy with investigating a murder in town and won't be able to make it."

"There are lots of rats in town," said Martin, walking up to join them with Grunt at his side. The page boy held a crust of bread, chewing as he spoke. "The Pied Piper tries to catch the rats, but I heard he really steals the souls of children." Grunt whined. Martin tossed him the crust of bread. The dog's jaws snapped, and he swallowed down the crust after a quick chew, proceeding to lick his lips.

"Stop saying that, Martin. It's not true," Zachariah told him.

"No one is stealing the souls of children. That is just gossip made up to frighten everyone and nothing else." Zachariah picked up his cup to take a drink.

"This man sounds very scary." Maria's hand went to her pregnant belly. "Cook and I surely wouldn't want our child near the man. I'm so glad we are protected in the castle."

"Good morning," came Vivienne's sing-song voice from behind him, and not a moment too soon. He didn't like this conversation and where it was leading. He wanted to leave before these nonsensical stories grew out of control.

"Thank goodness you are here," he said into his cup, turning to face Vivienne. His eyes opened wide and he spit ale in a stream from his mouth. "What in God's name are you wearing?"

Vivienne stood there dressed like a man. She wore breeches, boots up to her knees, and an oversized tunic with sleeves rolled up since they were much too long. She even wore a quilted gambeson over the ensemble that was meant for a man. It made her look ridiculous and as if she were drowning in those clothes. Her hair was actually braided and wound up, pinned to her head. She had a sword as well as a dagger attached to her belt and seemed like she was ready to fight anyone who even looked at her cross-eyed. Over the top of it all, she wore her lady's cloak of a purple hue, that only made it even more confusing and made her seem as if she were losing her mind.

"I'd like to return your wife's gown to you." She handed him Margaret's gown folded into a neat square. "Thank you for the use of it, but I won't be borrowing any more of her clothes."

"I see." He stood up with the gown tucked under his arm. Leif plucked his lute and wandered across the room, singing to the nobles. "Why not?" he asked her, not disappointed in the least, but just wanting to hear her reasoning.

"I know how hard it must have been for you to see me in

Margaret's gown. I'm sorry about that, but Nairnie insisted I get dried off from the rain."

"Nairnie does have quite a way about her that makes it hard to say *no*."

"I'm glad you understand." She flashed him a quick smile, looking a little more like herself, but only for a second.

"Why don't you get something to eat and we'll be on our way? I have a full day of investigating planned," he told her. "Plus, I have other duties as sheriff that cannot be ignored much longer."

"I already ate. I came through the kitchen on my way down here and grabbed some food along the way. I'm ready to go right now, Sheriff." Her smile lit up the room. Even dressed like a man she held all the grace and elegance, as well as beauty of a noblewoman. How the hell she could do that, he didn't know. But it truly impressed him in an odd, twisted way.

"Good God, Vivienne, do you really have to wear those clothes in public?" Her uncle complained as he approached with his wife holding on to his arm.

"Gilbert, please lower your voice," warned Lady Mablethorpe. "You are creating a scene."

"*I'm* creating a scene?" he asked, anger flaring his nostrils. "Ellen, are you blind as to the addled way your niece is dressed? She is the one causing brows to lift, not me."

"I'm quite aware of Vivienne's attire," said his wife. "I honestly don't see anything wrong with it." She smiled, and Vivienne nodded and smiled back.

"I figured I would blend in better this way while I'm on Rotten Row investigating. I can't very well do that if I'm dressed like a lady."

"You're heading to Rotten Row?" That caused a bigger stir with her uncle. "Nay. I won't allow it. You are not going anywhere near there, so get that idea out of your head right now."

"I've already been there, Uncle," Vivienne replied calmly. "Besides, we need to return since that is where the mayor's wife was found murdered."

"That is my exact concern," said Lord Mablethorpe.

"Grunt found the corpse on Rotten Row, didn't he?" asked Martin.

"Yes, that's right," she replied. "It was thanks to Grunt that we found the poor woman."

"I want to help you and Grunt today on Rotten Row," offered Martin.

"Nay. That is no place for a child," Zachariah answered for her.

"Why not, Sheriff?" Martin sounded so disappointed. "I have my new sword to fight with, just like you and Lady Vivienne." He raised the wooded sword in the air to show him.

"That's not even a real weapon," spat Zachariah. "Nay. Absolutely not. You'll only get in our way."

"But I have nothing more to do here at the castle for now. Can't I go with you, Lady Vivienne? Please?" begged the page boy.

"What about your chores helping Adam in the kennels?" asked Vivienne.

"I already finished those early this morning."

"Well, I'm sure you have more training as a page to attend to," said Zachariah.

"Finished that already too," answered Martin, holding up his wooden sword once more. "Sheriff Fitch do you want to see how I fight with a sword? I'm good at it."

He chuckled. "I'm sure you are coming along well with your training, and that is another reason you should stay here. Sir Guy might want to teach you more."

"Nay, he won't," said Martin. "Sir Guy and his squire left an hour ago to go serve his required time fighting for King Edward."

"Is that right?" Vivienne looked over at her aunt and uncle.

"Aye," Lord Mablethorpe confirmed it. "All knights need to take their turn putting in time for the king. Sir Guy and his squire won't be returning to Mablethorpe for at least a few weeks."

"See?" said Martin. "Mayhap I can train with Lady Vivienne until they return. She can wield a sword better than most of the knights anyway."

"Martin! Please don't say that," scolded Vivienne, her gaze flitting over to her uncle, waiting for him to explode.

Just when she was sure her uncle would be angry again, her aunt spoke up, stopping him from saying a thing.

"I will watch Martin until they return," offered Lady Mablethorpe.

"Nay! You are lady of the castle and it is unheard of to be tending to a page boy," snapped Lord Mablethorpe. "I'll send a missive to his parents and have him taken back to his home until Sir Guy's return."

"Nay!" cried Martin. "Please, don't do that. My father will be angry and think I did something wrong. He'll beat me again." His worried eyes turned to Vivienne. "Please, my lady. Don't let Lord Mablethorpe send me home. I'm so scared of my father."

Vivienne looked over at Zachariah for help.

Zachariah cleared his throat. "I suppose Martin could stay with me for a few weeks. I mean, until his training can be resumed." Vivienne smiled and nodded at him, thankful for his help in this matter.

"Stay with you? Hah!" Lord Mablethorpe made a sour face.

"Sheriff, do you really think a nobleman is going to agree to have his son staying in town with a commoner?"

"Why not? I think it's a grand idea," said his wife. "However, it would be best if Martin just went there during the day and came back to the castle to sleep each night where he is safe. We wouldn't want anything to happen to him since we are responsible for the boy while he's here."

"Yes! I want to show Starah how I can protect her from the Pied Piper with my new sword." Martin waved his wooden sword through the air. Vivienne reached out and took it from him.

"Martin, this might be made of wood, but it isn't a toy," she told him. "It is a symbol of a weapon and you need to treat it with respect."

"That's right," agreed Zachariah. "Real swords are sharp and can kill people."

"I'll be careful. Please give it back to me." Martin held out both hands.

"Well, I suppose so." She handed it to him and he carefully took it from her, sticking it through his belt. Grunt sniffed it curiously.

"Careful, Grunt. It's not a toy," Martin told the dog. It was precious watching Martin's enthusiasm. He was normally a very happy boy. But whenever his father was mentioned, he became fearful. Now, Vivienne understood why. It made her wonder about Martin's home life. It couldn't be easy living with an abusive father. No child should have to endure that.

"I think it's a good idea for Martin to stay with the sheriff and his daughter during the day," Vivienne spoke up. "Starah is on edge because of all the stories of the Pied Piper. Having Martin there will make her feel comfortable, I'm sure. Besides, Sheriff Fitch has a nursemaid now. Nairnie will keep a close eye on the children, even when the sheriff is away working."

"What about the boy's parents? What am I going to tell them?" grumbled Vivienne's uncle.

"We won't tell them a thing," Lady Mablethorpe said, lifting her chin in the air. "As far as they know, Martin's training isn't paused at all. Besides, Martin will return at the end of each day, so it isn't as if we'll be lying."

"Nay. I don't like that idea," protested Lord Mablethorpe. "If Lord Collingham finds out I'm deceiving him regarding his son, it'll only cause trouble for me."

"Then mayhap you can find Martin another knight to train with until Sir Guy's return," suggested Vivienne.

"Nay, I need every knight's attention right now. I am starting a new training session for the tournament I will be hosting soon." It seemed her uncle was already planning another event. Why should that surprise her?

"A tournament? Here, at Mablethorpe Castle?" asked Vivienne. This was the first she'd heard of his plans and she couldn't say it disappointed her in the least. Even though she didn't like all her uncle's grand gatherings, this was different. She had never attended a tournament competition before but always wanted to do so. There would be knights from near and far coming to compete. She adored watching the joust as well as the hand-to-hand combat, sparring with swords. The whole idea was exciting to her.

"Aye," said her uncle. "I have been planning to host a tournament for a while now and word about it has carried all the way to the king. This morning, the king's messenger arrived here with a missive for me."

"The king sent you a missive?" Vivienne's heart sped up at hearing this. "What did it say?"

"It said that King Edward has chosen to visit during the tournament at Mablethorpe Castle. It seems since his son, the Black Prince, has been sickly and is now an invalid, that Edward is trying to make more of a presence among his lords. Apparently, his son's absence has upset everyone."

"When will this tournament take place?" asked the sheriff.

"It'll be happening in a month or two," Lord Mablethorpe answered. "Mayhap sooner. It will take me some time to send out invitations and plan a tournament fit for a king, but I will have an actual date soon."

"Uncle, that has to be very expensive to host such an elaborate event. How will you fund it?" asked Vivienne.

"It's no problem, Vivienne. The king offered to pay for it, so there are no limits to how grand this tournament is going to be." Vivienne watched her uncle's face light up with pride. And greed. She knew him too well to think he'd be anything but extravagant since it wasn't his money being used to pay for it.

"How exciting." Vivienne's hand went to her chest where she wore the king's ring hidden under her tunic. It was her birth father's ring that her mother gave her just before she died. The ring of King Edward. Mayhap she'd have a chance to actually meet the king and to tell him that she was his daughter. The thought overwhelmed her. But since King Edward had found enough favor with her mother to make her his mistress at one time, then mayhap he'd find it in his heart to help Vivienne find her mother's murderer.

"Lady Vivienne, we really need to go," said the sheriff, dragging her from her daydreams.

"Yes, of course. I'm ready to leave." Right now, she decided she needed to forget about the king and the tournament. Her job was to focus and find Florence's murderer. Thinking about her mother and the king was only going to distract her.

"So, can I stay with the sheriff and Starah?" asked Martin with hope showing in his big blue eyes.

"I don't see why not, but only during the day as Lady Mablethorpe suggested." Vivienne didn't even look at her uncle when she answered. She took control of the situation like she usually did, because in her mind it was the right thing to do. If her uncle didn't start adamantly objecting, all would be fine. Besides, she had Aunt Ellen there to support her. "Martin, you have been working hard and deserve this. You are going to be taking a short respite from work, and taking some time to have a little fun."

"Yay!" shouted the boy, waving his arms in the air, happy like any child would be to be able to play instead of tending to his chores.

"Vivienne, can you assure me that it'll be safe for Martin to stay in town during the day?" Her aunt might be on her side but she was always prone to worry.

"Of course it will be safe, Aunt Ellen. Martin will be staying with the sheriff. He'll also be watched over by the nursemaid, Nairnie. I hear stories that Nairnie can wield a mean ladle." She giggled at the thought. "I assure you that everything will be fine. After all, what on earth could possibly happen?"

Chapter Ten

After leaving Martin at the sheriff's house with Starah and Nairnie, Vivienne and Zachariah rode their horses through the streets of town on their way to Rotten Row.

"I think you should really close the town gates at night," she told Zachariah. "With the murder that happened, it might be a good thing to consider."

"I told you, the gates are being repaired. Besides, if it was an intruder who murdered Florence, then you might have a point," he answered. "However, if the killer is already inside the town walls, which I believe is the case, what does it matter?"

"If that's true, wouldn't you want to keep the killer here so he can't escape?"

"What makes you think the murderer hasn't already left? Or that he might leave during the day when the gates are open for anyone to enter? You see, it doesn't matter, Vivienne. Now please stop telling me how to do my job."

"I'm sorry," she apologized. "Sometimes I can't help myself."

"And so I've noticed."

"I suppose there is no real way to control things since the rat-catcher has been hired to do a job here in town."

"And he's not leaving until he's finished his job and been paid."

"Do you want him to leave?"

"I want to find out if he's a murderer before he disappears. Therefore, it is best if he stays in town where I can keep an eye on him."

"I get the feeling the killer is still here." She thought about the Pied Piper again. "We need to expose him and arrest him before he strikes again."

"My sentiments exactly. Did I tell you that I found out from Constable Dorson that the Pied Piper and his assistant, Wymond, are now living right here in town and not sleeping in the woods during the day as I expected."

"Really?"

"Yes. I guess they have been here for days and I didn't even know it."

"Where are they staying?"

"It seems that they've been sleeping at the far end of the church's graveyard. Behind all that unruly brush that needs to be cleared away."

"Does Father Francis know about this?" she asked in surprise.

"He's the one who gave them permission to stay there. He said the rats were getting out of control in the graveyard. If they could take care of the problem, he was happy to give them the yard where they could sleep."

"Then I was right when I told you I saw the Pied Piper in the graveyard. He was the one who left the rats on Florence's grave, just like I said!"

Grunt ran alongside the horses, getting distracted every once in a while to chase a squirrel up a tree.

"Lady Vivienne, I thank you for your kind words earlier at the castle."

"What do you mean?"

"I am talking about when you told Lord and Lady Mablethorpe that you thought it would be good for Martin to stay with me until Sir Guy's return. And that he'd be safe."

"I do think that."

"I know. So do I. It'll be welcome for Starah to have a friend with her. She's not been her happy self ever since the death of her mother. The only thing that seems to make her happy is being around Grunt and Martin."

"I agree," said Vivienne, feeling that she understood exactly what he meant. She'd never been the same since that awful day that her parents were murdered and her brother and baby disappeared. "Everyone deserves some happiness in life, and those children seem to enjoy being together so who are we to stop them?"

He chuckled softly. "Aye, just like us when we were children."

"Yes. I suppose you are right."

Vivienne didn't feel comfortable talking about the relationship between her and Zachariah. She'd been feeling attracted to him lately, and longed to be around him and his daughter. Even with Nairnie there. It confused her since she swore to never marry or want a family again. She didn't want or need any more heartbreaks in her life. By keeping everyone at a distance, it was her way of stopping grief, sadness, and heartbreak from ever finding her again. All she wanted now was to find justice for the death of her parents. But lately, seeing Zachariah and his daughter and being around his family life made her feel even lonelier than she ever had felt before. "Grunt, where are you?" she called out, looking around. The dog had been running alongside them when he suddenly disappeared a minute ago.

"I'm sure he's just off chasing a rabbit or another squirrel," said the sheriff. "I wouldn't worry. Grunt has a good nose and he will find us when he's finished with his exploration."

"I suppose you're right." Vivienne took in her surroundings as they turned a corner and headed for the low part of town. 'Rotten Row' was printed on a wooden sign atop a post, even though most of the people who lived here were uneducated and couldn't read or write at all. Like entering through a doorway to the underworld, everything quickly changed and turned undesirable. They rode down Rotten Row, the buildings blocking most of the sun from the sky and making it feel eerie. She quickly pulled some fresh mint out of her bag and held it up to her nose.

"What is that and what are you doing?" He looked at her oddly.

"It smells so awful on Rotten Row that I decided to bring some fresh mint with me from my garden to mask the odors." She took a deep sniff of it and smiled. "Would you like to try it? It helps."

"Nay," he said, acting as if she were bothering him.

While the streets in the good part of town were covered with cobblestones, once they got to Rotten Row, the street was just dirt. It was embedded with many deep ruts, puddles, and even trenches that were filled with human waste and scraps of rotting food. The wind blew the piles of rubbish, putting everything in disarray. Stench filled the air, making it hard to breathe. Filthy children with bare feet played in the puddles. Old women carried baskets filled with things Vivienne couldn't identify as she trudged through the mud, barely able to move. Small fires gave rise to white smoke every so often on the street in front of the rundown homes. Women and men stayed near to the fires, looking up in curiosity as they rode by.

"Stay close to me," instructed the sheriff. "We'll stop by the crime scene first and then question those in the tavern again to see if we can learn anything new that we might have missed."

"All right," she agreed. "We should try to talk to that whore named Joy as well. The one that the mayor was with the night of the murder."

A shiver swept up her spine as a cool breeze brought forth the putrid smell of the tannery from the far end of the row. Tanners used animal feces and urine and sometimes even rotten flesh to tan the leather. Outside their establishment, they tossed into the street, the horns and hooves of the animals that they skinned. How could anyone ever want to live here, she wondered. It was a sad as well as a very frightening place. She secretly couldn't wait to leave.

"Fresh fish! Buy my fish," called out a man in bare feet and tattered clothing. He lifted a piece of brown paper with a fish upon it, wanting Vivienne to take it. She looked down from her steed, realizing the fish was old and covered with maggots and flies. Most of its flesh was gone and all that was left was the head, tail, and spine. The man eyed her up in a lusty manner, and when he grinned she saw his broken and brown teeth.

"You're a wench, not a man!" he exclaimed, having just noticed. "Why are you wearin' those clothes? I'd like to see your legs, wench." His hand snaked out toward her as he tried to touch her.

"Get out of here!" commanded Zachariah, riding in between the man and Vivienne, kicking out his foot from atop his horse as he rode. He tried to keep the fishmonger from reaching out to touch Vivienne, and she appreciated his protection.

"Sheriff, I've got somethin' for you that you're goin' to like." A whore stood in a dark doorway with her hand under her gown between her legs. She made lewd noises and swiveled her hips in an alluring manner.

"Oh!" gasped Vivienne, looking away and to the other side of the street, but things didn't get any better.

"I've got even more to offer over here. I can please both of you at once," crooned a second whore competing for attention. She leaned on the wall of a bug-infested cottage that was made of wattle and daub and seemed to be falling down around her. Vivienne noticed several rats running in and out the open door. The whore pulled down her bodice, displaying her large, bare breasts as she licked her lips and leaned forward shaking her shoulders.

This time, Vivienne was too shocked to even say a word.

"Don't look, Vivienne," warned Zachariah, bringing his horse closer to hers as they continued to ride down Rotten Row. "That is nothing that a lady should ever have to witness."

"Too late. I've already seen it, and I'm sorry I did. I'm not sure I'll ever be able to get that out of my mind now."

She was trying not to look around, but only to focus on the road ahead. However, she couldn't help but notice two men jumping atop a third man and bringing him to the ground. While one man sat atop the first, punching his fist into the victim's face, his friend went through the poor man's pockets.

"Get up, let him go, and give him back his things, right now!" hollered the sheriff. "Unless you all want to end up behind bars." The men all got to their feet and ran off to hide in the shadows.

"I'm now starting to question having come here at all," Vivienne spoke her thoughts aloud. "Of course when I was here in the cover of darkness, this area didn't seem half as bad as it does. now."

"Now, you understand what I'm saying, Lady Vivienne? You are not safe here and this is no place for a lady. It's not too late. I can still take you back to my home. Just say the word."

"Nay," she answered stubbornly. "This is something I have to do."

"Somehow I knew you'd say that," he mumbled, shaking his head as they rode.

They turned down the narrow alley alongside the tavern. It was the place where they found the corpse. It was barely wide enough to fit the horses and they had to get off and walk them. They might try this now in the daylight, but it would be too risky in the dark.

They stopped at the back of the building. Large empty wooden barrels were stacked up and leaning against the tavern. There were broken boxes and remnants of rotten food scraps all around them. The air smelled strongly from urine today. Vivienne had no doubt in her mind that the drinking men came out back to relieve themselves, and she looked down, careful not to step in any puddles. Once again, she raised the handful of mint to her nose and breathed in its aromatic scent.

"You get used the to the odor eventually," the sheriff told her.

"Never," she mumbled into the green small leaves of the bundle of fresh mint.

The sheriff stopped her as they came to the back door of the tavern. The vision of poor Florence dead on the ground and being eaten by rats was embedded in her mind. She shuddered remembering how the rats had eaten away her eyeballs first. No one deserved to die in that manner! Her heart went out to the mayor and his daughter, Maleine. A man's wife and a girl's mother was taken from this world by murder unjustly. It was up to her now to help the sheriff bring peace of mind to them, and find and punish the killer. She thought she heard the sound of Grunt's howl and then she heard some shouting. It sounded like a male's voice.

"That was Grunt. I'm sure of it," she said, looking around as she held on to the reins of her horse. "He's howling the same way he does when he corners an animal on a hunt."

"I heard shouting as well." The sheriff stretched his neck, looking down the passageway. "It sounded like it came from down there. I'll investigate. You stay put and don't leave the horses unattended." He handed her the reins of his horse. "You never know when we might need to make a fast departure." He pulled his sword from the sheath and started walking slowly down the alley, making sure to look behind every barrel and box. Vivienne watched anxiously, her eyes scanning the area for anyone who might be hiding in wait in the shadows.

"Be careful, Zachariah," she called after him in concern, not using his title, but instead, speaking to him as a true friend.

"I will." He walked with his sword at the ready but didn't get far before he stopped. She heard the sound of running feet and the sheriff jumped to the side as Grunt sped past him and came right up to her with something in his mouth. Behind him was Wymond, the Pied Piper's assistant. The boy had something he held on to as he ran after Grunt.

"Come back here!" shouted Wymond, waving one fist in the air, sidestepping the sheriff.

"Don't move!" commanded the sheriff, causing Wymond to come to a screeching halt.

"Stop your dog from hurtin' Snuff!" screamed Wymond, pointing at Grunt.

"What?" Vivienne looked down to see Grunt proudly holding one of the rat-catcher's ferrets in his mouth. It was a slim, light brown animal with darker patches over his eyes. She remembered seeing the animal that first night that she'd met the rat-catcher. "Oh, my dog has your weasel?"

"He's a ferret." Wymond threw her a nasty look. "That hound would have Chomp too if I hadn't picked her up in time."

He referred to the ferret under his arm that was almost completely white and had a pink nose and red eyes.

"Grunt, put him down at once." Vivienne gently took the ferret from her dog's mouth. She quickly inspected him. "He didn't hurt Snuff, don't worry. Grunt just wanted to play, that's all." She handed the ferret back to the boy. He snatched him away from her and stepped back from the dog, keeping a wide berth.

"Mr. Piper isn't going to be happy about this." Wymond looked down and gave the ferret a kiss on the nose before sticking him under his free arm.

"Do you make those poor little ferrets hunt and kill rats?" she asked, seeing Zachariah slowly lowering his sword and walking over to join them.

"Snuff and Chomp don't kill rats often," Wymond explained. "They usually just flush out the rats from their small hiding spaces so Demon can get them."

"Demon?" Vivienne raised a brow. "Do you mean The Pied Piper?" If anyone was considered a demon, she was sure it was that man!

"Nay, although Mr. Piper does catch and even kill rats with his bare hands. I was talkin' about his cat."

"Ah, the big black cat with the two different colored eyes that my daughter is infatuated with and calls Midnight," said the sheriff with a nod.

"Yes, that sounds like the one. Have you seen her?" Wymond looked around the ground. "It's goin' to be time to start huntin' rats again soon and Mr. Piper gets so mean when Ebony disappears."

"Ebony?" asked Vivienne in confusion. "Now, who or what is that?"

"The cat. The black cat with the two-toned eyes," said the boy.

"I thought you just told us her name is Demon," said the sheriff.

"That's what Mr. Piper named her, but I don't like calling her Demon so I just call her Ebony instead."

"I do like that name better as well," agreed Vivienne.

"Ebony is pretty lazy and doesn't catch a lot of rats at all. Mr. Piper kicks her a lot and then he ends up kicking me, as if it is my fault the cat doesn't want to hunt rats anymore for some reason."

"Mayhap it's because my daughter keeps feeding the cat and she isn't hungry enough to go after vermin," suggested Zachariah.

"Ah. Yes, I'm sure it is." Wymond looked down at the ferrets in his arms. "Mr. Piper basically starves my ferrets so they'll be hungry enough to go after the rats."

"Your Mr. Piper doesn't sound like a very nice man at all," said Vivienne. "By the way, I don't think we've been properly introduced. I know your name is Wymond. I am Lady Vivienne."

"You're a noble?" He eyed her up and down.

"Yes. I know I'm not dressed properly right now, but I find it easier to ride and even move when I'm wearing breeches."

The boy snickered.

"I am helping Sheriff Fitch to find whoever murdered the mayor's wife, Florence," she continued.

"I know that. You already made it quite clear the last time we met." His smile disappeared.

"Did you or the Pied Piper dump a bunch of rats on top of Florence's grave?" she wanted to know.

Wymond looked down and pet his ferrets. "I did it," he admitted softly.

"What would possess you to do such a thing?" snapped the sheriff. "It's downright disrespectful to the deceased one and their family. Not to mention the priest and anyone else visiting the graveyard."

"I told him to do it, that's why," came a voice from behind them. Vivienne spun on her heel to see the rat-catcher standing there with his tall wooden pole with the cage mounted at the top. The live rats in it squealed and tried to squeeze through the wooden bars to escape. Sadly, Vivienne couldn't blame them. She wanted to escape this horrible man as well.

"That's an act that can be considered punishable by the law." The sheriff slowly lifted the tip of his sword and took a step closer to Vivienne to protect her.

"Are you going to arrest me, all-powerful sheriff?" the Pied Piper asked in a mocking tone.

"I'm considering it at the moment. However, it might be better if you just left town and never returned. You are frightening the children and most of the townsfolk too."

Vivienne wasn't sure why Zachariah was telling the man to leave when in her mind he was the number one suspect in the murder.

"Am I frightening you too, Sheriff?" The Pied Piper's gaze drifted over to Vivienne next. "Or is this just a heroic act to impress the wench?"

"That's enough!" shouted Zachariah.

"Listen. If I had wanted to hurt her, I would have done so by now," the rat-catcher continued. His voice was low and groggy and sounded sinister to her.

"One more comment like that and I'll have no choice but to arrest you right here where you stand," snapped Zachariah.

"Then I'll tell you exactly what I told that rotten mayor. When he pays me for the work I did, I'll leave, but not until then. We had a deal and agreed on a price. He is not keeping up his end of the bargain."

"Mayhap the reason he doesn't want to pay you is because

he thinks you are the one who murdered his wife," Vivienne spoke out. "I can't say I blame him since the evidence is pretty clear that you did it."

"Oh, you think so, do you?" The rat-catcher took a step closer to Zachariah. Vivienne started to fear for their safety. She rested her hand atop the hilt of her sword. She didn't want to use the blade, but would do so if she felt it was needed. She had failed to protect her parents seven years ago, and she would be damned if she failed Zachariah as well.

"Mr. Piper, mayhap we should go," said Wymond.

"Shut your mouth before I make you shut it," snapped the Pied Piper.

"Aye," Wymond muttered, looking down to the animals in his hands.

"Mayhap the sheriff and the haughty lady need to open their eyes a little more."

"Why do you say that?" asked Vivienne, trying her hardest to be brave and at the same time get answers.

"You two need to find different evidence if you think I killed anyone," the rat-catcher told them. "I only murder rats. Not people. Although, the mayor is a rat too so mayhap I'll have to start hunting him down next if he doesn't pay me soon."

"Talk like that is not helping your case any," warned the sheriff.

"Then tell the mayor to pay me our agreed upon price," hissed the rat-catcher, towering over the sheriff and glaring down at him. He was frighteningly big and Vivienne was sure very strong by the looks of him. She wouldn't be surprised if he could strangle a man with one hand only around the victim's neck. "I do not work for free!" he bellowed, his voice echoing off the buildings in the alley passageway.

"What price did you agree upon?" asked Zachariah.

The Pied Piper hesitated before he answered. "That is between me and the mayor and none of your concern."

"I'm the Sheriff of Mablethorpe and anything that goes on in my town is my concern."

"Then why don't you ask the mayor that question instead of me? And while you're talking to that rat, you can tell him I am not a patient man. I will not wait much longer. I'll give him until tomorrow at midnight to pay up, but that's it."

"What if he doesn't pay you?" asked Vivienne, not quite certain she wanted to know the answer to that question, but still she had to ask. "What will you do if he refuses to give you the money?"

The Pied Piper's head turned and his dark eyes seemed to penetrate her. He was a scary man and she didn't like being anywhere near him. "If he refuses, he's going to be payin' me in a totally different way," he warned them. "And believe me, the mayor will end up wishing he hadn't crossed me in the first place. No one cheats the Pied Piper and gets away with it." He turned his attention to the sheriff again. "Make the mayor hand over my money."

"You are in no position to be telling me what to do."

"Do it, Sheriff, I warn you. Because if you don't, you'll end up paying for his mistake as well in the end."

Vivienne drew her sword in one motion. She didn't like the way things were going. The sheriff lifted the tip of his sword and rested it right under the rat-catcher's chin. The man did not even flinch. Instead, he had the nerve to actually smile and chuckle.

"If you keep spewing threats, you're the one who is going to be sorry," Zachariah told him through gritted teeth. "You should be thankful that the little lady is standing here right now or I might not be so hesitant to use my sword on you at this moment."

"In my profession, I've learned not to be afraid of death, Sheriff," said the Pied Piper in a low and gruff voice. "The real question is ... are you?" He started laughing like a madman then, shaking his pole and causing the rats inside the cage to run in circles, banging against the wooden bars. Then he reached into a bag at his side and pulled something out. It was a conglomeration of dead rats all bloodied and tied together by their tails, much like the one she'd seen atop Florence's grave. "Come boy," he said to Wymond. "We've got a lot of rats to catch so get those ferrets movin'."

"Yes, Mr. Piper." Wymond put the ferrets on the ground and they slithered away into the dark corners of the alley.

Grunt's ears perked up and he looked as if he was about to run after them again. "Nay, Grunt. Leave them alone," warned Vivienne, reaching down and grabbing the dog's collar to keep him from darting away.

The Pied Piper ambled down the alleyway with dead rats swinging from his belt. He used the staff with the cage of rats atop it as his walking stick. He picked up a small horn attached to his belt by a cord and brought it to his mouth. With one big breath he blew a sequence of notes. The ferrets heard it and ran out of the shadows and followed him down the alley. Wymond turned to go as well but Vivienne stopped him.

"Wait, Wymond," she said, stopping him from leaving.

"What is it?" he asked, looking over his shoulder at her.

"You seem like a nice boy. Why are you even working for such a horrible man?"

Dismay darkened his face. "I'm an orphan, my lady," he told said, being respectful enough to use her title now that he knew she was a noblewoman. "I was livin' on the streets alone and hungry when Mr. Piper found me and took me in. He said I could work with him and he'd feed me in exchange."

"Still, there must be a better place to go. Won't you consider staying here in town? I'm sure the sheriff could find a job for you."

"Nay," snapped Zachariah, glaring at her. "No one in town would ever accept him."

"But it wasn't his choice to catch rats," stated Vivienne. "He's just a poor boy trying to survive."

Wymond looked back at the rat-catcher walking away. Then with frightened eyes, he glanced back at her. "There's somethin' I need to tell you," he said in a mere whisper.

"What is it? You can tell me anything," she said, urging him on.

"Boy! Get your ass over here right now. If you say another word to those two I'll have to cut out your tongue," threatened the Pied Piper, not even bothering to turn around.

"Oh!" gasped Vivienne, fearing for Wymond's safety.

"I'm sorry. I have to go now." He turned on his heel and sprinted down the alley to catch up with the horrible man.

"I feel so bad for Wymond." Vivienne let go of Grunt and sheathed her sword.

"Don't even." The sheriff put his sword back in its sheath.

"What do you mean?"

"You are always taking in orphans and that bad habit has got to stop right now."

"Why? I have no children of my own, and these orphans that you are referring to have no parents. I am only trying to help them."

"You keep doing that and someday it is going to catch up with you and cause you a lot of trouble."

"How so?"

"Just stop doing it, Vivienne. Please."

"*Lady* Vivienne," she corrected him, not liking to be told

what or what not to do. "I don't see anything else here at the scene of the crime that looks suspicious. I'm going inside the tavern to talk to the whore."

She heard him groan from behind her and it made her smile.

Chapter Eleven

"Yes, I was with the mayor that night, just like he told you," the whore named Joy told them as they sat in a dark corner of the tavern. She looked down and played with the cup containing wine rather than to look them in the eye. The sheriff had paid a man well to guard their horses in the alley until they finished up with the questioning.

"And what time was that?" asked the sheriff.

Joy leaned forward and covered her mouth partially with her hand. "He came to me after his council meeting, so mayhap nine o'clock."

"How long was he with you?" asked Vivienne.

"He was in my room when you both came into the tavern and announced you'd found a dead body in the alley," said the girl. "So whatever time that was. I don't know for sure."

"The council meeting ended at nine, so that checks out," said the sheriff. "The body was found at a little past eleven o'clock. So, you're saying the mayor was with you for the full two hours?"

"Yes." She sat upright and scratched her nose. Then she

started drumming her fingers on the table. "I have clients, Sheriff. So if we're done here, I need to get back to work."

"Can't it wait?" asked Vivienne. "This is important."

Joy looked down her nose at Vivienne. "Some of us are not wealthy nobles. I am a working woman and need all the money I can get."

"Go on," said Zachariah, getting to his feet. "But if you think of anything that is suspicious, please let one of us know."

"I'll not tell the likes of her anything," answered Joy with a sniff, her daggered look directed toward Vivienne. She stood and faced Zachariah. "However, if I think of anything, I'll be happy to tell you, Sheriff." She smiled and reached out, running her fingers down his chest. "In the privacy of an upstairs room, mayhap?" She smiled and her gaze flashed to the stairs leading to the whore's bedchamber.

Vivienne didn't like the way Joy was acting toward Zachariah. And since he wasn't pushing her away, it made her wonder how well the sheriff really knew the wench.

The girl started to leave, but Vivienne stopped her.

"Wait," she said, getting to her feet and walking toward her. "Have you ever had ... relations with any of the town's councilmen?"

"Like who?" asked Joy. "There are lots of them, you realize. I usually end up taking any man who can pay up to my bed. I don't make a list of who they were. I basically bed every man who comes into this tavern."

Zachariah cleared his throat. "Not all of them," he muttered.

"What about those councilmen?" she asked with a nod, seeing the chamberlain, the market inspector, the bailiff, and the town clerk sitting at a table together drinking.

Joy stretched her neck to take a look. "All but one of them," she answered.

"Not the town clerk, right?" She figured the mouse of a man wouldn't have the nerve to bed a whore.

"Nay, the bailiff." Joy laughed. "Why would you think I wouldn't be coupling with Maurice?" she asked about the town clerk.

"Because he's so quiet and timid."

That made her laugh even more. "Oh, my lady you are so naive. Maurice might seem timid to you, but I assure you he is the loudest and wildest of all of them in bed. He was the one I used to enjoy the most. Until recently."

"What happened recently to change things?" asked the sheriff.

She shrugged. "Maurice told me he found someone else and wouldn't be spending time with me anymore."

"Who was this girl?" asked Vivienne.

"He didn't say and I didn't ask. But it's most likely one of those tarts that display their goods right on the street." She fixed her gown, acting as if the thought disgusted her. "Now if you'll excuse me, my clients are waiting." She turned and wiggled her hips as she walked up the stairs. Vivienne had no doubt that Maurice had taken up with one of the two whores who solicited themselves to Zachariah on their way here today. The thought disgusted her as well.

"What do you think?" asked Zachariah.

"I think she has quite a business since she's been bedding most of the council and as she says every man who comes in here."

"I never sought out her services."

"I never asked."

"I know. But just in case you were wondering."

She was, but it wouldn't do her any good to let him know she cared. "I think Joy was lying when we asked her about the mayor."

"Why?"

"Didn't you see how she touched her nose and partially covered her mouth with her fingers when she answered? That usually means someone is lying or isn't telling the whole truth."

"What makes you think so?"

"I've studied people's reactions and actions a lot in the last seven years, Sheriff. I am still searching for my parents' killer and have to be alert and observant. That is what I discovered."

"So, what part do you think she was lying about? And why?"

"I'm not sure yet. I need to think about everything she said."

"Let's go back to my home and discuss this. I don't want you lingering here any longer."

"Don't we want to question more of the patrons? Or perhaps the councilmen again?"

"I'll do that on my own time with my constable. Right now, I can see the way these drunkards are eyeing you up and I don't like it. All I want to do is to get you to safety. Plus, I'm not sure how much I can trust the man I paid to watch our horses."

"Grunt is out there. Plus, you paid the man quite well. I'd hardly think he'd want to risk losing the horses."

"It doesn't mean a thing here on Rotten Row and you should know that by now. All it takes is someone else to come along and either pay the man more to let him steal them, or they could be stolen by force."

"Yes, you're right," she said, thinking of the men fighting earlier in the street and all the grubby, disreputable people walking the row. She still clutched the fresh handful of mint, bringing it to her nose once more when she saw a man vomiting across the room and another urinating into a bucket that was meant for spit. "I'm ready to leave. Let's go now." It took all her strength to walk out of there slowly instead of bolting up and running out the door.

By the time they arrived at the sheriff's home and handed over the horses to be stabled, Vivienne was tired, nauseated, thirsty, and hungry.

"Allow me," said Zachariah, opening the door for her. Grunt sprinted inside ahead of them.

She was about to walk into the house when she heard a soft mewing coming from behind a bush. Midnight, as Starah called her, stuck her head out, watching them with her two different colored eyes. The black cat mewed again and licked her paws.

"Oh, It's Midnight. I think the poor thing is hungry," said Vivienne, meaning to pick up the cat.

"Fast, get inside." Zachariah yanked her into the house, followed her in, and slamming the door behind them.

"What did you do that for? I said the cat looked hungry. Didn't you hear me?"

"Shhh," he said. "I heard you. But I don't want my daughter to hear you. Besides, if the cat is hungry then she can go hunt a few rats like she's supposed to be doing."

"You can't mean you want Midnight to have to eat rats."

"I don't want or need the rat-catcher at my door looking for his cat, so let it go."

"Ah, there ye two are. Just in time for some of my vegetable cheese tarts, fresh bread, and some fruit," said Nairnie, placing wooden plates on the table. Martin and Starah were already seated and eating. "I would have liked to make somethin' with meat, but to do that the sheriff is goin' to have to give me some money to go to the butcher's shop," she complained.

"Oh, it smells so good in here that I don't even need this anymore." Vivienne walked over to the table and placed her handful of mint down.

"What's this?" asked Martin, reaching out and picking it up.

"It's mint," she told him.

"What's it for?" asked Starah with big, curious eyes.

"Lady Vivienne used it to mask the stench of Rotten Row," explained Zachariah, reaching out to the table for an apple.

"Nay!" Nairnie was putting a hot tart on the table, but reached over and swiped her long wooden spoon at him. The sheriff moved his hand just in time and the spoon banged down on the table instead. "Ye need to wash up first. And no weapons at the table. I swear ye're no better than the pirates aboard the Falcon. None of ye have a lick of manners."

"What's the Falcon?" asked Vivienne, following Zachariah over to the wash basin before Nairnie started swinging her serving spoon at her too. She and the sheriff removed their swords and hung them on hooks in the corner.

"The Falcon is the pirate ship she was on with her grandsons," said little Starah.

"Nairnie, I thought I asked you not to fill my daughter's head with silly made-up stories about pirates anymore. She'll start having nightmares about them if you don't stop. " He washed then dried his hands on a cloth while Vivienne washed up as well.

"Hrmph," Nairnie said with a sniff, picking up a long knife and slicing the loaf of freshly baked brown bread. "I dinna make up stories. They are all true. And they are far from silly."

"Well, can we just forget about them for now? I don't want pirate talk at the table." Zachariah pulled out a chair for Vivienne and she sat down. He followed the same action. Instantly, Grunt's chin was on his lap. "Why the hell does this dog always come to me begging for food when I never even give him anything?"

"Mayhap that's why," Vivienne answered with a giggle. "Grunt is sociable and likes to eat with everyone."

"Lady Vivienne, can I keep this mint?" asked Martin, sniffing it and then letting Starah smell it too.

"Sure," said Vivienne. "But you might want to put it in water so it doesn't die." She helped herself to a slice of bread, taking a bite and almost moaning aloud it was so tasty.

"Can you eat mint?" asked Starah curiously. "Because it smells yummy."

"You sure can," Vivienne answered. "And if anyone wants more mint, I have an entire garden filled with it back at the castle."

Martin tasted a leaf and made a face. "I'm not sure. I think I'll just use it to sniff instead of actually eating it."

"Did ye find out anythin' new with the investigation?" asked Nairnie, pulling up a chair and sitting down to join them.

"Not much," Zachariah answered, picking up his spoon and digging into the hot tart.

"We saw that nasty Pied Piper again and he really scared the daylights out of me." Vivienne heard the sheriff clear his throat at her comment. She looked over to see him slowly shaking his head, warning her not to talk about the rat-catcher in front of the children. Vivienne didn't want to scare them but she also didn't want to shield them from reality. She figured they should know all about the Pied Piper and be warned not to go near him. If not, they might be considered naïve, the way Joy referred to her. In Vivienne's mind, everyone, even children, needed to be informed and prepared for whatever life threw their way. Still, she decided not to talk about it now since it seemed to upset Zachariah.

"So, what did you children do today?" asked the sheriff, continuing to eat.

"Not much," said Martin with a shrug.

"Martin showed Starah his wooden sword and how to use it," Nairnie answered for them.

The sheriff's head snapped up. "He did? Martin, I don't want my daughter using a sword so please don't do that again."

"For heaven's sake, it's not dangerous, it's only wooden," said Vivienne. She couldn't believe how over-protected the sheriff was with his daughter. "Besides, girls need to know how to defend themselves too so what's the harm in it?"

"That's right, Father," said Starah. "Lady Vivienne uses a sword so why can't I?"

"Because I said so, that's why," he answered. "Besides, Lady Vivienne does a lot of things that I don't exactly find appropriate for a girl to do. I can't say she's being a good example."

"I'm not sure I like the sound of that!" It was one thing to hear Zachariah reprimanding his daughter, but she was only seven. However, when he started acting that way to her, she wasn't going to put up with it. She stood up and walked over to collect her sword. "Martin, I think it is time we get back to the castle."

"Already?" Martin frowned. "But it's not even getting dark yet. Can't we stay a little longer?"

"I'm afraid not. I have things that need my attention at the castle and so do you." She strapped on her sword and opened the door. "Thank you for the food, Nairnie, it was delicious."

"But ye didna even eat much of it," said the old woman, eying up Vivienne's plate with the half-eaten tart.

"I'm sorry, but I really need to leave now. Come, Martin."

"Aye my lady," said the boy with a sigh, leaving the mint on the table and shuffling his feet as he headed for the door.

"Mayhap tomorrow ye'll like the food better," said Nairnie, getting up to clear Vivienne's plate from the table. But not before the sheriff reached out to scoop up and eat her leftovers. "I'm goin' to the marketplace to buy some food tomorrow, as well as some actual meat."

"Oh, is the market taking place tomorrow?" This interested Vivienne. "I'd like to go."

"We can all go together, but it'll have to wait until afternoon," the sheriff told them. "I have some things to attend to in the morning that cannot be ignored any longer."

"What things? Things that have to do with the investigation?" asked Vivienne. "Because I thought we were doing that together."

"Nay. I have to collect taxes from the business owners in the morning. It is part of my duty as town sheriff."

"Oh, that's a shame. I hoped to get to the market early before all the best things are gone," said Nairnie sounding very disappointed.

"What time does the market open?" asked Vivienne.

"The market opens in the square at nine," Zachariah told her.

"Then Nairnie, I'll be here before nine to go with you and the children to the town square. That is, unless the sheriff disapproves of shopping for some odd reason."

He looked up at her with tired eyes. "Nay, Lady Vivienne, I don't disapprove of shopping. I think you are taking my concerns and twisting them all out of proportion, as usual. I was only being cautious and thinking of my daughter's safety."

"Sheriff Fitch, you don't have to worry about the children at the market. I am well able to protect them from any overzealous fruit vendor who might start throwing apples at them." Vivienne was purposely being snide, but she didn't care. Sometimes Zachariah was hopeless about changing his ways.

Nairnie and the children laughed, but Zachariah didn't.

"I'd welcome yer company at the market in the mornin', Lady Vivienne," said Nairnie.

"Me too," added Starah. "I like you, and enjoy being around you."

"Lady Vivienne is the best," said Martin, yanking open the door.

"Thank you. All of you," Vivienne told them, feeling pleased by all the admiration she was getting, even if none of it came from the sheriff. "It is nice to know when I'm truly wanted and appreciated. Come, Grunt. You'll get no food from the sheriff, so stop begging." Grunt whined and padded across the room and followed Martin to the door. "The sheriff believes animals should hunt for rats if they're hungry. Good night, all," she told them, leaving and closing the door before Zachariah had a chance to defend his words or actions.

Chapter Twelve

"Martin, what do you have there?" asked Lady Mablethorpe the next morning as Vivienne was preparing to leave to go to the market in town.

"This is mint from Lady Vivienne's garden." The boy held up a huge bunch of it proudly to show her. He had his wooden sword hanging from his belt. "It's to smell good in case I go to Rotten Row."

"Oh my," said Lady Mablethorpe laughing and holding her hand to her chest. "Are you trying to smell good for anyone special?"

"Huh?" He looked at her and wrinkled his nose.

"Aunt Ellen, I think Martin just wants to share the pleasant scent of mint with the sheriff's daughter, Starah."

"Aye, she wants to smell good too," said Martin, not understanding that he was being teased.

"And Martin is never going anywhere near Rotten Row," added Lady Vivienne. "I've been there and it's not a place for children. Or anyone with morals or respect," she added under her breath.

"We're going to the market with Nairnie," said Martin, reaching out and petting Grunt who was by his side like always. "I'm going to buy Grunt a bone."

"You are?" asked Lady Mablethorpe. "Where did you get the money for that?"

"I don't have any money," said Martin, looking up through his long bangs at Vivienne. "Mayhap someone can give me some?"

"I'll buy Grunt a bone," said Vivienne, swiping Martin's bangs from his eyes.

"Thank you," said Martin. "Did you hear that, Grunt? Did you want a sniff of my mint too?" Martin held the mint in front of the dog's nose. Grunt tried to take a bite and Martin pulled it away. "Nay, it doesn't taste good so just sniff it." He shoved it up against the dog's nose, causing Grunt to sneeze.

Vivienne chuckled. "I think mint tastes good," she told him.

"So do I," stated Lady Mablethorpe. "Cook puts it in a lot of his food and you eat it, don't you?"

"Like what?" asked Martin.

"Like the sheriff's favorite, roasted lamb with mint sauce," Vivienne answered.

"Oh, I do like that," he said in thought. "Mayhap I'll give some of this mint to Nairnie then so she can make the lamb and mint sauce for the sheriff and he won't be so grumpy all the time."

"I think that's a splendid idea," said Vivienne. "One good meal might be all it takes to make Sheriff Fitch smile again."

Zachariah purposely got up early to collect the rents and was finished before the marketplace even opened. He wanted to investigate some more on Rotten Row but didn't want to tell

Vivienne. He was sure she'd insist on going with him, and he didn't feel good about her being down there. This way, he could ask some more questions and hopefully find some answers to the murder case since he felt as if they were at a standstill and never going to catch the killer. Why was this so hard?

Constable Dorson accompanied him today. They went to the tavern even though it was early and not opened yet. He'd requested that Joy meet them downstairs.

"What is it, Sheriff?" asked the whore, walking downstairs scantily clad as usual. She held a blanket wrapped around her and had bare feet. Her hair was messy too. The tavern proprietor had just paid his rent and busied himself behind the drink board, pretending not to listen.

"Constable Dorson and I just want to ask you a few more questions."

"I told you everything I know yesterday. Did that noble-woman who dresses like a man send you back here?"

"Who is she talking about, Sheriff?" asked the constable.

"She means Lady Vivienne," he told the constable. Then he looked back at the whore. "And no, Lady Vivienne doesn't tell me what to do. I came here because I need to know each man you bedded the night of the murder."

"What does it matter? Are you going to tax me on it?"

Zachariah saw the tavern owner, Philip watching them. "Philip, please join us," he called out.

The man hurried over, wiping his hands on a towel. "Sheriff? Is something wrong?"

"I'm guessing you get a percentage for every man Joy services, don't you?"

"Well ... I ..."

"He does," said Joy, sticking her nose in the air. "So what of it?"

"If that's the case then I suppose Philip knows exactly who you sleep with, doesn't he?"

"Sheriff, I don't get much from it, honest I don't." Philip held up his hands in surrender. "Please don't arrest me for it. I am only trying to make a living."

"I should charge both of you taxes on those nightly visits. I'm sure the king would want to know what you're doing."

"How much do you want?" Philip pulled a pouch from his side, eager to get matters cleared up.

"I don't want money, just information at this time," said Zachariah. "But if I don't get it, things are going to change around here. And not for the better." Being sheriff, Zachariah could make all their lives miserable if he so wanted, and they knew it. He held a lot of power in town. There was nothing they could do to stop him either.

"What do you want to know?" asked Philip.

"I want the names of the men that were serviced by Joy from nine at night until I arrived here and found the body a little after eleven, the night of the murder."

"I told you, I was with the mayor," said Joy with a roll of her eyes.

"The whole time?" He saw Philip's gaze meet Joy's eye and the man looked worried.

"Tell them, Joy. It's not worth it," begged Philip.

"Oh, all right," she said, plopping down on a chair and pulling her feet up, covering them with the blanket too. "I was with a total of three men that night. At that time, I mean."

"Three men? In two hours?" asked the constable, his mouth hanging open.

"It's my profession," she told him with a shake of her shoulders and a dip of her brows. "What can I say? I'm good at what I do."

"Who were they?" asked Zachariah.

"Well, let's see." She put her hand to her mouth in thought. Zachariah remembered Vivienne saying that meant she was lying.

"You tell me, Philip. And no lying, or I'll know."

"All right, Sheriff. Anything you want." Philip was only too glad to do what was asked of him. "She was with the mayor right after the town council meeting ended," said the man. "That was a little after nine o'clock when the council members all arrived."

"How long did Joy's little rendezvous with the mayor last?" asked the constable.

"Well, I'm not sure," said Philip. "Hammond went upstairs about half an hour later."

"So that is when the mayor came down then?" asked Zachariah.

"Nay," said Joy. "I left the mayor in one room sleeping while I used a different room to be with Hammond."

"Hammond? The chamberlain?" asked the constable.

"That's right," she said. "A half hour later, Hammond left and I serviced Elias."

"The market inspector," said Philip, even though Zachariah knew who she meant.

"So that was about ten-thirty then?" asked the constable.

"I suppose so."

"What about the mayor?" asked Zachariah. "Where was he at this time?"

"He was still snoring away in my bed in the other room," Joy answered.

"Why would you leave him there and use another room?" he asked. "I don't understand."

"His time was paid for ahead of then so I couldn't very well kick him out," said Joy. "You know, I do have morals."

"Nay. I didn't know that," mumbled Zachariah. "So the

mayor paid for several hours ahead of that night, just so he could sleep there?"

"Nay," she answered. "The mayor wasn't even aware that his time was paid for. All right, I'll admit I got paid twice for him that night."

"You did?" asked Philip.

She shrugged. "I was going to tell you, Philip. Don't worry, I will give you your cut."

"I don't understand," said the sheriff. "If it wasn't the mayor, then who paid you to spend several hours with him?"

"It was his wife."

"What?" asked the constable. "The murdered woman?"

"Yes. Before she was murdered of course," said Joy.

"Florence paid you to keep her husband here?" This was news to Zachariah and it didn't make any sense at all. "Why would she do that?"

"I'm not sure," said Joy with another shrug of her shoulders. "When I went to the market in the morning, I passed by her house. She saw me out her window and opened the door to talk to me. I guess the mayor wasn't home or she never would have done that."

"What did she say to you?"

"Florence knew her husband was bedding me."

"Did she seem angry about it?"

"Nay, not at all. She actually said she wanted to pay me to keep him up in my room that night until at least eleven o'clock or so. She knew he came to see me a little after nine after each council meeting."

"Did she say why she wanted you to do that?" asked the constable.

"Why do you think? She obviously didn't want the man at home sniffing around her I guess. I didn't actually ask her, but neither did I care. All that mattered to me is that she paid me well. I'll do anything for money."

"Yes, it seems so," said the sheriff. "So then, you can confirm that the mayor was here at the tavern and in your bed from a little after nine until when I arrived two hours later and saw him coming down the stairs?"

"Yes. I finished up with Elias just before you came in. I went back to the mayor's room and he was just waking up, all ruddy and ready to rut once more."

"Ruddy?" asked Zachariah.

"His cheeks get red when he's excited," she explained. "I knew as soon as I walked in and saw him that he wanted me again. However, that's when you arrived so we couldn't do it after all. Just the once when he first got there."

"Did the mayor know his wife paid you to keep him upstairs that night?" Zachariah asked her.

"No." She scratched her nose.

"You're lying," snapped Zachariah.

"Oh, all right. I might have let it slip, but what does it matter? He was the one who told me that he thought his wife was having sexual relations with another man anyway. I suppose that just proved it. Once he knew Florence was going to most likely be meeting with her lover that night, Randolf wanted me to tell him who it was, but I couldn't since I didn't know."

"What did he say to that?" asked the constable.

"What could he say? No man likes to hear that kind of news about their wife, but it's a part of life. I pointed that out to the mayor and he said he agreed. Then he rolled over and went to sleep, so it couldn't have bothered him that much."

"Why didn't you tell all this to me yesterday?" asked Zachariah.

"I didn't want to talk about my personal business with that

haughty noblewoman looking down her nose at me. She would never have understood."

"Nay, I can't say she would," answered the sheriff.

"Is there anything else or can I go back to bed now?" she asked with a yawn. "I have a busy night planned and need to keep up my energy."

"That's all for now," said the sheriff. "But if either of you remembers anything else about that night, come to me or the constable with the information."

Zachariah and Constable Dorson exited the tavern and were about to mount their horses and leave when the Pied Piper stepped out of the shadows, surprising the both of them.

"Sheriff, the mayor still hasn't paid me so I left a little surprise on his doorstep this morning," said the rat-catcher.

"What did you do?" growled the constable.

"I just left a little present of dead rats, that's all."

"Sheriff, we should arrest him," said Constable Dorson. "He has all our children frightened out of their minds and he's terrorizing the entire town."

"I'm not terrorizing anyone. I am only doing my job and want to be paid for it. Remember, Sheriff, the deadline is by midnight tonight." The rat-catcher smiled, showing his decaying teeth.

Zachariah saw Wymond watching from the shadows, holding the staff with the cage of rats atop it. He shifted from foot to foot, and didn't seem like he wanted to be there at all.

"You murdered a woman and left her in the alley for the rats to eat!" shouted the constable. "How is that not terrorizing our town?"

"Constable, please," said Zachariah, holding out his arm. He didn't want any more trouble from the damned rat-catcher than they were already having. "There is no proof yet that he killed anyone."

"You have children, Constable, don't you?" asked the Pied Piper.

"Yes. I have three."

"And you have a fine little daughter, Sheriff."

"What are you getting at?" asked the sheriff through gritted teeth, not liking this strange man asking about their families.

"The mayor has a daughter too, and she is quite a looker," said the rat-catcher.

"Stop talking about our children," commanded the sheriff. "I want you out of town by tonight, whether you are paid or not."

"Why don't you pay me?" He looked down at the pouch at Zachariah's side that was filled with the taxes collected for the king. "It seems to me you've collected quite a sum today."

"This is the king's money and I am responsible for it. Your pay comes from the town. If the mayor made the deal, then you need to get your money from him, not me."

"Have you talked to him about it yet, Sheriff?"

"I haven't had the chance, but I will."

"Well, I'd suggest doing it quickly. After all, that deadline is tonight at midnight." He turned and disappeared into the shadows with Wymond following right behind.

"What do you make of that, Sheriff?"

"I'm not sure what to think."

"We need to arrest someone for Florence's murder and we need to do it fast."

"I agree." Zachariah's brain felt ready to explode from everything he'd just learned and what he'd just heard from the Pied Piper. "However, I cannot risk arresting the wrong man. Dammit, we need better evidence."

"Do you think the rat-catcher killed her? I do."

"Mayhap," he answered with a sigh. "But it could be anyone

really. After the information we just got from Joy, I could see this going in more than one direction."

"What do we do next?" asked the constable.

"I'm going to speak to the mayor again. I want you to go back to the coroner's office and question Gandalf and Torsten. Mayhap there is something about the corpse that they saw and forgot to mention. Right now, we need hard evidence or we are not going to be able to convict anyone for the murder of the mayor's wife."

Chapter Thirteen

Vivienne walked with the group to the marketplace, happy to be a part of this little outing. Nairnie was with her as well as Martin, Starah, and of course, Grunt. They'd joined up with Agatha Dorson, the constable's wife. Mrs. Dorson held her six-month-old baby, Aaron on one hip. Her ten-year-old son, Archibald, ran along as he played with Martin and Starah. Her five-year-old daughter, Anabel, held the hand of the mayor's daughter, Maleine, who was sixteen.

"What a beautiful day," said Vivienne, feeling happy to be with all the children. It somehow made her loss seem more tolerable. In a way, she felt as if Martin was her child, even though he wasn't. Still, she liked to have him around. He was such a cute and sweet little boy. And being with all these children, plus Nairnie and Mrs. Dorson, it gave her a true sense of family once again.

"Yes, it is nice that it isn't raining and the sun is shining," remarked Agatha. "Oh, I need to stop at the stall that has honey. I've been saving up for it and want to make the children a sweet treat."

"I want to buy some lamb for the sheriff," said Nairnie.

"Martin insists I make lamb with mint sauce so the sheriff won't be so irritable. The boy even gave me a huge bunch of mint from your garden, Lady Vivienne."

Vivienne giggled. "I don't think Martin remembers eating mint in any dish that he actually liked. At least he'll be able to watch how it's made so he knows mint can taste very nice indeed."

"Who is that boy watching us?" Maleine walked up next to Vivienne, still holding Anabel's hand.

"What boy?" Vivienne turned around and saw Wymond standing under a tree watching them. She got a very odd feeling about it. "Children, stay close to the adults," she instructed.

"Is somethin' wrong?" asked Nairnie.

"It's Wymond," she said with a nod to where he stood. "He's the rat-catcher's assistant and he seems to be watching us."

"Hmm," said Nairnie, cocking her head to get a good look at him. "He doesna seem dangerous at all. Mayhap he just wishes he could play with the other children."

"I hope that is all it is, but the knot in my stomach is saying differently."

"Good morning, Lady Vivienne."

She turned around to see the town clerk standing silently behind her, his hands clasped in front of him.

"Maurice. Good morning," she greeted him. "Are you here shopping at the market as well?"

"Nay. The mayor called a surprise meeting. I am headed to the town hall now to join the others."

"Surprise meeting? Does the sheriff know about this?"

"I doubt it. He left early this morning and no one has seen him since."

"Yes. He had to collect the rents. He told me."

"My husband went with him before sunup to do that," Agatha told her, having overheard the conversation. "I had hoped he'd meet me here in the town square to help carry groceries home, but I don't see him anywhere. They should be well done by now. I wonder where they are."

"Really," said Vivienne, her frustration growing. "Excuse me, please." She turned and headed right for Wymond. Grunt saw and followed at her side. When Wymond saw her, he turned, looking ready to run. "Wymond, wait!" she called out. "Don't be afraid. I just want to talk to you."

He stopped and slowly turned around. "Don't let that dog go after Snuff and Chomp again." Wymond had a canvas bag with a long strap over his shoulder. She noticed the ferrets poking their noses out and sniffing the air.

"Grunt, you be nice," she told her hound. "Sit." Grunt whined but did as told. "Wymond, have you by any chance seen the sheriff this morning?"

"Why?" he asked, looking frozen in fear.

"He was supposed to meet us here. I believe Constable Dorson was with him."

"Oh," he said, seeming to relax. "Aye. They were on Rotten Row earlier this morning."

"Oh, were they?" So it seemed the sneaky sheriff wanted her out of his way once again. Vivienne didn't like that. "What were they doing on Rotten Row?"

"I'm not sure. They came out of the tavern."

"The tavern? Is it open this early?"

"I don't think so."

"I see." She figured they were there questioning Joy again. It had to be. There would be no other reason.

"Who is that tall, dark-haired girl?" he asked, his eyes focused on Maleine. "She looks about my age and is really pretty."

"That is the mayor's daughter, Maleine. It's best not to look at her."

"What?" His arms had been crossed over his chest, but when he heard that, he dropped them.

"Does that upset you for some reason?"

"Nay. Why should it?" He had that look again like he was ready to bolt. She had to talk fast if she wanted to get any information out of him.

"Wymond, you were going to tell me something the other night in the alley. Before the Pied Piper stopped you from doing so. What was it?"

His eyes darted back and forth and he became instantly upset. "I can't say. He'll hurt me if I do."

"Who will hurt you? Who is it you're afraid of? You can tell me."

"I need to go," said the boy, turning and running off, leaving her feeling worthless since she wasn't able to get a single shred of information from him when she honestly thought she would.

"Lady Vivienne?"

She turned to see Zachariah heading toward her from across the town square. He approached with Constable Dorson. "Good morning, Sheriff Fitch."

"Was that the rat-catcher's assistant I just saw you talking to?"

"Yes. His name is Wymond in case you've forgotten."

"I didn't."

"Sheriff, my wife is trying to get my attention," said the constable. "I believe she might need my help carrying her purchases, or perhaps with the children."

"Go on," he told the constable. "We've done all we can for now."

"Thank you, Sheriff." Constable Dorson ran across the square. Scooping up his son Archibald, he held him close in a hug. He made sure to kiss his wife and greet his other two children as well.

"That's sweet," she said. "Constable Dorson really seems to love his family."

"I think he's just a little spooked after talking with the Pied Piper this morning."

"Oh, really. Where did you see him?"

"Outside the tavern."

"I hear you two were questioning Joy again. Without me." She crossed her arms over her chest.

"Who told you that?" He followed her gaze, taking the path that Wymond had taken. "Ah, it was Wymond. What did he say to you?"

"Nothing you'd want me to know, I'm sure. After all, I thought we were in this investigation together, but you seem to have forgotten that. Again."

"Now, just a minute, Vivienne. I only went back to Rotten Row with the constable because I didn't want you down there anymore. I could see how much it upset you yesterday. And don't say that it didn't because I'll know it's a lie if you do."

"Oh, all right," she said, blowing a puff of air from her mouth. "I admit I was a little uneasy on Rotten Row and I cannot say I'm sorry I missed the visit there this morning. But I feel if we worked together we'd be a lot closer to solving this case."

She was about to defend herself when he objected, but to her surprise he did just the opposite.

"I agree," he said. "Will you take a walk with me so I can tell you what I learned in the tavern this morning?"

"I'd like that," she answered softly. "Just let me tell Nairnie where I'm going. I'll leave Grunt with Martin as well. The hound tends to be a distraction."

Vivienne was sad to have to miss the market, but since it was so crowded it was nice to leave all the noise and commotion behind as well. She walked with Zachariah through the marketplace, out the town gates, and toward the beach that was nearby. Gulls cried out overhead as they made their way over the sand and to the water. It was such a beautiful day that she was truly enjoying this walk with Zachariah, even if they weren't saying much to each other and just exchanging pleasantries and small talk about the children. They sat down on the sand and Vivienne thought it felt so good that she even took off her shoes.

"All right now, tell me. What did you learn on Rotten Row this morning?" She kept her eyes closed and her face turned upward, soaking up the sun.

"I thought nobles tried to stay out of the sun," he commented. "After all, only peasants are tanned from working in the fields."

"I'm not good at following orders."

"So I noticed."

She peeked out of one eye. "Well?"

He told her everything they'd learned and also relayed how the rat-catcher seemed to be throwing out threats left and right.

"I stopped by to see the mayor but he wasn't home. The door was ajar so I entered and found a pile of dead rats inside his house," he added. "It seems this time, the Pied Piper actually entered the mayor's house, dumping the rodents right in the middle of his floor."

"That is scary," said Vivienne.

"It also proves that the Pied Piper knows how to get into the mayor's home."

"And he could have broken in and poisoned Florence's mead, just like the mayor thinks," she added.

"It wasn't a nice thing to find. I didn't want to leave the rats there in case Maleine returned so I hired a few men to help me remove them."

"The mayor must have found the rats and that had something to do with the emergency meeting he called this morning for the council members."

"What meeting?" Zachariah frowned and sat up straight. "I didn't know anything about this."

"Yes, I just saw Maurice a little while ago and he told me. Mayhap the mayor couldn't tell you since you and the constable disappeared so early without telling anyone where you were going. I am just glad that Maleine arrived at your home early this morning and didn't meet up with the Pied Piper in her house or see all the dead rats either. That would have been detrimental to her. Especially since she is still so upset about the death of her stepmother."

"Yes. I agree. I sent the constable back to the coroner's office earlier, hoping Gandalf could provide us with new information."

"Did he?"

"Nay. And I'm getting worried. I can't arrest anyone without proper proof."

"I think the mayor sounds pretty guilty after what you just told me."

"I agree. But then again, there were four council members at the tavern that night as well as many others. Any one of them could have killed Florence."

"Or even Joy," said Vivienne.

"I am not above suspecting the coroner or his scribe either. After all, you were the one to realize Florence was poisoned by arsenic and they seemed to have overlooked it. That's not like Gandalf at all. Plus, the Pied Piper says he didn't kill her, but he sure seems guilty. Mayhap it could even be Wymond if the rat-catcher told him to do it. That boy does whatever he is told to do."

"Wymond? Oh, nay, it wasn't him, I'm sure. He's just a scared boy."

"Don't let that image of him fool you."

"Which one of these people had the best reason to kill Florence?" she asked.

"I'm not sure."

"From what Joy said, it sounds like Florence was having a tryst with someone and Joy mentioned it to the mayor. He could have sneaked out of the tavern and killed his wife because of it."

"I suppose. But this seems to be so much more than just a jealous killing."

"Do you think the rat-catcher did it since the mayor won't pay him?"

"I think he has the best reason. In his mind, anyway. Either way, I think the Pied Piper is somehow involved," said Zachariah. "What was Wymond doing in the town square today? He doesn't belong there. Not during business hours."

"I'm not sure. He seemed to be quite interested in Maleine for some reason. He kept watching her and asking about her and saying she was pretty."

"Mayhap he's just being a normal lust-filled young man."

"Mayhap. I tried to get him to open up to me since he was about to tell me something the other day in the alley."

"Did he?"

"Nay. He was too frightened to do so. He said he couldn't tell me. That *he* would hurt him if he did."

"He? The Pied Piper?"

"I don't know. He left before I could get any more information from him."

"I'm concerned that the Pied Piper is going to try something if the mayor won't pay him by midnight."

"Then have the mayor pay him. After all, he did the job and deserves to be paid."

"I know Randolf and he is cheap as well as stubborn. As long as he thinks the Pied Piper killed his wife, he won't be giving anyone a single penny from the town's treasury until the case is closed."

"You're the sheriff. Make him do it. Or have the chamberlain hand over the funds. I thought he was in charge of things like that."

"He usually is, but this is different. The mayor hired the rat-catcher personally, not the town. It was a private deal."

"You need to do something! This is starting to get out of hand."

"I agree. I'll have to find the mayor and have a talk with him, however I can't say I really blame him. If my wife had been murdered, I'd want her killer punished too. Not paid."

"But we don't know for sure the Pied Piper killed her."

"Nay, we don't. However, the way the rat-catcher is acting is certainly suspicious."

"What do you think Florence was even doing on Rotten Row the night she died? Do you think her murderer killed her and just dumped her body there?"

"Nay. There would be too much risk of being seen. I think the murderer killed her right there in the alley."

Vivienne had a thought and sat upright. "I wonder if Wymond saw the murderer that night and he wanted to tell me who it was. He seemed upset about something and wanted to speak to me."

"If so, it must be the rat-catcher who murdered Florence. If it was anyone else, Wymond would have divulged the information. Or at least told the Pied Piper."

"Wymond does seem awfully frightened of the Pied Piper for some reason, I will agree to that. This all seems suspicious and is not in the rat-catcher's favor at all."

"I'll try to talk to the mayor again, as well as the rest of the council members. Mayhap one of them saw or heard something that could help to identify the killer and close this case once and for all."

"Good. I'd like nothing better." She put on her shoes and stood up. "I'm going back to the marketplace."

"Really? Why?"

"Because, I don't get to experience things like that often being locked away in the castle all the time. Besides, Nairnie has a special meal planned for you, and I am going to help her prepare it."

"You are? Why would you do that?"

"Why not? You know I like learning new things."

"But you're a noblewoman, not a commoner."

"I know that. I think I'll even invite some people to join us. How about Constable Dorson and his family? They seem so nice. Plus, Starah and Martin would enjoy playing with Archibald and Anabel."

"I think that's a fine idea. For my daughter's sake. But it's an awful lot of work for Nairnie."

"I'll help her, don't worry. Not that Nairnie needs help since she's cooked for an entire ship of pirates."

Zachariah groaned. "Please. Not the pirate stories again. They are getting old."

Vivienne could tell Zachariah didn't believe a word Nairnie said. It did seem farfetched, all her wild stories. But it entertained the children and Vivienne saw no harm in it. Actually, it all sounded real to her and she couldn't help believe that Nairnie was telling the truth. She didn't seem like a person who lied, but rather told things the way they were. No matter how harsh the situation. "What about inviting the mayor and Maleine to dinner as well?" Her heart went out to the girl with everything that was going on and the murder of her stepmother.

"I don't know if that's a good idea," he objected. "If the mayor is a suspect, then it might not be wise to invite him into my home. I can't be putting the children in the line of potential danger."

"I suppose you're right. However, I still want to invite Maleine. If her father is going to spend his nights in the tavern or in a whore's bed anyway, she shouldn't be alone at a time like this."

"Do whatever you want, since I know there's no stopping you once you've made up your mind."

"That's right. Glad you noticed." She smiled in a triumphant manner.

"Here. You'll need more money if I have to feed all these people." He started to reach for his pouch but she stopped him.

"Nay. I have money. And since it was my idea to invite them all, I insist on paying for the meal in full."

"Lady Vivienne, I don't know if I like that," he said, shaking his head.

"Why not? Because I am a woman and you, being the man, feel as if you should pay?"

"Nay. That's not it at all. I just don't think your uncle would like to hear his money is being spent on meals for commoners."

"It's not my uncle's money. It's mine."

"You have money? From doing what?"

"My parents had all their money in a trunk on the wagon the night they died."

"And the horses took the wagon with your brother, your son, and all your belongings."

"Unless you are forgetting, some of the trunks fell off the wagon and I salvaged them. One of them had all my parents' money in it. Not that it was a lot, but it was more than I ever expected them to have. It's been what I'm living on since their deaths."

"Oh, that's right. I forgot about the trunk with the money. Still, I can't let you spend your money on me."

"You can't stop me from doing so. I don't have much family left, except for my aunt and uncle. Let me spend it on your family instead, Sheriff."

"I appreciate that since my parents are gone too and I don't see my siblings much anymore."

"Why don't you ever even talk about your brother and your sisters?" she asked. "Every time I even mention them, you change the subject."

"There is nothing to tell, and it's nothing I want to talk about. You know that."

"You are pretending you don't even have siblings. I don't understand why."

"Vivienne," he said, forgetting to use her title. "You know my brother, Isaac, is a mercenary, my sister, Magdalena, is a nun, and my younger sister is ... is dead."

"Cassandra is not dead! And it's terrible that you cannot even bring yourself to speak her name."

"She's dead to me."

"She's a Winchester Goose, so just admit it," said Vivienne, referring to the legalized prostitutes of London.

"I told you, I don't like talking about my family, now leave it be."

"If I had family still alive or any siblings at all, I'd not only be talking about them constantly, but spending as much time with them as I could as well."

"I've got to try to catch the mayor and the others before they leave the town hall." He didn't even respond to her last comment, and neither did she think he would. Zachariah Fitch was as stubborn as the day was long. He somehow felt responsible for how his siblings turned out after the death of his parents. It was apparent that he wasn't pleased by any of them, not even the sister who was a nun. This man was more than complicated, and she wasn't sure she would ever truly understand the way he thought or felt.

"Of course," she said, realizing he was running away from his problems again. But there wasn't much she could do right now to help him reconnect with his siblings. Therefore, she'd do the only thing she could to bring some happiness into his life. She'd get back to the market and find Nairnie and together they'd make Zachariah a meal he'd never forget.

Chapter Fourteen

"So you sell honeyed mead, I see." Vivienne picked up the bottle, uncorked it and took a sniff.

"Yes, my lady. This mead is the finest around." The merchant was an older woman named Wulfhilda. She smiled a lot and Vivienne got a good feeling from her.

"Did you sell any of your honeyed mead to the mayor's wife lately?" She corked the bottle back up and put it back down.

The woman's smile disappeared. "I did. Florence always bought her mead from me on market day to support me. But I didn't poison her if that is what you're thinking. I heard about her death, and it is a shame. She was one of the kindest people you'd ever meet, and I thought of her as a friend."

"I see," said Vivienne. The seller seemed to be sincere and she had no reason to doubt her. "Have you sold any mead to the rat-catcher by any chance?"

"The Pied Piper?" Wulfhilda's brows dipped, causing her forehead to wrinkle. "Nay! I wouldn't let that rat-catcher get anywhere near my table. He's the one who probably killed Florence."

"Really? Why would you say that?"

"For a few days, Florence hadn't been feeling well. She sent her daughter Maleine to purchase her mead on the last market day. Maleine paid me but had to leave with the blacksmith's family. She asked me to just leave the bottle of mead on her doorstep for her mother, and so I did. As I was leaving, I spied that rat-catcher hiding behind a tree. I was frightened, and ran back to the market and never even turned around."

"Thank you," said Vivienne. "You have been a great help."

"Didn't you want to buy my honeyed mead, my lady? Or are you too afraid it might be laced with arsenic and that you'll die too? Since the mayor's wife died and the gossip is that she perished from drinking my mead, I haven't been able to sell a single bottle today. I don't know how I'll survive."

Vivienne felt bad for the old woman, but at the same time she was hesitant to purchase the mead. What if it was really laced with arsenic? She didn't want to take the chance before they found Florence's killer.

"Och, ye have mead! I love mead," said Nairnie coming up behind her.

"The mayor's wife loved her mead as well," said Wulfhilda. "She couldn't get enough of it. She was the one who kept me in business and able to feed my family."

"Well, give me a bottle of it, lass," said Nairnie, plunking her coin down on the table. "Lady Vivienne, I'm sure ye want one too."

"I'm not sure. I rather prefer wine, actually."

"I have wine, too." The seller pulled out a few bottles and plunked them down on the table. Vivienne saw no way out of this now. "Red wine or white, my lady? My daughter is a nun at Maltby le Marsh Abbey and she makes both the wine and the mead with the monks and nuns there and gives it to me to sell. I'm allowed to make a profit. It is the best you'll ever taste."

"Really?" This interested Vivienne since she knew the sheriff's sister was a nun there as well. "I'll take a bottle of red," she told her, laying her coin on the table. After all, if it was made by the clergy, it had to be safe. The woman smiled again, scooping up the coin and sliding the bottle toward her.

"Thank you both. You have made an old woman very happy."

"I'm an old woman too," said Nairnie with a chuckle. "I'm glad I could help ye out."

"Yes. Me too," said Vivienne, picking up the bottle of wine. "Wulfhilda, did you say your daughter is a nun at Maltby le Marsh Abbey?"

"Yes. Her name is Sister Roberta. Do you know her?"

"Nay, I cannot say I do. But tell me, do you know Sister Magdalena? She is a nun there too and is the sheriff's sibling."

"Hmm," said the old woman in thought. "I can't say I know her, I'm sorry. But did you hear about the ghost that has been haunting the abbey's graveyard lately?"

"Nay, I didn't. A ghost, you say?"

"Yes. It is said to be one of the dead monks that used to live there."

"Really." Vivienne's heart skipped a beat. "I saw a ghost monk right here in Mablethorpe in the church's graveyard just yesterday. Mayhap it was the same one."

"Oh, my. The ghost monk must be traveling now," said the vendor. "Many people have seen him lately. His occurrences are becoming more and more frequent. It is downright scary."

"Och, ghosts are nothin' to fear," said Nairnie with a wave of her hand. She tucked the bottle of mead into her bag hanging over her shoulder. "If they're dead, they canna harm ye. It is most likely just a story to scare someone."

"Nay, it's true. Roberta wouldn't lie to me, and she saw this ghost. She said it was frightening." Her eyes grew wide.

"No more frightenin' than the Pied Piper we have here, I'll bet." Nairnie seemed to find amusement in all of this.

Vivienne noticed Elias, the market inspector at a table inspecting produce. "Excuse me," she said, walking over and tapping him on the shoulder.

"Lady Vivienne," he said in surprise, turning around with a tomato in his hand.

"May I speak with you for a moment, Elias?"

"Of course." He put the tomato back down. "You are fine. Your produce is of the right quality," he told the vendor before turning back to her. "What can I help you with, my lady?"

"Do you inspect all of the product being sold at the market each week?"

"Yes, of course."

"How often is there a market in the town square?"

"Three times a week in the summer. On Tuesdays, Thursdays and Saturdays."

"Can you tell me if you found anything wrong with the mead or wine at that woman's table during the past week?" She pointed to the table where she'd just been.

"Wulfhilda's product?" He laughed. "Oh, nay, her mead and wine is the finest and she brings it here from the abbey in Maltby le Marsh. It's made by the hands of monks and nuns."

"But you do check it, right?"

"Of course I do. It's my job. Every market day Wulfhilda gives me a sip of her mead as well as the wine."

"And you checked it the day that Florence was murdered?"

"Yes. I told you, I always do. It is my job."

"So, you didn't become ill from it at all?"

"My lady, are you implying that I might have been slacking on my duties? Because I assure you, I am loyal to my job and would never put any of the townsfolk in danger by allowing tainted product to be sold."

"I'm not saying that at all. I am sure you do a fine job, Elias. I just wondered if you became ill afterwards. That's all."

"Nay, not in the least. Now, unless there will be anything else, I have more tables to stop by and inspect."

"Aren't you going to the emergency council meeting?"

"What meeting? I didn't hear of any."

"Maurice said the mayor called one this morning. I believe it is happening now."

"Then it is going to have to happen without me. The mayor knows how busy I am on market day. There is no way I can go."

"Just one more thing, if you don't mind."

"What is it?" Elias seemed impatient and irritated by her questions. She supposed she couldn't blame him. She was taking up quite a bit of his time.

"Wulfhilda said she dropped off a bottle of mead on the mayor's doorstep since Florence hadn't been feeling well for about a week. The last time she did so was the day she was murdered."

"Aye. And before you ask, I inspected the mead before she did that. Actually, I watched over her table for her while she went to the mayor's house to leave the mead there."

"What was wrong with Florence? With her illness and all."

"I'm not sure, but she'd been having stomach cramps and diarrhea. I suppose she ate or drank something that didn't agree with her."

"How do you know that? Did the mayor tell you?" The mayor didn't mention this information to her or the sheriff, so she thought it odd that Elias would know about it.

"Nay, the mayor never said a word about his wife to anyone. I swear that sometimes he even forgot he was married. I heard the information from Maurice."

"Maurice? The town clerk?" This surprised her since the man seemed so quiet and afraid to speak up about anything.

"That's right. Like I said, Maurice."

"How would he know about Florence's health if the mayor never said a word about it?"

"My lady, I am not prone to gossip, and I cannot say for sure, but think about it. If Maurice knew, than Florence had to be the one to tell him. Now, if you'll excuse me, I have work to do."

"Yes, by all means. Thank you for your time." She watched Elias walk away, the information she'd just discovered swarming her head. Things were starting to fall into place but she needed to think on this before she brought it up to Zachariah. The last thing she needed was to make accusations that weren't true.

"Lady Vivienne, Nairnie tells me that I am invited to the sheriff's home for a meal tonight." It was the mayor's daughter, Maleine. She was a pretty girl with dark hair and dark eyes. She looked nothing like her father so Vivienne realized she must have gotten her good looks from her birthmother. She was always smiling and very respectful. Vivienne liked her a lot.

"Yes, Maleine, you are invited and I hope you will join us."

"Is Father invited as well?"

Vivienne paused, not sure how to answer. She didn't want to insult the girl by saying he wasn't, but Zachariah warned her against having the mayor there since he was a suspect in the murder case.

"If so, Father won't be able to make it," Maleine told her. "He always goes to the tavern on Saturday nights and doesn't return until very late. Actually, he goes right from work and I won't even get to see him beforehand."

"That's what we thought and why we didn't extend the invitation to him as well." It was a lie, but well needed in this situation.

"I'll be there, though. I am happy to have somewhere to go

so I won't be alone at night. Now that my stepmother is ... gone." Her smile disappeared.

"I'm so sorry about all this, Maleine." Vivienne reached out and took the girl's hand. "It must be so hard for you to endure, having lost two mothers."

"My birth mother died from the plague," she told her. "My father sent me away to stay in a convent during the plague so I wouldn't get it. When I returned, Mother was already buried. A few months later he married Florence. She seemed to be a nice woman, but I never became that close to her."

"Why not?" asked Vivienne, being curious as to the home-life she had.

"Father kept sending me away to work for the blacksmith's family, so I suppose I never had the opportunity to do so. I had hoped we'd become closer and that is why I bought her that hand cloth with her initials stitched on it."

"Do you like working for the blacksmith, watching his children while his family travels?"

"I enjoy being part of their family while I'm with them, but I admit I do miss my life here in Mablethorpe. I feel as if I have no friends at all. Especially not ones my own age."

"Are you close to your father?"

"I was when I was young. But things changed over time," the girl admitted.

"How so?"

"Father started working more and more and was never home. We never did anything as a family anymore. Sometimes, he didn't even come home nights. Or at least that is what Florence told me happened when I was not here."

"I am looking forward to seeing you tonight, Maleine. Nairnie and I are going to cook up a real feast."

"I cannot wait," said Maleine, her eyes lighting up with excitement. "I am so happy to have somewhere to go."

Martin ran up with Starah and two of the constable's children. "Maleine, we're going to go look at the bunnies for sale at the other end of the square," he told her. He wore his wooden sword proudly at his side. Grunt was next to him, panting. "Want to come with us?"

"I'd love to," said Maleine. The constable's daughter, Anabel reached up and took Maleine's hand. "I'll watch over the children," she told Vivienne.

"Thank you. I'll let Mrs. Dorson know."

Vivienne watched them walking away, smiling and laughing. Little Starah was so happy that she skipped and turned full circles with her arms extended.

"They're like a family," said Nairnie, walking up behind her. "It's a good feelin' dinna ye agree?"

"I do, Nairnie."

"I can tell ye want a family of yer own, lass. Ye are old enough, so why aren't ye married with children by now?"

"I was married. Once. It was a long time ago. I also had a son. But not anymore."

"What happened?"

"They are all gone now, Nairnie, and I miss them with all my heart. Even my parents and my brother, Adrian, were taken away from me."

"Ye'd better tell me about it."

Grief tugged at Vivienne's heart and she suddenly felt like crying. But she wouldn't. She was stronger than that. With a quick sniffle, she managed to blink away her tears. "Some other time, perhaps. Right now we have a big meal to plan, Nairnie. Do you have everything we need?"

"Everythin' but yer smile, lass. I can see how sad ye are and I dinna like it at all."

"I'll be fine, I promise. I am a survivor and always will be."

"Aye, she said in her all-knowing way. "But dinna ye think it is time to stop just bein' a survivor?"

"What does that mean?"

"It means, I can see how badly ye want a family of yer own. Ye should be a wife and a mother. That's what ye were meant to do."

"I don't agree, Nairnie. If God wanted me to be a wife and a mother then he wouldn't have punished me by taking away everyone I ever loved."

"Did ye ever think that mayhap it is time to find new people to love in yer life? After all, I see how fond ye are of that page boy, Martin."

"Yes," she said, watching the children off in the distance. Martin was showing Grunt a baby rabbit and holding Grunt back as the dog sniffed the animal in curiosity. "I have grown quite fond of Martin, but unfortunately he'll never be the son I lost. He has parents, Nairnie. I can never be his mother. I am saddened to think that his father beats him. I wish I could protect Martin forever."

"Ye are a kind soul with a good heart, lass."

"Enough with all this talk, we have work to do. And I am going to help make this the most memorable dinner that the sheriff has ever had."

Chapter Fifteen

Zachariah shuffled into his home later that day, feeling tired, hungry, and like a failure since he still hadn't been able to find enough evidence to convict and lock away Florence's murderer, whoever that may be. He had his suspicions, but it wasn't enough to make an arrest. If only someone could have given him something ... anything he could use. Instead, his hand came up empty. By the time he'd gotten to the hall for the meeting, no one was there. He ended up helping out at the marketplace since a few brawls broke out, and he never even found the mayor or other council members to talk to them.

"Father!" cried Starah when he opened the door.

"Just in time to eat. Hurry, the meal is ready," said Nairnie, putting the food on the table. Everyone was there and waiting for him. The constable and his wife and children, Maleine, Martin, Starah, Nairnie, and of course Vivienne.

"How did it go?" Vivienne put down a platter of what looked like lamb chops smothered in a green sauce. She hurried over to talk to him as he washed his hands in a basin of water.

"Not well," he told her, softly so the others couldn't hear.

"Oh, I'm sorry. So you couldn't find out anything at all that could help us with the case?"

"Nay. How about you?"

"I discovered a few things that might be beneficial to us, but I'll tell you about them later. Right now, everyone is waiting for you and the food is getting cold."

"It does smell delicious," he said drying his hands, feeling so tired that he really just wanted to sleep.

"Well, hurry up." She grabbed the towel from him and threw it down. "Martin is excited to taste the mint sauce. He's been sniffing a handful of mint all evening and wouldn't let Nairnie throw all of it into the kettle. He was so cute."

"I'll bet," he said, his mind on other things. "Vivienne, we've run out of time."

"No, we haven't. The meal is just getting started." She held out her arm to the table of people and all the food atop it. He couldn't help noticing Grunt already sitting next to his empty chair, ready to use his lap for a chin rest again.

"That's not what I mean." He took her arm and lowered it, looking deeply into her clear blue eyes that were lit up with happiness and excitement like he'd never seen before. "The Pied Piper warned us that if he didn't get paid by midnight, something bad was going to happen."

"So, he puts more dead rats on a doorstep again." She shrugged. "What does it even matter?"

"Nay, I'm afraid he might do something awful this time. Really bad."

"Oh." The smile and excitement washed away from her eyes and face. "You don't think he'll murder someone again, do you?"

"Anything is possible. I'm going to stay up all night and take Constable Dorson with me to Rotten Row."

"You're not going to spend the night on Rotten Row! Please, tell me it isn't true."

"I have no other choice. I need to keep an eye out for whatever the rat killer intends to do, and stop him from moving forward with his plan."

"I just wish you would pay him. If so, all of this could be over and we wouldn't have to worry about anything bad happening."

"I can't," he told her. "The mayor offered him a crazy amount and I don't have those kind of funds."

"Well, what about taking them from the town?"

"I can't drain the town's funds and leave everyone in a bad situation. Nay, there's got to be another way."

"I don't understand why the mayor ever made such a bad deal in the first place."

"Me either. It was more than enough to pay a man for killing rats. Even if he killed hundreds of them. However, the Pied Piper claims the mayor was supposed to pay him twice that amount."

"I don't understand. Why would the mayor even offer him an absurd amount of money? You told me Randolf was cheap. And he was paying this man out of his own pocket?"

"Yes, I don't understand it either. Something is very, very wrong here."

"If I have to call ye two to the table once more, I swear it'll at the end of my ladle hittin' ye over the head," shouted Nairnie. She stood at the table with her hands on her hips, giving them that squinty eye thing she did when she was about to become angry. Everyone waited patiently, their eyes focused on the food. He swore he could see them salivating. Grunt whined and lay down on the floor next to his chair, putting his nose between his paws and looking up with longing in his eyes.

"All right, let's eat," he called out, getting a cheer from the children. He looked back over his shoulder and talked softly to Vivienne. "We'll discuss this after the meal. We still have a few hours to figure this all out. I am hoping with your help we can do it."

"I'll try my best," she told him. "And to warn you, I did my best helping Nairnie cook, but I'm not that skilled in the kitchen since I usually have servants doing it all for me."

"I'm sure I'll love it since it came from you." He reached out and stroked the back of his hand gently over her cheek, watching as her eyes closed and a smile turned up the corners of her mouth. Damn, if everyone wasn't watching right now he'd be half-tempted to kiss her right on her beautiful lips.

Suddenly, he felt pain, realizing Nairnie's ladle had come crashing down atop his shoulder.

"Ow!" he cried, spinning around on his heel. The old woman's angry eyes and pursed mouth told him she was no one to mess with.

"I warned ye. Now both of ye get to the table because I didna work all afternoon cookin' to have to serve cold lamb."

"We're going, Nairnie. Hold back on the ladle," said Vivienne, taking his arm and pulling him over to the table. He sat down and looked around at all the smiling faces and it never felt so good. The aroma of roasted lamb, mint sauce, and an array of cooked vegetables wafted up filling the room with a delicious scent.

"Shall we pray?" asked Vivienne, getting a few groans and dirty looks from the children who were already devouring the food with their eyes.

"I'll lead the prayer," Zachariah offered. Everyone held hands with the people on either side of them. He was lucky to hold Vivienne's soft hand. It was such a difference from Nairnie's callused, dry skin since she was on his other side and he held her hand as well. "Thank you, God. For this meal, the roof over our heads, and your protection. Please watch over all of us, and keep us safe. Especially tonight."

"Amen," everyone answered and commotion started up as well as conversation and laughter as everyone dived into the feast laid before them.

It was good to be alive and to have a family. And friends. Zachariah looked down to see Grunt's chin on his lap and those big brown eyes staring up at him. "All right, Grunt. Just this once," he said, cutting off a small piece of his lamb chop and giving it to the dog. He got a hand squeeze on his arm from Vivienne and looked over to see her smiling at him. It made all of his problems momentarily disappear. Damn, this all felt so good and he hoped it would never end.

Sadly, he had a bad feeling that it wouldn't last. Because in the back of his mind, he couldn't stop thinking that tonight all hell was about to break loose and that there was going to be nothing he could do to stop it.

AFTER THE MEAL, Vivienne took Zachariah to the side and told him everything she'd learned today at the market while the rest of their guests were getting ready to leave.

"That's good information," he told her, making Vivienne feel valuable once again.

"I know we can't be sure, but I think Florence was having an affair with Maurice," she told him. "If not, how would Maurice know about her illness when the mayor wasn't freely sharing the information with anyone?"

"I agree," said the sheriff. "Plus, remember that Joy told us Maurice no longer used her services, so it makes sense that he was secretly seeing Florence."

"I still can't picture Maurice as a wild man in bed like Joy claims. He seems like such a shy man."

"If he's really that different behind closed doors, he could have killed Florence."

"Nay. Not if he was having an affair with her," said Vivienne in deep thought. "It is more likely that Florence was meeting with him the night she was murdered. Mayhap that is why she paid Joy to keep her husband occupied. She didn't want the mayor to find out."

"I don't know about that. Why would she go to the tavern to meet Maurice? She knew her husband was going to be there. It would have been too much of a risk."

"Then there must be another reason she was going to risk it," said Vivienne. "It had to be an important one. And mayhap it involved more people than just Maurice. Perhaps she was meeting with several men ... or councilmen that night."

"Florence doesn't seem like the kind of woman who would bed them all."

"No, silly. That is not what I meant. I think she might have been going there for a much bigger purpose. One that she was afraid her husband would find out about. And possibly, not agree with at all."

"You might have something there. Although without more evidence of why she was going and who she was meeting, we're never going to figure out the motive for her killer to want to do away with her."

"Good night, Sheriff," said Mrs. Dorson as her family headed toward the door. "We appreciate your invitation and the food was delicious. It was relaxing and a nice break from my normal routine."

"Yes, the children really seemed to have enjoyed themselves," said the constable. "So much so, that they don't want to leave."

"Why don't you let Anabel and Archibald stay here overnight?" suggested Vivienne. "I think Starah would really enjoy that."

"Yes, she would," agreed Zachariah.

"Well, I don't know. We've already been such a burden to you." Agatha looked over to her husband. "What do you think?"

"Before you answer, Mrs. Dorson, I have to tell you that the constable and I will be gone all night."

"You will?" Agatha looked up at her husband.

"I'm sorry, sweetheart, but the sheriff thinks the Pied Piper is going to try something tonight. We will be watching him on Rotten Row to stop him before anything bad can happen."

"Emery, I'm scared," said his wife. "I don't feel safe being alone with the children all night with that madman on the loose."

"That's why ye'll stay here as well, Mrs. Dorson. "Ye and that wee bairn in yer arms." Nairnie nodded at the baby that Agatha held to her chest.

"Yes, that's a wonderful idea," said Vivienne. "I can stay here with Martin as well."

"I don't know," said Zachariah, rubbing the back of his neck.

"There is safety in numbers," Vivienne pointed out. She was sure the sheriff was about to agree to it when there came a knock on the door. She followed the sheriff over to the door and he opened it. Vivienne was surprised to see one of her uncle's guards, Richard, at the sheriff's house.

"Richard? What are you doing here? It's still light and I didn't request you escort me home."

"Your uncle sent me, my lady," said Richard from atop his horse. "Something has happened and he requires you to bring Martin back to the castle at once."

"Oh, no. What happened?" asked Vivienne.

"He didn't tell me that information, my lady. All Lord

Mablethorpe said was that it was imperative that I bring you and Martin back to the castle. I will say right before he gave me this order, he received a missive from Lord Collingham, so it might have something to do with Martin."

"Martin's father?" whispered Vivienne, thinking of the man who beat his son. She didn't like this at all.

"I hope everything is all right," said Mrs. Dorson in concern, having overheard.

"I'll get Martin," offered Nairnie, heading over to where the children were playing with the dog.

"I'm sorry, everyone, but I guess I will not be able to stay here overnight with Martin after all," Vivienne told them.

"It's all right," said Zachariah with a nod. "You need to go back to Mablethorpe Castle with Martin just like your uncle said. It sounds important."

"I'll be back first thing in the morning. Oh, what about Maleine? Can she stay here overnight as well?"

"I'm afraid not," Zachariah answered. "Right before I returned home, one of my constables found me and told me that the mayor had a message for me."

"What was it?"

"He wasn't happy that Maleine was coming here for dinner. He probably was furious that I didn't invite him, actually. The constable said the mayor's orders were to bring her safely home afterward and to make sure she locked the doors once she was inside. He would be home later."

"Hrmph," sniffed Vivienne. "He means after he is done drinking and bedding whores at the tavern. I still think she should stay."

"He's her father, Vivienne. We have no right to overstep his wishes. Constable Dorson and I will escort her home and make certain everything is in order and that she is safe before we leave."

Vivienne felt her gut twist which was always a sign that something bad was about to happen. "All right then. I suppose." Vivienne's hand went to her stomach. Mayhap it was just the lamb not agreeing with her because there was no reason for her to feel so anxious. Was there?

"Here's Martin, ready to go," said Nairnie, hauling the boy to the door against his will.

"Nay, Nairnie. I want to stay here tonight too like the other children are doing."

"Not tonight," said Vivienne, taking him by the hand. "Tonight we need to get back to Mablethorpe Castle."

"Why?" he asked with a scowl, looking up through his long blond bangs.

"I'm not sure, but it is what Lord Mablethorpe ordered."

"Do we really have to listen to him?" Martin wouldn't give up. "You never listen to him at any other time."

"Martin, that is not true!" It more or less was, but she didn't want to give him more fuel for the fire. She supposed she hadn't been the best example to him when it came to showing respect toward a noble. Mayhap she'd have to be more careful around Martin from now on since he was young and impressionable.

"But I want to spend time with my new friends. I don't really have any friends back at the castle, Lady Vivienne. Can I stay here tonight? Pleeeeeease?"

Vivienne hated when Martin gave her that cute little look and acted this way. It was so hard to say no to the child. "We'll return first thing in the morning and you can be with your friends then," she promised. She said the words, but that gnawing feeling in her gut warned her that somehow it wasn't going to happen. God's eyes, all she could think of right now was that she hoped this time she was wrong.

Chapter Sixteen

Vivienne rode through the castle's gate with Martin sitting in front of her atop the horse. Grunt followed, stopping every so often to sniff around the ground. They dismounted and her aunt and uncle ran out of the keep and to the courtyard to meet them. This couldn't be good.

"There you are. Finally," complained her uncle.

"What's the matter?" she asked, helping Martin to dismount. The stable hand came to take care of her horse.

"Gilbert, mayhap we should go inside to the privacy of your solar first," said her aunt wringing her hands together.

"Nay, here is fine. The boy is going to find out sooner or later so what does it matter?"

"Find out what?" asked Vivienne. "Will someone please tell us what is going on?"

Vivienne's uncle started to open his mouth, but her aunt stopped him.

"Nay. I'll tell him." She came forward and took Martin's hands in hers. He looked back at Vivienne with scared eyes.

"It'll be fine," she assured him even though she had no doubt in her mind that was the furthest thing from the truth.

"Martin, we received a missive from your home today."

"From your father," intervened her uncle, gaining him a daggered look from his wife.

"Please, Gilbert. I told you I'd handle this."

"God's eyes, Ellen, just tell him already that his mother is dead."

"What?" Martin's gaze shot up to Vivienne, and she'd never seen him look so sad ... or frightened.

"That's right," said Aunt Ellen. "I'm sorry, Martin. Your mother died in her sleep. I guess the healer said she had a bad heart."

"My mother is dead?" came Martin's soft little wail. "I'll never see her again?"

"That's correct," said Lord Mablethorpe. "But don't worry, your father will be here to collect you and take you back home tomorrow, first thing in the morning."

"Nay!" Martin's body stiffened and his eyes grew wide. "I don't want to go home. I want to stay here with Lady Vivienne." He clung to Vivienne's side. She put her arm around him. Grunt came running over to nuzzle the boy.

"I'm sure it's just for the funeral and then you'll return to Mablethorpe," Vivienne told him. "You'll be back before you know it."

She looked up to see her aunt slowly shaking her head. Then her uncle's booming voice broke in again, only making matters worse.

"Your father decided you won't continue your training here at Mablethorpe," he announced.

"I won't? I'm not going to be a page anymore or a knight someday?" Martin's little fingers curled around the hilt of his wooden sword, almost like a sign that he wasn't about to let his dream go.

"You're finished," her uncle continued. "Your father thinks

you'll be better off in a monastery since he already has six sons that are training for knighthood."

Martin whimpered and started to cry. "I don't want to be a monk."

"That's absurd," spat Vivienne. "The poor child has just lost his mother and he's much too young to be sent to live with the monks."

"Nay, he's not," said her uncle. "He'll be considered an oblate. Sometimes they start at five or six years of age. It'll be good for him. The boy is already too obnoxious and not very good or devoted to his training. He'd never be a good knight, anyway."

Martin broke free and ran toward the kennels. Grunt followed. Vivienne's anger flared.

"Uncle, why did you have to say that? You've upset him. You had no right to say he'd never make a good knight. Why would you say such a thing after he's just lost his mother? What were you thinking?"

"Yes, Gilbert. You need to have a more gentle touch." Thankfully, Aunt Ellen stepped in to support her.

"God's teeth! The two of you will be the death of me yet." He waved them away and in a huff hurried back to the keep.

"I'll go try to comfort Martin," Vivienne told her aunt.

"I'm sorry, Vivienne. "I know how fond you are of the boy. But there is really nothing we can do. We have no choice but to respect his father's decision."

"Why can't we try to convince Martin's father to let him stay here with us? It's no secret he doesn't want anything to do with his son. You also heard Martin tell us that his father beats him. The poor child is frightened out of his mind."

"I'll try to talk to your uncle about it, but I don't believe the decision will be reversed. I'm so sorry, Vivienne." Her aunt left, making her way in to the keep.

Vivienne hurried to the kennels, wanting nothing more than to hug and kiss Martin right now. She longed to keep him safe from his father. She wished more than anything that Martin would be allowed to stay with her, because if so, she would show him the love he never knew. Yes, that is what she wanted more than anything right now.

"Martin? Are you in here?" Vivienne entered the kennels, being greeted by Adam, the kennel groom. He held a glowing lantern to light the area.

"He's in the empty kennel with Grunt," Adam told her, lifting the lantern so the light shined on them. Martin lay in the hay crying, hugging Grunt like he never wanted to let the dog go. "I heard what happened and have to say I'll miss the boy. So will the dogs."

"Thank you, Adam. We will all miss him," said Vivienne, feeling her heart breaking. "Martin, come back to the castle. It's time to sleep."

"Nay! I want to stay here with Grunt."

"You can both come into my room tonight," she offered, trying to help him feel more at ease.

"Nay. I want to be left alone. Go away!"

"The poor tyke," said Adam, shaking his head. "He's welcome to stay here and sleep in the kennel with Grunt tonight. As long as they don't disturb the rest of the hounds."

"Thank you, Adam. "Mayhap I'll leave him be for now and come back a little later to check on him."

"Get some sleep, my lady. I'll be staying here and will watch over the boy."

"Thank you, Adam. I appreciate it." She stuck her head over the top of the stall. "Goodnight, Martin. I'll see you in the morning."

Martin didn't respond. He was either ignoring her or mayhap had already fallen asleep, being exhausted from the day's activities. Either way, she decided she'd leave him alone for now. Mayhap being with him right now was only going to make things worse for the both of them somehow. He just lost his mother and tomorrow he'd lose her as well. This just didn't sit right with Vivienne. She decided she needed to do something about it, but first, needed a glass of wine and a hot bath to think about this entire situation. She also wanted to ponder over the information about the murder case, hoping she could figure out what they needed to know, and then get back to Zachariah so he could arrest the murderer.

After cooking and eating the big meal at the sheriff's home, she felt exhausted and could barely keep her eyes open. She had no idea how Zachariah and Constable Dorson were going to be able to stay awake all night long, hoping to stop the rat-catcher before he caused any harm.

It was about ten o'clock by the time Vivienne stepped into the hot bath that the servants had set up in her room. Sinking down into the water, she let out a small moan of delight. Yes, this was exactly what she needed after having traipsed around town all day long.

"Will there be anything else, my lady?" Maria, the kitchen maid was tending to her since Vivienne didn't have a handmaid at this time.

"Nay, Maria, thank you." She could see Maria rubbing her pregnant belly and realized she must be overly tired as well. "Did you and Cook set a date to get married yet?"

"Nay, my lady. We're both a little afraid to talk to Lord Mablethorpe about it. And since he needs to give us his permission, we decided to wait just a little longer. That way there might be less chance of him denying our request."

"Don't worry about my uncle," she said, sinking down deeper into the hot water. "I'll talk to him soon in your behalf."

"Thank you, my lady." Maria handed her a goblet of wine

which Vivienne sipped as she tried to relax. She didn't drink the wine that she'd bought at the market, but some that they had at the castle instead. Part of her was still a little wary about drinking wine from Wulfhilda. After all, for all she knew, it could be laced with arsenic just like Florence's honeyed mead. There was still no proof that Wulfhilda wasn't the one who poisoned the mayor's wife. Vivienne didn't feel as if the woman was capable of such a violent act, but she didn't know her and supposed anything could be possible at this point.

"Good night, my lady," said Maria, leaving the room and closing the door behind her.

"Yes, good night," Vivienne replied, her eyes already closing as she leaned her head back on the edge of the wooden tub that was lined in linen so she wouldn't receive splinters from the wood. There was one nighttime candle burning in the room. A small fire also blazed on the hearth across from her. It felt good to be in the comfort of her own room again. Mablethorpe Castle held all the luxuries a noble would ever want. After spending so much time with the commoners in town lately, she started appreciating things more, wondering how they could live that way. While being at the sheriff's small house wasn't all that bad, she decided that after having visited Rotten Row it was probably the worst place she'd ever been in her life. Too tired to care about anything right now and too exhausted to think about Martin or even the murder, she allowed herself to relax and slowly drifted off to sleep. Sleep should have brought her solace and well-needed rest. But instead of having pleasant dreams, her turmoiled mind filled with troubles brought her back to continue her recurring nightmare from seven years earlier ...

The fighting frightened the horses, causing them to rear up and paw at the air, whinnying loudly. The wagon jerked and her brother fell back in the hay with his feet in the air. Then the horses took off down the road at a run, pulling the wagon along with them. The sound of Vivienne's crying baby from the bench seat inside the basket caused her to panic and become furious all at the same time.

Her baby was gone! She had to save him. She needed to help her mother and also save her brother. Everyone needed her, but she felt frozen and as if she couldn't move to do anything to help.

The crying of her baby echoed loudly in her ears. The screaming of her brother and the look of terror in his eyes as she watched him head down the road being pulled by the frightened horses, made her feel useless. Her father was dead. Her mother ... where was her mother? God's eyes, she needed to find her baby. Her helpless, newborn baby who depended on her for his life.

Even in her weakened state from just having given birth, Vivienne's motherly instincts kicked in and she fought like a lion. She started swinging the sword wildly at her attacker as she lunged forward, stabbing at him over and over again. All the while she grit her teeth. No one was going to kill any of her family and get away with it! She was so angry right now, that she wasn't even scared. She wanted both of these bandits to die.

"You bastard! I'll kill you for what you've done," she shouted, causing him to actually back away from her now. His sword dangled from his fingers as he gripped his bleeding sword arm which she had injured. God's eyes, she wished she had severed his arm altogether.

"Let's go," called out the man's friend from his steed. "Someone's coming."

The man she'd struck mumbled something under his breath that she couldn't decipher, but it sounded as if he said the words, 'too soon.' He then turned and ran, mounting his horse, and then taking off with his friend, leaving her stranded all alone.

"Vivienne," came her mother's soft cry from the ground. Vivienne spun on her heel and ran to her mother, dropping the sword and falling to her knees at her mother's side.

"Mother!" she cried, cradling the woman's head atop her lap. "They killed Father. And the horses ran off with Adrian and my baby." Tears gushed from her eyes as she looked down at her mother bathed in the scant light of the partial moon that broke through the clouds. "Mother, please don't die too! Do not leave me, I beg you. I need you!" Vivienne said the words, but knew that all the wishing in the world wasn't going to change what happened here tonight. Blood covered her mother who clutched her abdomen and moaned in pain. There was no use denying that she was not going to live. Her mother lifted her hand, yanking at a chain around her neck until the chain released. Then she slowly held out her closed fist to Vivienne.

"Take ... this ... Daughter. For you ... and the baby."

"Mother, what are you doing? What do you mean?"

"Listen ... to ... me."

"I need to get you help. I think I hear horses coming down the road. I'll signal to the riders." She started to stand, but her mother's hand on her arm stopped her.

"Too ... late," came her mother's soft reply as her eyes started to close. "Go to ... your father. He ... will protect ... you ... and the ... babe."

"Mother, didn't you hear me? Father is dead!" she screamed. "I can't go to him for help. It's too late! I need to find Adrian and my baby."

"Wait." Her mother opened her fist and Vivienne looked down to see a gold ring with a ruby gemstone embedded in it dangling from the chain. It was something her mother had been wearing around her neck, although Vivienne had never known it. "This is ... your father's."

"Mother, what you saying?" Vivienne cried. "You are delirious from the pain. Father doesn't have a ring like this. He is only a poor foot soldier." She picked it up with two fingers, taking a better look at it in the moonlight. "This is gold. With a *ruby! It must belong to a very rich noble, or mayhap even a king."*

"Yes. King ... Edward. He's your ... father. Don't ... tell ... a ... soul."

"M—my father?" Vivienne thought for a moment that she had heard wrong. "Mother, what did you say? You are hurt and talking nonsense. Mother, can you hear me?"

Her mother became deathly still. When the light of the moon broke through the clouds once again, spilling over her, Vivienne saw that she stared up at her with open eyes that held no life at all within them. Just like her father. Now her mother was drained of all life too. There was no doubt in Vivienne's mind that she was dead. She had just lost both her parents in a matter of minutes. This couldn't be happening. She had to find Adrian and the baby. Bid the devil, her stomach ached and her body started shaking. She looked down to see blood on her gown and it wasn't from her parents or the man she'd stabbed. It was a result of giving birth and still not being healed. Her head dizzied. The sound of approaching hoofbeats pounding on the earth echoed in her head. Then, she felt as if she couldn't breathe and everything went black around her.

"Vivienne! Vivienne, wake up!"

Her eyes snapped open with her heart pounding wildly in her chest from her horrible dream. It took her a moment to realize that she was sitting in a tub of cold water in her room. The candle had burned out but there were enough glowing embers on the hearth for her to see the goblet floating in the water from her wine. She must have dropped it when she fell asleep.

"Vivienne? Did you hear me?" The door opened and her aunt stuck her head inside the room. "Good God, girl. Are you still sitting in the bath?"

"Aunt Ellen? What time is it?"

"It's midnight." She turned and talked to someone outside the room. "Go fetch a servant to help her from the tub and to get dressed. Hurry." She quietly closed the door and walked over and lit a candle to brighten up the room. "You must be freezing sitting there for hours in that cold water."

"Aye. It is frigid," she said, getting up and stepping out of the tub. She took the towel her aunt handed to her. "I guess I was so tired that I fell asleep in the bath. I suppose I should dry off and get into my night rail." She yawned as her aunt helped her to dry off with the towel.

"Nay, you can't go back to sleep. You need to get dressed, quickly."

"At this hour? Why on earth would I do that?"

There was a small knock at the door and Maria stuck her head inside. "Lady Vivienne? The kennel groom said you needed my help?"

"Yes, come in, quickly, Maria." Her aunt hurried over to the door. "Find Lady Vivienne something to wear from the wardrobe. Something that won't hamper her from riding or moving quickly."

"Aunt Ellen, what is going on?"

"It's Martin," she said, wringing her hands in worry.

"Martin?" Her head snapped upward. Finally dragging herself from her half-asleep state, she remembered the boy was upset and sleeping in the kennel. "Oh, I need to check on him. Wait a minute. Weren't you just talking to Adam?"

"Allow me to help, my lady." Maria walked up with her clothes and started to aid her in dressing in a gown.

"Nay, not that gown, Maria," called out Aunt Ellen. "Give her that tunic and the breeches instead. She needs to move quickly and the gown is too cumbersome."

"Aye, my lady." Maria hurried back go the wardrobe and returned with Vivienne's clothes that were meant for a man.

Actually, they were made for a young squire and were closer to Vivienne's size.

"You are actually encouraging me to wear breeches?" Vivienne asked her aunt. "Now I know something is really wrong. Tell me, what is it?"

Aunt Ellen's worried voice conveyed what was going on. "Vivienne, I was woken by Adam who told me that after he returned from drinking in the great hall he went to check on Martin."

"Oh, good. Is Martin feeling any better?" she asked, as she started to dress, keeping her back turned at first so Maria wouldn't notice her ring. "I hope he isn't still crying. The poor boy was so upset."

"We don't know. Martin was gone," said her aunt.

"Gone?" Vivienne quickly turned toward her aunt. "Did he perhaps go to sleep in the great hall after all?"

"Nay. Or if he did, no one can seem to find him. Adam said Grunt came to get him, barking like crazy. That's what alerted Adam that something was wrong, and he made his way back to the kennels to check on the boy."

"Oh, no. If Grunt isn't with Martin, then something is really wrong. Quickly, Maria, bring me my boots," she told the kitchen maid as she finished dressing.

"Here you are, my lady." Maria helped her don the boots. Vivienne hurried over and strapped on her weapon belt with her father's sword and her dagger on it. Then she rushed over to the hook on the wall and grabbed a cloak, throwing it over her shoulders.

"I've got to find Martin." Ripping open the door, she exited the room, only to find Grunt waiting for her. He barked anxiously, urging her to follow him.

"My lady, I'm so sorry." Adam ran down the corridor to join her. "I told you I'd watch over Martin and I let you down."

"Don't blame yourself, Adam. At least Grunt alerted you that Martin left. I have a feeling he was so upset about losing his mother and having to go back home to his father that he might have run away." She hurried down the stairs with the others following and the dog leading the way out to the courtyard.

"Where do you think he'd go?" asked Adam, hurrying to keep up with her pace.

"I'm not sure." She stopped for a second, seeing Grunt trying to direct her to the stable. "This way." When she got to the stable, the commotion woke the stableboy sleeping within.

"Saddle my horse," she instructed.

"Aye my lady." The boy ran to the stall and stopped. "Your horse seems to be missing, my lady. I don't understand this at all."

"Martin. He took it," she said. "Quickly, saddle another."

"Aye, my lady," said the boy, doing as ordered.

"Where do you think he went?" asked Adam.

"I have a good idea of the only place he'd go. It is somewhere he feels safe."

"Vivienne, where are you going?" asked her aunt, finally catching up to her.

With the horse saddled, she quickly mounted, talking to the others from the top of her steed. "I am sure that Martin must be on his way back to town. To the sheriff's house."

"You're not going to town alone, young lady," scolded her uncle, entering the stable in his nightclothes. Richard, the guard, was with him.

"Uncle, you can't stop me. I fear for Martin's life. No child should be out there alone in the dark. Especially not headed for town with that mad Pied Piper on the loose. I am going to look for Martin so get out of my way."

"At least take Richard with you. Richard, go with her," ordered her uncle.

"Aye, my lord." Richard ran for his horse.

"I won't be back until I find him." Vivienne exited the stable. "Grunt, show me. Where did Martin go? Find him."

The hound bayed at the moon and ran over to the castle gate scratching at it to get out.

"Raise the gate and lower the drawbridge," yelled her uncle. "Fast! We're in a hurry."

"Martin must have left hours ago. Before the gate was closed for the night," said Vivienne, wondering how no one saw him go. "I hope I can get to him in time."

"In time for what?" asked her uncle.

She looked down at the others, the gnawing and twisting sensation in her gut so strong now that she felt as if she would retch. This was a sure sign that something really bad was about to happen.

"In time to save Martin. Before another child disappears from my life forever."

Chapter Seventeen

Vivienne rode like the wind, making it to the sheriff's house quickly, Richard at her side. She jumped off her steed, seeing her horse standing nearby in the bushes.

"It's my horse," she told Richard. "Good. Martin must be here."

"I'll secure your steed so she doesn't run off," offered Richard, dismounting and going to grab the reins.

Vivienne hurriedly headed to the door, stopping suddenly when she saw the rat-catcher's black cat with the two-toned eyes sitting outside the house.

"Midnight? What are you doing here?"

Grunt saw the cat too and tried to go after it, but Vivienne was fast enough to reach down and grab him by the collar as the cat disappeared into the night.

"Nay, you don't, Grunt. You need to stay here with me tonight." She was about to walk up to the door when a horrible odor attacked her senses. She looked down at her feet and almost screamed. A large pile of dead and bloodied rats littered the area directly in front of the sheriff's door. "Richard! Come quickly," she cried, feeling things growing worse by the minute.

She released Grunt and he sniffed around the ground trying to find the cat's scent.

"My lady, what is that?" Richard hurried to her side, staring down at the rats as well. "Did that cat I just saw run off, bring those rats here?"

"Nay. There are too many of them. Besides, Midnight is no good at hunting rats at all. She'd rather beg for scraps of food instead."

"Then how did they get there?"

"It's the Pied Piper's calling marker. He's been here tonight, I have no doubt."

"The town rat-catcher? Why would he come here?" asked Richard. "I thought he stayed down on Rotten Row. And why would he dump dead rats on the sheriff's doorstep? It makes no sense at all."

"Actually, it makes perfect sense, Richard. It means the mayor didn't pay his fee in time. The Pied Piper warned them if he wasn't paid by midnight, the sheriff as well as the mayor would be sorry."

"It is at least half past midnight now, my lady."

"Yes. I fear we might be too late!"

In the scant light of the moon, Vivienne's gaze traveled up to the sheriff's door. It was open a crack and she knew Nairnie never would have left it this way before they all retired to bed for the evening.

"God's eyes, nay!" She stepped over the dead rats and pushed open the door, peering into the dark house. "Martin?" she called out. "Are you in there?"

No answer.

Grunt sneaked around her and ran inside.

"I get a bad feeling about this," she said over her shoulder to Richard, stepping further into the house. "Nairnie? Agatha?

Anyone? It is me, Lady Vivienne. Wake up! I fear something bad has happened."

"I'll light a candle, my lady." Richard found one on a table next to the door and lit it. The room brightened in a soft glow. Vivienne's heart dropped when she realized no one was inside. Still, nothing seemed to overturned or amiss, so mayhap they were all asleep upstairs. As much as she wanted to believe this, she knew better. The pain assaulting her stomach was a sure sign of trouble.

"Blethers, lass, what are ye doin' here at this late hour?" Nairnie shuffled down the stairs in her night rail, a lit candle in her hand. Her hair was tousled and her eyes half shut. Grunt barked and ran halfway up the stairs to meet her, and then turned around and descended once again.

"Nairnie? Who is shouting at this hour? They woke the baby." Constable Dorson's wife appeared at the top of the stairs with her baby, Aaron, in her arms. The infant cried softly.

"I'm no' sure what's goin' on," said Nairnie, yawning and making her way to the bottom of the stairs. "But if Lady Vivienne is no' quiet, she is goin' to wake all the children soon."

"Nairnie, the children. Where are they?" asked Vivienne looking around the empty room, her heart about beating out of her chest. "Please tell me that they are all upstairs safely sleeping."

"Nay, they wanted to sleep down here by the hearth, my lady. I didna see any harm in it so I agreed." Nairnie looked over to the glowing embers on the hearth, stretching her neck. "Children? Where are ye? Dinna play silly games with us by hidin'. Show yer faces right now."

"I'll check up here," said Agatha, trying to hush her crying baby as she went to look in the upstairs rooms. "Nairnie, the children are not up here!" she screamed.

"God's eyes, where could they be?" cried Nairnie. "The

three of them were here when I locked up and went to bed, I swear." She was talking about the sheriff's daughter Starah, and the constable's children, Anabel and Archibald.

"Nairnie, I hate to have to say this, but I think they were taken by the Pied Piper," Vivienne told her. She heard Agatha scream and hurry down the stairs with her baby clutched tightly to her chest.

"My children! We have to find them," cried the constable's wife.

"Och, Lady Vivienne, this is my fault I fear." Nairnie reached for a chair and sat atop it without looking back.

"What do you mean, Nairnie? Did something happen earlier regarding the children?"

"Aye. Right before bedtime we heard some kind of music comin' from outside. Like it came from a horn. The children were excited and ran to the door and opened it to see if it was perhaps a jongleur."

"At that time of night?" asked Vivienne, knowing no one but bandits or thieves traveled the streets in the dark.

"We didna see any musicians, but that is when they found that black cat sittin' just outside the door."

"The rat-catcher's cat?" asked Richard. "Are you sure?"

"It had two different colored eyes," said Nairnie. "And Starah kept calling her Midnight."

"That's the one," Vivienne confirmed. "We just saw it on the stoop when we arrived."

"Did you let the children go outdoors?" asked Agatha. "In the middle of the night? How could you?"

"Nay, of course no' Agatha, I am no' daft! Just the opposite, actually," stated Nairnie with conviction. "I ken how much the sheriff despises that cat, so I told the children we had to leave Midnight outside. I closed and locked the door and instructed them to get to sleep. Starah wasna happy about it. She wanted to let Midnight inside to feed her." Nairnie sighed. "I dinna ken what her infatuation is with that cat."

"You did the right thing, Nairnie," Vivienne assured her. "None of this is your fault, I'm sure. Tell me, what happened after that."

"Nothin'." Nairnie shrugged, staring at the ground. Grunt came over and rested his chin on her lap, looking up at her with sad eyes. Her hands automatically went out to pet him. "The children settled down atop the blankets near the fire. When I was sure they'd go to sleep, I headed upstairs to try to help Agatha calm little Aaron."

"I'm so frightened," said Agatha, rocking her crying baby, and weeping along with the young boy. "We have to find them. We just have to!"

"I'll get dressed anon." Nairnie sprang to her feet, and Grunt ran over to the door.

"Nay. Richard and I will search for them," Vivienne announced. "You two stay put in case the children return."

"Lady Vivienne, why did you say you think the Pied Piper took them?" asked Agatha, tears streaming from her eyes now. "Why would anyone do such a horrible thing?"

"The rat-catcher left his marker of dead rats on the stoop," she explained, not wanting to hide any information from the others since they were all in this together. "He warned us that if the mayor didn't pay him by midnight, something was going to happen, but no one could expect this. My guess is that since the children heard the sound of the Pied Piper's horn earlier, he was nearby and watching, just waiting for his opportunity to snatch them away. With the sheriff and constable down on Rotten Row looking for him, this was his perfect opportunity. I'm sure Starah must have opened the door again to see the cat once you went upstairs, Nairnie. That had to be when he snatched the children away."

"I feel like such a simpkin," said the old woman hitting herself in the head. "I should have realized Starah wouldna leave that cat alone."

"We should find the sheriff and notify him right away," suggested Richard.

"Yes. Find my husband too, please," begged Agatha. "He needs to know about our missing children."

"We will. Don't worry." Vivienne headed across the room to where Grunt was standing and staring at the door intently. "By the way, did Martin come by here tonight?"

"Nay," said Nairnie. "The last we saw him was when ye took him back to the castle with ye earlier. Why do ye ask?"

"Martin received the news tonight at the castle that his mother died and his father is coming to take him home. He was so upset by it that it seems he ran away."

"So he's missin' too?" asked Nairnie, shaking her head in disgust.

"Yes." Vivienne's heart ached. If anything happened to Martin or any of the children, she would never forgive herself for not having been here to protect them. "Martin stole my horse from the stables to get here. We found it wandering around right outside the sheriff's door, so I am sure he was here."

"Then the Pied Piper must have taken Martin too," said Richard. "Time is of the essence, my lady," he reminded her. "We should start looking for them at once."

"I agree. We need to go. Nairnie and Agatha, please stay here with the baby where you'll be safe until we return."

"But what about the children?" asked Agatha. "Do you think the Pied Piper will harm them?"

That terrible twisting sensation heightened in Vivienne's gut once again. She put her hand on the hilt of her sword. "No one is going to hurt them, because I won't allow that to happen. I will fight off the Pied Piper single-handedly if need be, but I promise I will bring all the children home alive and unharmed. Every single one of them. Even if I have to give my life to do it."

She opened the door and left with her guard. Grunt went with them.

"Where would we find the sheriff?" Richard asked her once they'd mounted their horses once again.

"Sheriff Fitch and Constable Dorson are spending the night on Rotten Row waiting for the Pied Piper. They figured he'd try something tonight since the mayor obviously didn't give him his pay. However, they are looking in the wrong place it seems."

"I don't understand. Why wouldn't the mayor pay him?"

"He thinks the Pied Piper killed his wife. I guess it is his way of rebelling against a possible murderer."

"I know how he feels, but is it a known fact that the Pied Piper killed his wife?"

"Nay, not yet. The sheriff and I are not sure who did it."

"Why didn't the sheriff just pay the man instead? I mean, at the expense of innocent children?"

"No one knew this would happen, Richard," she told him, suddenly wondering about something else. "Before we ride to Rotten Row, I want to go past the mayor's house."

"Why?"

"Because, the Pied Piper is mostly upset with him, and the mayor has a daughter. I fear Maleine may also be in danger. Let's go," she said, kicking her heels into the sides of her horse and heading toward the mayor's home. Something told her that when they got there, Maleine was going to be missing as well.

As they neared the mayor's home, she saw someone in the street, lying on the ground.

"Who is that?" she asked Richard.

"It's too dark to see. But I think whoever it is, he is hurt. And also trying to summon us."

"CALM DOWN, Randolf, and tell us exactly what happened." Zachariah and Constable Dorson stood inside the mayor's house after hearing him screaming about something when they approached his front door to question him tonight. They'd been on Rotten Row tracking the Pied Piper until they turned down an alley and found the body of the town clerk lying in a heap. He'd been stabbed by a sharp wooden staff and was dead before they even had a chance to save him. Damn, this night was going from bad to worse. They hadn't yet solved the first murder, and now there were two to contend with.

"Look!" The mayor pointed to the pile of dead rats on the floor right inside his home. "I returned from the tavern and found this. *Inside* my house! And my daughter is missing. I thought you were watching over Maleine."

"We delivered her home safely a few hours ago," Constable Dorson told him. "We even made sure she locked the door before we left."

"That's right," said the sheriff. "Mayhap she got lonely or frightened and returned to my house to spend the night with the other children after all." He suggested this, but knew by the piles of dead rats inside the house that it most likely wasn't the case.

"Nay, Maleine is not there." Vivienne barged into the house with Grunt leading the way. "I just came from your home, Sheriff. It seems that the Pied Piper has paid a little visit to you tonight as well."

"What do you mean?" Zachariah's heart jumped into his throat. "God's eyes, don't tell me Starah is missing too."

"Not only her, but two of your children as well, Constable Dorson," she said. "Plus, Martin ran off from the castle and he is missing now too."

"Dammit, we should have arrested that rat-catcher and put him in custody," swore the constable pacing the floor.

"Why didn't you?" snapped the mayor. "If you would have done so like I asked you to do in the first place Sheriff, we wouldn't be standing here looking at dead rats instead of my daughter right now."

"If you had stayed at home instead of inhabiting a stool and an upstairs room at the tavern, mayhap your daughter as well as all our children wouldn't be missing right now, so don't blame us," shouted the constable.

"You should have paid the Pied Piper. That's why he did this, Mayor," added Vivienne.

"Pay the man who murdered my wife? Never!" The mayor crossed his arms over his chest.

"We've been trailing the Pied Piper for the last few hours but he somehow managed to lose us at every turn," said the sheriff.

"You're the law in this town, how the hell could that happen?" The mayor glared at him.

Zachariah saw Grunt go over near a table holding drinks, sniffing around and pawing at the floor.

"Cursing isn't going to solve anything," said Zachariah. "Mayor, did you know that Maurice, the town clerk, died tonight?"

"So the Pied Piper murdered two people in alleyways now. What are you going to do about it, Sheriff?" The mayor's arms flailed about as he spoke.

"I never said Maurice was murdered, so how did you know that?"

"I heard a rumor. At the tavern. That there was another murder."

"If so, you or anyone in that tavern should have contacted me."

"I thought someone had." The mayor shrugged.

"We found Maurice stabbed to death with a wooden staff in an alley on Rotten Row, although it is not yet public knowledge. Why don't you tell us the truth, how you really knew?" Zachariah glanced over at Vivienne, but she for some reason didn't even react. Instead, she was more interested in what her hound was doing.

"I didn't know for sure. I just assumed he was murdered when you mentioned his death. Murdered by the Pied Piper, of course. The wooden staff proves it. It is the same staff the rat-catcher carries around."

"Well, I don't agree with you, Randolf," said Zachariah. "Because, I think you murdered Maurice because he was your wife's lover."

"Me?" the mayor's hand thumped against his chest. "That's the most absurd thing I've ever heard. I didn't murder anyone. I was in the tavern drinking. And bedding that whore, Joy. You can ask her if you don't believe me."

"We already did and she said you stopped by but didn't stay. She also told us that when she told you that Elias revealed to her that Florence was having relations with Maurice, that you stormed off angrily."

"Damn that whore," muttered the mayor.

"When we were out tracking the rat-catcher we found you slinking around the alleys instead," said Constable Dorson.

Zachariah was sure that the mayor was Maurice's killer, even if he still didn't have the proper proof. He was going on a hunch, but something told him he was right. "The constable and I both saw you earlier tonight in the area where Maurice was murdered. We stayed hidden in the shadows and didn't make our presence known. If we hadn't been following you, we might have never found Maurice."

"And if we'd stayed on the trail of the Pied Piper instead, all our children might be safe and at home right now," added Constable Dorson.

"You can't blame his murder on me," said the sheriff. "Joy was lying. I mean, did you actually see me do it?"

"Nay, we did not," answered Zachariah. "However, I think we have enough evidence to prove it's true. Especially since you knew all about Maurice's murder and where he'd been found, although it wasn't public knowledge."

Vivienne walked over to add to the conversation. "Mayor, why did the Pied Piper suddenly demand twice the amount of money you originally offered him to catch rats? After all, that is what happened, isn't it?" She seemed calm right now, and that surprised Zachariah. Especially since she'd just informed him that Martin was missing, too. He knew how fond she was of the page boy. Right now, he was about to explode with anger and was feeling like a nervous wreck at hearing the news about Starah being abducted. He needed to find his daughter and wanted more than anything to leave here right now. However, there was something he needed to do first as town sheriff. He needed to arrest the mayor before he could kill again.

"Lady Vivienne, not now," he told her.

She continued speaking without bothering to listen to him. "I think the reason is that the Pied Piper knew something that could incriminate you, Mr. Mayor. Isn't that right?"

"Of course not! Sheriff, what is this nonsense?" screamed the mayor. "We have to find our children and that murdering Pied Piper. I demand you shut her up right now."

"Nay, I'd like to hear what she has to say. Please continue, Lady Vivienne."

"First off, we'll find the children, because I won't let anything happen to them," she promised. "However, before we do, there is something that needs to be addressed." Grunt whined and pawed at the floorboard, continuing to sniff the wood.

"What do you mean?" asked the mayor.

"I had some time to think about things in the tub earlier," she told him, walking over toward Grunt. "The sheriff and I also discovered some information that shed a little light on the situation. Not to mention, I believe we now have proof that you murdered not only the town clerk but also your wife."

"Please, Vivienne," Zachariah said under his breath. "We don't have proof of that yet."

"On the contrary, I think we do." She hunkered down and pried up the end of a floor board where Grunt had been sniffing and pawing at it. There was a space underneath and she pulled out a small wooden box, throwing it on the floor. Many coins spilled out and rolled around, causing the room to go silent.

"Mayor, do you mind telling us what that is?" asked the sheriff.

"I have no idea." The man was obviously lying.

"Then let me take a stab at it." Zachariah walked over and kicked at the pile of coins. "Lately, the vendors in town don't seem to have enough to pay their full taxes for some odd reason. I also went over the town clerk's books earlier this evening and found the records lacking and the chamberlain's coffers quite low too."

"Those councilmen are both stealing from the town. Arrest them for it," snapped the mayor.

"*They* are stealing?" He looked back down at the coins that had been hidden in the floorboards. "I think you are the one stealing, and thanks to Lady Vivienne we know have the proof we needed."

"Thanks to Grunt," Vivienne mumbled.

"Nay, I know nothing about that money or how it got there.

It's not me cheating anyone. It must have been Florence. That is probably why someone killed her in the first place."

"I thought you said the Pied Piper killed your wife," broke in Vivienne. "Changing your mind about that now?"

"Nay. I'm sure he did. Arrest that rat killer, Sheriff." The mayor's story was starting to waver and weaken quickly.

"Nay, Mayor, I won't arrest the rat-catcher for this, however I will arrest a rat. That is, you! You are under arrest for swindling, stealing, and extortion. Constable, tie him up."

"With pleasure, Sheriff." The constable did as told, tying the mayor's hands in front of him.

"You can't arrest me! You have no proof," shouted the mayor. "It was Florence who did it, not me. She must have hidden the money in the floorboards."

"Convenient for you to say that since your wife is dead and cannot defend herself," said the sheriff. "I might not have proof yet that you murdered two people, but that box of money and the discrepancy in the records are proof enough of your attempts to extort everyone in this town. As soon as word gets out, I am sure the council members, as well as the shop owners, will all happily come forward to divulge the information to me that you were threatening them to keep them quiet, making them pay you however much you wanted. What did you do? Threaten to take away the jobs of the councilmen and have them replaced? And what about the shop owners? I'm guessing you told them they were paying you protection money and if they said a word to me or to anyone about it, you'd have their businesses or homes burned down or something of that sort."

The mayor didn't say a word, which also proved his guilt.

"Maurice was your wife's lover, like the sheriff said, wasn't he?" asked Vivienne. "Florence must have found out what you were doing and she was going to expose you by telling Maurice about it."

"Yes, I see it all clearly now," said the sheriff. "Florence must have approached you about your extortion. Or mayhap you just overheard a conversation or intercepted a missive as she tried to contact Maurice to tell him about it."

"Florence knew that the council members always went to the tavern after the town meetings," added Vivienne. "Since Maurice was so timid, my guess is that she wanted more assurance that you'd be caught in case he wouldn't speak up. She was going to meet with the council members, not just him, and tell them all at the same time."

"Aye," agreed the sheriff. "That is why she paid the whore named Joy to keep you up in her room longer that night. So you wouldn't come down and catch her and she'd have the time to expose your doings to all four of the councilmen. Of course, she didn't know that you were blackmailing them as well."

"I might have been doing that, but you will never prove I killed anyone. It was the Pied Piper who did it, I tell you." The mayor wouldn't confess to the murders, and that is what they really needed him to do. Zachariah had to keep trying. The only problem was, he wasn't sure how to make him talk. Not until Vivienne spoke up once again.

"That's funny that you'd say that, Mr. Mayor." Vivienne walked over to the door. "Since I have an eyewitness who says he saw you kill not only your wife, but also Maurice."

"You do?" Zachariah looked over at her in question. "That's great. That is all the proof we need to put him away for a long time. Who is it?"

"Richard, bring him in," she called out the open door.

"Yes, my lady." The castle guard walked in, holding Wymond, the rat-catcher's assistant. The boy looked to have been beaten. He was covered in blood and seemed to have a broken leg. He leaned on Richard just to walk. With each step he winced in pain.

"What's this?" asked Zachariah.

"On the way here tonight, we found Wymond lying in the street, trying to crawl away to safety with a broken leg to find someone who would listen to him," she explained.

"Does he know anything about the children?" asked the sheriff, hoping he could tell them where to find them.

"The Pied Piper took them," said Wymond. "He forced me to help him abduct them, but I didn't want to do it, honest I didn't. He threatened to kill me if I disobeyed."

"As we can see," said the sheriff. "Go on."

"He also said he'd kill me if I said a word about what we saw. When I wouldn't agree to help him or stay quiet any longer, he beat me up and tried to kill me. I would be dead already if he hadn't heard someone coming and rushed away with the children tied up in the back of the wagon."

"What exactly did you see?" asked Zachariah.

Wymond looked over at Vivienne.

"You need to tell him, Wymond. A lot of people are counting on you right now," she said softly.

"All right. I will," said Wymond. "The night the woman was murdered, me and the rat-catcher were in the alley huntin' down rats. Like we usually do. We saw him hit her over the head with a rock and leave her there to die."

"Him who?" asked Zachariah. "I need a name."

"Him. The mayor," said Wymond, pointing at him. "He killed his own wife."

"Nay, that's not true," snapped the mayor. "My wife was poisoned by arsenic. Poison just like the rat-catcher uses."

"Mr. Piper's arsenic went missing about a week ago," said Wymond.

"That's right," said Zachariah. "He did tell me that."

"He thought at first he misplaced it," continued Wymond. "Then when word was that the woman was poisoned by arsenic, we figured out it was stolen by the mayor. He killed his wife, no matter what he says."

"Why didn't you try to help Florence?" asked the constable. "Or at least tell someone she was there?"

"I wanted to, but the Pied Piper wouldn't let me."

"The Pied Piper saw an opportunity to make more money and decided he'd blackmail the mayor, didn't he?" asked Zachariah.

"Yes. That's right," confirmed Wymond. "He wanted more money from the mayor to keep quiet about what we saw."

"It all makes sense now." Zachariah was starting to see a light at the end of the tunnel regarding this case. "It's over, Mayor. You've been caught and might as well confess."

"Florence wasn't going to stay quiet about my extortion so I had to kill her!" shouted the mayor. "She found my secret hiding place with the money and said she was going to turn me in. I threatened her to stay quiet. I accused her of having an affair. I didn't have proof but I had a feeling about it so I took a chance and it paid off. I reminded her that adultery for a woman was a serious offense and that there could be severe consequences if I told the sheriff about her actions."

"That must be why she was going to the council members instead of the sheriff," said Vivienne. "You were the one who poisoned her mead, not the Pied Piper, weren't you? You hoped that would kill her, since you knew how much she liked the drink. You planned on blaming it on the Pied Piper all along, and thought no one would ever find out about any of your secret doings."

"I did, only I didn't know how much arsenic to use," admitted the mayor. "I stole it from the Pied Piper and put some in Florence's bottle of mead but I didn't use enough. It was taking too long. It made her ill but the woman just wouldn't die! I should have used the whole damned bottle, I know that now.

When I heard from Joy that Florence had paid her to keep me in her room that night, I realized my traitorous wife was going to tell her lover what I did. She needed me out of the way when she did so. However, I didn't realize at the time who her lover actually was."

"So you snuck out of the tavern when Joy was servicing the other men, and you went back home to find Florence and kill her," said the sheriff. "Then you snuck back up to the room afterward and was there when I entered the tavern."

"Yes, but I didn't have to go far. I found Florence in the back alley of the tavern. She was sick and throwing up and could barely walk. But she was still alive and could still give someone a message. I couldn't take the chance. I realized if she was there on Rotten Row then it had to be her meeting place. She was dying anyway so I just helped her along with the rock to the head. It worked beautifully." The mayor chuckled. "The rats eating her body before you found her was just an added stroke of luck. It turned out looking like even more evidence pointing to that damned rat-catcher being the murderer."

"You disgust me," hissed Vivienne. "You killed an innocent woman. Your wife! How could you?"

"Florence wasn't innocent," sneered the mayor. "She was coupling with another man behind my back."

"Well, you were sleeping with whores so what's the difference?" Vivienne stood up to him.

"As a man, I have the right to kill my wife if she is cheating on me."

Vivienne's gaze flashed over to the sheriff.

"Not in my town, you don't," growled the sheriff.

"I wanted to tell you about this sooner, Sheriff," said Wymond. "But the Pied Piper is greedy. He thought the mayor would pay him more money to keep quiet about what he did so he demanded a high amount."

"Why didn't you try to help Florence instead of leaving her there to be eaten by rats?" the constable ground out.

"I did sneak away from the rat-catcher and try to help her, but I saw she was already dead." Wymond shook his head, his face showing his despair. "I didn't know what to do. I was scared and had no one to talk to. I am an orphan and Mr. Piper is the closest thing I have to family. I have no one but my ferrets, and now he has taken them too."

"Do you know where he took the children, Wymond?" asked the sheriff.

"Nay. He tied them together with rope so they couldn't escape and put them in the back of a horse drawn wagon he stole. He made me help him grab the four children at your home, Sheriff. It was right after he knocked out the mayor's daughter and abducted her. He made me leave the dead rats inside the mayor's house and outside your home as a message to all of you."

"Four children? So was Martin with them?" asked Vivienne.

"If you mean the little blond boy with the wooden sword, yes." Wymond smiled. "He was so brave and tried to help me fight off the Pied Piper when I was being beaten. He used his wooden sword to try to reach the rat-catcher, even though he was tied up."

"Yes, that sounds like Martin," said Vivienne with a sad smile.

"Constable, put the mayor behind bars while the rest of us search for the children," ordered the sheriff.

"What's going to happen to me now?" asked the mayor in fear.

"For now, you'll go to jail. After the trial you'll be sentenced," said Zachariah. "With the charges of extortion on top of a double murder, I'm sorry to tell you that you will be executed."

"Nay," he said. "I only wanted more money to help raise my daughter."

"You sealed her fate by doing this, didn't you?" he asked. "Because of you, Maleine will never be accepted in town again."

"Maleine is all alone. She has no relatives. You can't kill me. I'm all she has. Please," begged the mayor.

"I don't think she'll want you as a father anymore after what you did," Wymond told him. "Maleine seems like such a nice girl, and I feel sorry for her. She deserves better than you."

"Let's go," said the constable, yanking the mayor toward the door. The mayor broke free and fell to the ground, grabbing for something in his pocket with his tied hands.

"Watch him! He might have a weapon," shouted Zachariah.

VIVIENNE WATCHED in horror as the mayor pulled something out of his pocket. She thought it might be a knife but instead it was a small bottle. He pulled the cork out of the bottle with his teeth and looked over to her, his eyes interlocking.

"Tell Maleine I'm sorry and that I still love her," said the mayor. "Tell her I am sorry I was such a bad father. Take care of her, my lady. Please. She has no one now. I didn't mean to ruin her life." He brought the bottle to his mouth, and with a big swig, downed the contents in two gulps.

"What's he doing?" asked the constable, trying to get him back on his feet.

"That's one of the bottles of arsenic that he stole from the Pied Piper," said Wymond.

"Arsenic?" Zachariah hurried over to the mayor, but it was too late. The mayor's body twisted and contorted on the ground as he choked on his own vomit. His eyes rolled back in his head and he gasped for breath. Then he stopped moving altogether. His eyes were open and he stared up at them in horror.

Zachariah hunkered down to check him for signs of life and slowly shook his head. "He's dead. The mayor killed himself," he announced, getting back to his feet. "There is nothing we can do now. We have all heard his confession and it will be recorded. We have our murderer, and now we need to go after the children."

Grunt barked and headed for the door as if he knew what was said.

"Richard, will you stay here with the body and Wymond until we return?" asked Zachariah.

"Aye, I'd be happy to do that for you, Sheriff."

"Constable, Lady Vivienne, let's go. I only hope we're not too late." They all hurried to the door.

"Mayhap try looking at the docks, since he headed in that direction," shouted Wymond from his position, sitting down on a chair, nursing his broken leg. "The Pied Piper might think Rotten Row is the first place you'd look for him so he is trying to make distance between you and him. I am sorry I can't be more of a help."

"Thank you, Wymond," said Vivienne. "You have already been a great help in more ways than you know."

Chapter Eighteen

"Zachariah, I am so frightened," said Vivienne as she rode with the constable and the sheriff, looking for the missing children. She hadn't used his title, and neither would she at a time like this. She thought of him as a friend and confidant right now, and that was all that mattered.

"You're not the only one," he answered. "I can't believe this is even happening."

"Should we head to the docks, Sheriff?" asked Constable Dorson.

"I suppose so. Although I'm not sure the Pied Piper could have made it that far without being spotted. Plus, the docks are spread out. If he takes them on a boat out in the water we'll never catch them."

Grunt barked, trying to get Vivienne's attention, stopping and looking at something on the ground.

"Hold up," she called to the men. "I think Grunt might have found something."

They rode over to join her as she dismounted and hunkered down to look at the object in the dark.

"What is it?" asked the sheriff.

She picked up the greens and held them to her nose. "It is the bunch of mint I gave to Martin. I think he might have dropped in purposely, hoping we would find it."

"Well, we know they came this way. Keep your eyes open for anything that might lead us to them."

They traveled toward the docks quickly, but yet keeping their focus on the ground. After a little while, she thought she saw something else and stopped them once again.

"What now, my lady?" asked the constable as they gathered in a circle. They stayed atop their horses while Vivienne got down on her knees and picked up something from the mud, holding it up for them to see.

"That looks like one of the ribbons Starah wears in her hair," said the sheriff.

"Grunt, sniff this," she told her hound, holding it out to him. The dog sniffed it up and down. "Find her," she commanded.

"Egads, Vivienne, you can't really think—" The sheriff stopped in mid-sentence as Grunt ran off barking. He led the way, looking over his shoulder, waiting for them to follow.

"God's eyes, he's doing it," said Zachariah.

"He's a bloodhound," Vivienne reminded him, climbing back atop her horse. "It's his job and what he does. Why should it surprise you?"

"You're right," Zachariah answered, shaking his head. "Why should anything you or that blasted hound do ever surprise me?"

When they got to the docks, Vivienne realized there were many fishing boats in the harbor as well as larger trade ships moored further out. Small transport boats were tied up at the shore that would be used to load and unload the ships. Running in a long row along the coast were warehouses and taverns for the sailors, and even some rundown houses. The breeze blew the salty sea air around them. There were boxes and barrels up and down the wharf as well as docks men and beggars sleeping right out in the open. There would be so many places where the Pied Piper could hide the children. It could take all night to find them. If they were even here at all.

"Mayhap we should split up," suggested the sheriff. "Constable, you go north and Lady Vivienne and I will go south. Holler if you find them."

"Aye, Sheriff," answered the constable with a nod, heading away.

"Mayhap we should start waking some of the bilge rats and ask them if they saw anything," he commented.

"Bilge rats? That's not even funny in this situation," she told him.

"Sorry. I wasn't thinking."

"What if we don't find them?" she asked, looking out to the water. "The Pied Piper could have them far out on the water by now."

"Nay. All he wants is ransom money, most likely. I don't believe he really wants to hurt them."

"I hope you're right," she said, putting her hand on the hilt of her sword. "I don't want to believe that anyone would intentionally want to hurt children." Her emotions got the best of her, thinking about her infant son and younger brother who went missing. She hoped in her heart that someone had found them and taken them in. Tears filled her eyes and she could barely see as they rode looking for the children. She couldn't lose one more person she cared about in her life. "Please, God. Let us find them," she whispered, even though she'd shunned God and hadn't prayed at all since that awful night seven years earlier. "Don't punish me again," she begged. "I have to find them. For the constable and the sheriff. And for Martin's sake. Don't let them die."

"Did you say something?" Zachariah asked, looking back

over his shoulder as they continued to ride slowly over the docks.

"Nay. I'm fine." She used the back of her hand to wipe the tears off her cheeks.

Grunt ran around sniffing everything. Every so often he barked, leading them farther away from their starting point.

"Mayhap we're looking in the wrong place," said the sheriff after a little while. "I think we should go back to town. I don't believe the Pied Piper would have come this far. Not when he wanted money. I think Wymond misled us."

"Nay, I don't believe that. Wymond has eyes for Maleine and I am sure he wants the children found as much as we do."

"Damn it, where are they?" he growled, every minute that went by seeming to make him more anxious and upset. "We wasted too much time at the mayor's house. Why didn't we leave there right away?"

"Take a deep breath," she told him, digging down deep to find the strength she needed to continue. "We are going to find them, I know we are."

Finally, as if God was listening to her requests, she saw something in the moonlight scurry by and then one more.

"It's Snuff and Chomp!"

"What?" He looked over at her and frowned.

"Wymond's ferrets. I just saw them slink by. We've got to be getting close now. Wymond said the Pied Piper took the ferrets with him."

"All right. So where are the children? I don't see them." He stopped his horse and looked around from atop. There was moonlight, but the night was still dark and it made it hard to see anything clearly.

Then Vivienne spotted something the same time as Grunt. The Pied Piper's cat sat atop a barrel down by the water. Grunt saw her and took off at the run after the cat.

"Fast! This way," she shouted, directing her horse to chase after the dog. Midnight weaved in and out around wooden boxes, barrels, and skeins of rope. Grunt was right on her tail. Then the cat took a strange turn, heading back in the direction of town but veering off toward the beach instead.

"Are you sure about this?" the sheriff shouted from behind her. "There is nowhere to hide in this direction."

"I'm just following Midnight, like you are," she called back. "That cat knows your daughter. Since Midnight is too lazy to catch rats, you can be sure she'll head right to Starah hoping to get some food."

"Let's hope you're right. For all our sakes. I'd hate to think we're blindly following a damned cat that is only running for her life."

"We're doing it for the children. For their lives," she told him. "I have faith. Don't give up. I'm sure Midnight will lead us right to them."

Just when Vivienne was about to stop and admit to Zachariah that she'd possibly been wrong, she saw something on the beach up in the distance in the moonlight. It was a small fisherman's shack that looked to have been abandoned years ago. Still, that is where the cat ran, slipping under one of the wooden walls that had partially rotted out. The shack was covered by a thatch roof.

Grunt stopped at the door, barking like crazy. Then her heart jumped when she heard children crying and calling out for help.

"Zachariah, I hear them! They are in the fisherman's shack. I'm sure of it." As she rode closer, she looked up the beach to the strip of land and saw a horse and wagon half-hidden in some brush. This was the place, she was sure of it. The Pied Piper had the children hidden in the shack. She stopped the horse and jumped down, running to the shack.

"Nay, Vivienne. Wait! He could be in there waiting for you to enter," warned Zachariah.

She stopped abruptly, waiting for Zachariah to join her, never having considered this. Grunt still barked, pawing frantically at the side of the shed, trying to get to the cat.

"Grunt, we're in here," shouted Martin. Relief washed through her to hear the boy's voice.

"Martin, is the Pied Piper in there?" she called out.

There was a pause before he answered.

"No."

"Good," said Zachariah, about to open the door but she grabbed his arm to stop him.

"The rat-catcher is in there with them," she whispered.

"Nay, he isn't. Martin just said he wasn't."

"He was lying," she said softly. "I can tell by the way he paused before he answered and also by the tone of his voice. I'm telling you, the Pied Piper is in there and probably has a knife to Martin's throat, making him answer that way."

"Damn it." Zachariah ran a weary hand through his hair. "We need to get in there. I wish Constable Dorson had come with us."

"I have an idea," she said, looking back at the horse and wagon up on the hill. "Draw him out somehow. But take your time." She got back atop her horse.

"Where are you going?"

"Trust me."

ZACHARIAH HAD to hold himself back from throwing open the door and killing the man who was holding their children hostage. But if he did, one or more of the young ones could be killed. Just like Vivienne said. He had to trust that she knew what she was doing and had a plan. In the meantime, he needed to think. What would lure the man out? His hand brushed against his money pouch and gave him an idea.

"Pied Piper, I know you're in there," he called out. "I have ... your money. From the mayor. Hand the children over to me, unharmed and it's yours and you are free to go."

"You lie, Sheriff," came the Pied Piper's deep voice. "You won't let me go. You think I killed that woman and probably that man now too."

"Nay. Nay, we know you didn't. Wymond told us the truth and the mayor confessed. You will not be arrested for murder. We know you didn't do it. Take the money. Take it, and then go. I won't stop you."

"I don't see no money."

He realized the rat-catcher must be looking out a crack in the shack. Zachariah's bluff wasn't going to work unless he could convince the man he really had what he wanted. Suddenly, he remembered something. He'd collected the rents yesterday and still had the money in his pouch. It wasn't near the amount the rat-catcher demanded, but he didn't have to know that.

"It's right here." Zachariah untied the pouch and held it up, shaking it, jangling the coins inside. "Look," he said, taking a handful of coins and throwing them down on the sand. Then he tossed the bag with the remaining money atop it.

The door slowly squeaked open. Zachariah's fingers closed around the hilt of his sword. He'd be ready for the man and take him down as soon as he was far enough away from the children. He couldn't risk that any of them would be hurt.

"Throw down your sword. Into the water. As well as your dagger," came the Pied Piper's demand.

"And why would I do that?"

"Because, if you don't, I'm going to kill your daughter." The Pied Piper stepped out onto the sand and when he did,

Zachariah almost died from fright. The rat-catcher had his dagger pressed up to Starah's throat as he held her tightly against his body.

"Starah," Zachariah said in a mere whisper, too scared right now to even move.

"Father, I'm frightened. I don't want to die," she cried. The fear on her face was so disturbing that it made him want to retch, not to mention want to kill the man holding her.

"All right," he said, holding his hands in the air. Grunt continued to bark, pawing the side of the shed. "I'll do what you ask. Just please, don't hurt her." Zachariah slowly removed his sword and tossed it into the water of the North Sea.

"Now the dagger," said the Pied Piper, moving closer to the coins, still holding tightly to Starah.

Zachariah tossed his dagger to the side as well, still holding his hands in the air. "All right. I did what you wanted. Now release my daughter as you promised."

"Hah! Not before I have the coins and know you aren't trying to fool me. Send out the blond boy," yelled the Pied Piper. Slowly, the door to the seaside shack opened and Martin walked out, his wooden sword swinging from his belt. "Pick up the bag and the coins and hand it to me," he told Martin.

Martin's eyes met with Zachariah's. "Do it, Martin. Do as he says," the sheriff told him.

"All right." Martin hurried over to the pouch, falling to his knees in the sand. He scooped up the coins, shoving them inside the pouch.

"How many are there? Count them," the Pied Piper ordered.

Martin looked at Zachariah again, but this time Zachariah very slightly shook his head, hoping Martin would understand what he meant. He didn't want the rat-catcher to realize the amount he requested was not all there.

"I can't. I don't know how to count," Martin called back, making Zachariah relieved. He knew damned well the boy could count better than any seven-year-old because Vivienne had personally taught him that as well as how to read and write. Martin was smart and had understood his silent signal.

"Bring the pouch here. Quickly."

Martin did as told.

"Open it. Let me see what's inside."

Martin looked back at Zachariah but didn't do it.

"Do it now, or your little friend here dies," warned the rat-catcher, pushing his blade closer to Starah's throat. The sheriff's daughter wailed, crying and fearing for her life.

"Wait. I'll do what you say. Don't hurt Starah. She's my friend." Martin opened the pouch and the Pied Piper stretched his neck to see inside, grabbing the pouch from him.

"What? There's barely anything in here. You lied to me, Sheriff! You lied and now you'll pay because I'm going to kill your daughter since you deceived me."

"Nay!" shouted Zachariah, rushing the man, knocking him to the ground. He heard lots of barking and the sound of wagon wheels crashing over the sand, getting closer. He struggled with the Pied Piper on the ground, doing all he could to keep the man's sharp blade from piercing him since Zachariah had no weapons now. "Martin, get Starah out of here. Hurry!" he shouted, trying to hold the rat-catcher off, but it wasn't easy. The man was big and very strong with arms the size of tree limbs.

The Pied Piper managed to get atop Zachariah, his big body pinning him down in the sand. The rat-catcher's weight on his chest started to cut off his air. "You die, Sheriff," he hissed, but instead of his blade he used one hand to uncork a bottle. "You'll die now just like the mayor's wife did."

"Arsenic," Zachariah said with a gasp, barely able to speak.

He recognized the bottle as being identical to the bottle of arsenic that the mayor had used to take his own life. He couldn't help thinking how quickly it had killed the mayor.

"That's right, it's poison. And you are going to drink it." The Pied Piper tried pouring it down Zachariah's throat, but he struggled to hold the man back and turn his head at the same time, clamping his mouth closed. Then Vivienne seemed to fall from the sky, jumping from the wagon as it approached. Her sword was drawn and ready to strike. She landed on top of the rat-catcher, pushing him away from Zachariah.

"You will not hurt anyone I care about!" she shouted. "I won't let that happen ever again."

It was just the distraction he needed to try to escape. Zachariah rolled out from under him and got to his feet. "Children, get in the wagon. Hurry," he shouted, punching the Pied Piper in the jaw, although the man didn't even flinch from the force of his fist. Zachariah used all his strength to pull the man away from Vivienne, trying to give her a moment to get free.

"Vivienne, throw me your sword. Hurry," he ordered, holding out one hand.

"Nay. I'm going to kill him for what he did. No one is going to take my family away from me again."

"Do what I say, sweetheart. Give me the damned sword." He shook his empty hand but still she wouldn't give up her weapon.

Like a woman possessed, Vivienne continued to fight. But she wasn't strong enough to go up against this powerful man. The Pied Piper grabbed Vivienne's sword by the blade, groaning loudly as the sharp edges dug into his flesh and caused his hand to bleed. He pulled the sword to him and then yanked Vivienne against his chest. Before Zachariah could even stop him, he had Vivienne's own sword to her throat.

"That was stupid," said the Pied Piper, laughing. "And now, I'll be on my way with not only the coins, but also your little lady, Sheriff. I'm taking her sword as well." He headed for the wagon with Vivienne struggling to get out of his hold, but to no avail.

"Vivienne, don't fight him. He'll kill you," Zachariah warned her, hoping to hell she would listen to him this time.

"Sheriff, here's your sword."

"And your dagger."

He spun around to see Maleine handing him his sword that she'd picked up out of the water. Archibald gave him his dagger. Maleine, Anabel, and Archibald were tied together with rope around their hands and legs. Starah ran across the sand to Zachariah, clinging desperately to his leg.

"Father," his daughter wailed, tears streaming down her cheeks. "I'm so scared."

"Thank you, children," he said, taking his blades from them and then quickly reaching down to give his daughter a quick hug and a kiss on the cheek, thankful she was alive. "Starah, stay here with Maleine and the other children. Do you hear me? It's very important. I have to save Lady Vivienne from the Pied Piper."

"Nay, I don't want you to leave. Stay with me." Starah continued to cling to his leg, making it impossible for him to go to Vivienne's aid. He turned his head to see the rat-catcher leaving in the wagon, his arm still around Vivienne. The blade was still pressed to her throat as he headed down the beach along the water's edge.

"Sweetheart, I can't let Lady Vivienne die," he told his daughter, feeling time slipping away. Every second could be the difference between life and death. "You need to listen to me. I love you and I'll be right back. But right now, you need to stay here with the other children."

"Nay! You're going to die," cried Starah. "I know you're going to leave me, just like Mother did."

"Look at me," he said, hunkering down and holding her chin in his hand, staring directly into her big brown eyes. "Have I ever lied to you before?"

She shook her head.

"And I'm not lying to you now, either. I swear. I promise I will be fine and I will return. Now please, Starah. Do as I say. I have work to do."

"I'll watch her, Sheriff. Come on, Starah." Maleine pulled Starah to her, which allowed Zachariah to run over to his horse. He followed the wagon at break-neck speed, trying to catch up to the rat-catcher before something awful happened. Grunt barked, running ahead of him to lead the way as they chased the wagon heading down the beach at the water's edge.

VIVIENNE STRUGGLED with the Pied Piper, and probably could have broken away and jumped off the wagon, but at the last second she saw Martin from the corner of her eye. He was hiding in the back of the wagon.

Fear crashed through her as history seemed about to repeat itself. Her stomach clenched and she felt as if she would swoon. All she could see in her mind right now was her younger brother Adrian and his scared expression as the horse and wagon ran off with him still in the back while she helplessly watched him go. That same fear she'd seen in her brother's eyes seven years ago was in Martin's eyes right now. There was no way she would ever even consider saving herself and leaving Martin behind. She wouldn't let his fate be determined by the Pied Piper, not even if she had to give her life to try to stop it from happening.

"Vivienne," shouted the sheriff, riding his horse fast, trying to catch up to them. "Get off the wagon. Do you hear me? Jump into the water. Jump, I say."

Once again, she looked back at Martin who was creeping forward toward them. He gripped his little wooden sword with two hands.

"No," she said, looking at Martin and shaking her head. "Don't do it."

"Who are you talking to?" The Pied Piper turned slightly to look behind him. When he did, Martin brought the wooden sword crashing down over the rat-catcher's head. It was just the distraction she needed. She managed to yank her sword away from the Pied Piper at that moment, holding the tip of it under his throat now. She was so angry and the blood pumped through her so furiously that she would have no regret taking this man's life. Her only thought was that she didn't want Martin to see her kill him.

"Whoa, whoa!" shouted Zachariah, turning his horse enough to grab the reins of the horse pulling the wagon, managing to make it stop. From the jolt of the quick movement, Martin's little body lunged forward over the back of the wagon against the bench seat. He smashed into the rat-catcher, knocking the tip of Vivienne's sword away. The Pied Piper pushed Vivienne out of the wagon and she and her sword fell into the sea.

"I'll kill you, you little whelp!" Still atop the wagon, the Pied Piper stood up, his hands fastened around Martin's throat as he lifted him up by the neck and the boy's feet dangled in midair. He was trying to choke Martin to death! It was a true nightmare come to life once more.

As if in slow motion, Vivienne crawled through the shallow water to grab her sword, but she could barely move. The intensity of the situation, her knees sinking into the wet sand, her own fear, and her grief of the past weighed heavy upon her shoulders and held her down. She saw Zachariah leap off his horse. He ran across the beach with his sword held high, making his way to the wagon quickly. Then Martin stopped struggling under the Pied Piper's hold and his eyes closed. The page boy's face quickly started turning an eerie shade of blue.

"Naaaaay!" screamed Vivienne, not believing what she saw. Martin couldn't breathe. He was going to die. She couldn't allow this to happen. Nay, she wouldn't lose another person she loved.

Struggling to get to her feet, she ran toward them, gripping her sword tightly. That's when Midnight jumped from the back of the wagon up to the top of the bench seat. Then the sound of Grunt barking echoed in her ears. She watched in amazement as her hound leaped through the air and up to the wagon, trying to get the cat. Grunt knocked into the Pied Piper, causing him to drop Martin's limp little body right into the water.

"Martin!" she cried, releasing her sword and forgetting about the Pied Piper momentarily. All that mattered right now was to help Martin. She got to her feet and ran across the beach to retrieve him. The waves crashed over his body, quickly pulling him out to sea. She dove into the water, taking a hold of him, and quickly swimming back to the shore, laying him down in the sand.

"Sheriff! Did you get him?" cried the constable, riding his horse down the beach after them.

"Aye," Zachariah called back, having the Pied Piper face down on the ground and his foot atop his back. His blade was pressed up against the rat-catcher's neck. While the constable and the sheriff worked to tie him up, she leaned over Martin, hoping and praying that he was not dead.

"Martin, can you hear me? Wake up," she cried, shaking the boy by his shoulders. His eyes remained closed, his body limp, and his head tilted back. When he didn't awaken and didn't even move, she took his cold little body into her arms. Holding him tightly up against her, she rocked him back and forth as she would a baby, and cried. "I love you, Martin. Please, please, don't die on me. Come back to me, I beg you."

Then the most miraculous thing happened. Just when she thought she'd lost him, too, the little boy coughed and spit up water. He wheezed, trying to take a breath.

"You're alive!" she shouted, hugging him and kissing him. His head lifted and his eyes opened. Those beautiful, bright blue eyes stared directly into hers and she saw the life shining forth within him once again. A large smile slowly spread across his face.

"Did I get the Pied Piper, Lady Vivienne? Did I save you with my sword?"

"Yes, sweetheart, you certainly did." She laughed and placed kisses all over his face and on the top of his downy head. "You were such a brave boy and will make a fine knight some-day. Thank you from the bottom of my heart, Martin. Not only for helping me, but for coming back to me as well."

Grunt ran over with his tail wagging. His big nose sniffed the boy and then he licked Martin's face, causing him to giggle.

"Hello, Grunt. Good to see you." Martin reached up and gave the dog a big hug around the neck.

"Vivienne, let's go!" shouted Zachariah from down the beach. "All the children are in the wagon and I've got the Pied Piper tied up on my horse. Is Martin all right?"

"Yes, he's fine," she called out to him, pushing back a wet strand of hair from Martin's eyes. Even sopping wet, nothing or no one ever looked so good to her as seeing Martin alive did right now.

"Glad to hear it," called out the sheriff. "I want to get back to town quickly to put the Pied Piper behind bars where he belongs before he tries to hurt anyone else, so hurry."

"Of course. And everyone will want to know that we found the children and that they are unharmed," she called back to him, not able to stop smiling. "Come on, Martin. It's time to go home." She stood up and held out her hand.

"Wait, I lost my shoe in the water, Lady Vivienne." Martin crawled over the sand, reaching into the water to get his shoe. Vivienne looked down at the little boy as he sat in the water and lifted up his foot to put on his soggy shoe.

She froze, her heart almost stopping when she spied the bottom of his bare foot. His left foot. There, in the moonlight like a message beaming down from the heavens, was a brown birthmark shaped like a heart. In her mind she heard her mother's voice clearly, saying her son had been kissed by an angel. Her infant son had this same heart-shaped birthmark on the bottom of his left foot. It wasn't a coincidence, she knew that now. She'd felt an attraction or connection to Martin ever since he'd showed up in Mablethorpe to be mentored. He had the same blue eyes as she, and the same blond hair. There was no doubt in her mind or her heart that he belonged to her.

"My son," she said in a mere whisper, reaching down to pick him up, holding him in a protective tight hug as his legs wrapped around her waist. Her rapidly beating heart seemed to meld with his, their two bodies pressed closely together. Once again she felt the same connection she'd had with her newborn son just after giving birth. Just before she lost him. "I found you. Thank God, you are alive. I am never going to let you out of my sight ever again. I love you, Martin!" Tears flowed from her eyes like a waterfall, but they were happy tears and she didn't mind them.

"Thanks for coming to get us from the rat-catcher, Lady Vivienne. But why are you crying?" Martin had no idea she was his mother since he already had parents. That is, a dead mother who had raised him, and a live father who beat him and seemed to want nothing to do with him. Now that she knew he was her son, all that would change. She would do everything in her power to make sure of it. No one was ever going to hurt her baby again.

In the deep darkness of her grief, a tiny crack formed and light burst through, bringing hope back into her life. In that very moment, part of her horrendous nightmare had vanished. She felt blessed for the first time in seven years. She had found her lost baby and he was alive! Vivienne was a mother once again. The son she'd lost and who she believed to be dead was alive and now she'd found him. That was a miracle, and one that would change both of their lives forever.

Chapter Nineteen

Vivienne drove the wagon carrying the children while the sheriff and the constable made sure the rat-catcher didn't escape. Their first stop was to the sheriff's office to lock up the Pied Piper where he'd await trial. Martin had asked them for the Pied Piper's horn before they took him away. She wasn't sure why Martin wanted it, but the sheriff said the rat-catcher would no longer need it so he gave it to the boy. Once the Pied Piper was locked up and the sheriff gave orders to the other constables, both he and Constable Dorson walked back out to join them.

Constable Dorson got atop his horse, letting both Anabel and Archibald ride with him. The sheriff, however, scooted next to her on the bench seat of the wagon. The rest of the children were in the back with Grunt. Starah held Midnight tightly in her arms while Martin held Grunt's collar so he wouldn't frighten the cat and make her run. Maleine sat between the children, helping to keep the cat and dog separated.

"Father, can I keep Midnight?" came Starah's question from behind them as the sheriff took the reins.

When Vivienne was sure he was going to object, she cleared her throat.

"The Pied Piper will most likely be locked up for some time, won't he?" she asked.

"Aye. He has some serious offenses that will need to be considered," Zachariah answered as he headed the horse and wagon back to his home. "With the kidnapping of five children, and all the attempts to murder, he will most likely end up hanging or being beheaded."

"So, he won't be returning to Mablethorpe," she said.

"Nay, I'm happy to say he won't."

"Then the cat will need a home, don't you agree?" she asked him.

"Vivienne? What are you doing?" he said under his breath, knowing she was up to something.

"Wymond said that Midnight was never any good at catching rats, and Starah adores her," she told him. "You realize that if you say no, she'll just keep going out to look for the cat."

"I suppose you have a point. We don't want anything like what happened here tonight to ever transpire again."

"Then can I keep her, Father?" Starah was standing in the wagon, still coddling the cat and looking over their shoulders now.

"Starah, sometimes you act a little too much like Lady Vivienne," he told her.

"What does that mean?" asked the little girl.

"I think it means you can keep Midnight. Doesn't it, Sheriff?" Vivienne smiled triumphantly.

"I suppose so," he answered, getting shouts of joy from all the children. "But if Midnight doesn't learn to hunt rats soon, I might change my mind. If there's going to be a cat living in my house, she needs to be useful."

"Martin and I will teach her to hunt rats, Father. We promise." Starah kissed the cat on the head. Midnight looked up with her eye of green and eye of yellow and mewed softly, sounding so content.

"Sheriff, stop the wagon! Stop right now," shouted Martin. "Maleine, hold on to Grunt."

"What's the matter?" Zachariah looked back but kept going.

"Stop," said Vivienne when she saw Martin climbing up the side of the wagon, ready to jump out. "Martin, what are you doing?"

"I just saw Snuff and Chomp. I'm sure I did."

"Who?" asked the sheriff, finally stopping the wagon.

"He's talking about the rat-catcher's ferrets," Vivienne explained.

"It's too dark to see anything. I'm sure he's mistaken," Zachariah grunted.

"Nay, he's right. I see them too." Vivienne jumped out of the wagon to help Martin.

"Sheriff? Is everything all right?" asked Constable Dorson from atop his horse. His children both sat in front of him and he had his arms around them.

"I want to see Mother," whined little Anabel, rubbing her eyes.

"Go on back to the house and tell Agatha and Nairnie that we found the children," instructed Zachariah. "We'll be there as soon as we're finished with this nonsense."

"Aye, Sheriff." Constable Dorson left with his children, heading back to the sheriff's home.

"Maleine, quick. Throw me the rat-catcher's horn," shouted Martin, holding up his hands. His clothes were still wet and his hair dripped with water, but he didn't seem to care. "I'll call the ferrets to me, the way the Pied Piper did."

"So that's why you wanted the horn," said Vivienne, feeling proud that Martin even thought about the ferrets and their fate.

"God's eyes, nay," complained Zachariah from the front of the wagon. "We're not going to be bringing those rodents back too, are we?"

"They are not rodents, they are ferrets," Vivienne corrected him. "They are also pets. Wymond will be looking for them. We have to help him since his leg is broken and he won't be able to go out searching for them." Vivienne reached for one of the ferrets, but he was spooked and slipped right through her fingers.

When Maleine tossed the horn to Martin over the side of the wagon, she had to let go of Grunt to do so. The dog put his front paws up on the edge of the wagon, looking down to the ground with his tongue hanging out.

Martin blew a few notes on the horn, and sure enough the ferrets both ran right to him, the same way they did when the Pied Piper had summoned them. He bent down and picked up the brown one at the same time that Grunt jumped over the side of the wagon barking, chasing the white one around in circles.

"Grunt, stop that," cried Vivienne, but she realized her dog was only helping them after all. Grunt picked up the white ferret with the pink nose and trotted over to her with the animal in his mouth, proudly presenting it to her. "Well, good boy. You brought me Snuff. Or is this one, Chomp? I'm not really sure."

"The white one is Chomp," Martin told her. "She's a girl. Snuff, the brown one is a boy."

She gently took the ferret out of Grunt's mouth and inspected her to make sure she wasn't harmed.

"All right, everyone back into the wagon," commanded the sheriff. "There will be no more stops to collect anything tonight. So if any animal darts off, consider them gone for good."

"Can I hold Chomp?" asked Maleine.

"Sure," said Vivienne, handing the white ferret to her.

When they got back to the sheriff's home, the constable was

waiting with his wife and their baby and the other two children. Nairnie was with them. They all stood outside the house.

"Thank goodness, ye are all back and look to be all in one piece." Nairnie waddled over to the wagon and her eyes opened wide when she saw Martin. "Laddie, why are ye drippin' wet?"

"I fell in the water when I saved Lady Vivienne from the Pied Piper with my wooden sword," Martin told her. "And we saved Chomp and Snuff too." He proudly held up the brown ferret to show her.

"Och, dinna tell me that rodent is comin' into the house." Nairnie wrinkled her nose.

"Nay, Nairnie," Zachariah answered with a chuckle. "But unfortunately the cat is staying with us from now on."

"Och, ye found Midnight?" Her expression changed to one of happiness now. "I'm glad. I like that cat. Well, come on inside, all of ye. I have prepared some food for ye to eat. I'm sure the wee ones must be hungry."

"I'm starving," said Martin. "It's a lot of work being a knight, you know." He tapped the wooden sword at his side and smiled.

"Knight or no, we'll need to get you into dry clothes before ye get sick in this night air. Come on," said Nairnie, reaching up to help Martin out of the wagon.

"I'll take Snuff," Maleine offered, taking the ferret from Martin so she held both of them now.

"Come on, Starah. You need to get to bed." Zachariah helped his daughter out of the wagon since she was still holding tightly to Midnight. Then he glanced over at Vivienne. "You're going to the mayor's house with me to finish up there, right?"

Vivienne wanted to stay with Martin, but when she looked over at Maleine snuggling the ferrets it about broke her heart.

"My father will be worried about me. I'm sure he can't wait to see me," said Maleine.

"Yes. I'm coming too," Vivienne told him, knowing it would

be hard for Maleine when she found out the truth about her father. As much as Vivienne didn't want to leave her son after finally finding him, she also couldn't let Maleine go through this horrible time alone.

"I'm coming along as well, Sheriff. You'll need me," said the constable, kissing his wife and children before mounting his horse.

"Starah, you be good until I return." Zachariah hugged his daughter and handed her over to Nairnie. The cat meowed and actually licked him on the hand. He, in turn, quickly pet the cat on the head. Vivienne smiled, thinking there was hope yet that Zachariah and Midnight might actually end up being friends.

"Can Grunt stay here with us?" asked Martin, looking up eagerly. "I'm sure he's hungry too."

Vivienne wanted more than anything to jump out of the wagon and kiss and hug her child the way the men did theirs. But she hadn't told anyone yet what she'd discovered. And she wasn't sure what to do since Martin's father was arriving tomorrow at the castle to take him home. She needed to be alone with Zachariah and tell him about this. He'd know what to do. However, she wasn't going to be alone with him for a while yet. Not until things were settled pertaining to the mayor and his daughter.

"Sure, he can," said Vivienne. "Grunt, go on in the house with Martin."

The dog jumped over the side of the wagon and ran through the open door.

"Just keep the dang cat away from him and keep the door to the house closed," called out the sheriff, climbing back atop the wagon.

"Sheriff," said the constable. "Should we leave the horse and wagon here in the stable until we find out who the Pied Piper stole it from?"

"Nay, not yet." Zachariah shook his head. "We'll need it to go to the coroner's."

"We'll need to use it to take Wymond to the doctor since he's broken his leg," Vivienne said quickly, not yet having told Maleine that her father was dead.

As they made their way back to the mayor's house, they didn't talk much. Then, Maleine spoke up from the back of the wagon.

"Is there something you're not telling me?" she asked.

The sheriff was about to speak, but Vivienne gently touched his arm and shook her head, wanting to be the one to tell her.

"What do you mean?" she asked.

"When the Pied Piper had us locked in the shed on the beach, I heard the sheriff tell him that Wymond told him the truth and that my father confessed. He said the rat-catcher wouldn't be charged with murder."

"That's right," said the sheriff. "Wymond is at your house right now. He came to us, wanting to help save you and the rest of the children."

"I know. Wymond is nice. He shouldn't be punished for only doing what the Pied Piper forced him to do," said Maleine.

"You have to understand that Wymond is still an accessory to the crime," said the sheriff.

"Not really," Vivienne spoke up. "After all, he only helped kidnap the children because he said the Pied Piper threatened to kill him if he didn't. He was just trying to save his own life."

"That's true," said Maleine. "He even tried to help us escape, but the Pied Piper beat him and broke his leg. We all saw it. Please, don't put Wymond in jail or execute him."

"Maleine, don't worry, he won't be executed. Will he?" Vivienne asked, looking over to the sheriff.

"Most likely since he was a witness to both murders and came forward, as well as told us where to find the children, his sentence should be lighter," said Zachariah. "However, I can't say for sure yet. It all depends on how his trial goes."

"Wymond saw my mother murdered?" Maleine seemed very upset to hear this.

"Yes, Maleine, he did," Vivienne told her. "And the town clerk was also murdered tonight and Wymond saw the killer do that too."

"I'm confused," said Maleine. "So, if the Pied Piper didn't do it, then who did?"

Vivienne and Zachariah exchanged glances as they pulled up to the mayor's home and stopped the wagon.

"It was my father, wasn't it?" asked Maleine. "He murdered both my mother and that town clerk." She was a bright girl and figured it out on her own.

"I'm sorry, Maleine, but yes, it is true," Vivienne told her in a soft voice, hurriedly getting out of the wagon. The sheriff got out and helped Maleine to the ground. She still held on to the ferrets.

"Are you going to execute my father for what he did?" asked Maleine, tears flowing from her eyes. Vivienne's heart went out to her. This poor girl had lost two parents in a matter of days. Vivienne knew how that felt and it was a horrible feeling indeed. She walked over to put her arm around her, but Maleine stepped away from her. "I want to see my father. I need to tell him goodbye before he goes to jail." Still holding the ferrets, she ran into the house.

"Zachariah, we've got to stop her. We can't let her see her father lying there dead," said Vivienne, about to run after her.

"It's all right," he told her, putting his hand on her shoulder. "She's going to find out sooner or later."

Vivienne ran into the house anyway, stopping when she saw Maleine's gaze drop to the floor and the body of her dead father.

"Father!" she cried, her entire body trembling.

"Maleine! You're all right." Wymond hobbled out of his chair, holding on to furniture to get to her. "You found Chomp and Snuff. Thank you." He took the ferrets from Maleine.

Maleine walked forward as if in a trance, dropping to her knees and throwing herself over the corpse of her father. She cried so hard that Vivienne felt she needed to do something to help her but didn't know what.

"Lady Vivienne," said her guard, Richard, looking up helplessly as well.

"Why did you kill him?" Maleine looked up with anger in her eyes. "I didn't even get to say goodbye."

"We didn't kill your father." Vivienne got down on the floor and took Maleine's hand in hers. "Maleine, your father couldn't live with himself after the bad things he did. He drank a bottle of liquid with arsenic in it, killing himself instantly."

"The same way he killed my stepmother," said Maleine.

"Yes," she answered. "But before he did it, he told me that he only wanted the best for you. And that he loved you, Maleine."

"Oh, Lady Vivienne, what will I do?" Maleine threw herself into Vivienne's arms. "I have no one now, and nowhere to go."

"You have me, Maleine," Wymond said from his chair. His broken leg stuck out in front of him at an odd angle. He cradled his ferrets in his lap. "Mayhap we can get married. Then you and I and Snuff and Chomp can live together."

"Really," said the sheriff, shaking his head. "And where would you live? In the graveyard? And what would you do for money? Hunt rats? Wymond, you're in no position to make her any promises. You're going to trial soon and I can't honestly say what's going to happen because of your part in all this. After all, you kept valuable information pertaining to the murders from me."

"But I came to you, Sheriff. I told you what I saw. I tried to help the children and to help you find them."

"That's right, he did," said Vivienne, cradling the crying girl in her arms. "And Maleine confirmed that it was true about not wanting to kidnap them and how Wymond tried to stop it, almost getting killed because of it."

"Vivienne, please. You're not helping matters any," said the sheriff, looking less than pleased with her comments. "Constable, Richard, can the two of you take the mayor's body out to the wagon and bring him to the coroner's? Constable Dorson will deliver the corpse and then you can get back to the castle, Richard. Thank you for staying here until we returned."

"Aye," said Richard. "I'd be more than happy to help in any way I can."

"Your assistance is appreciated. I'll be sure to mention it to Lord Mablethorpe."

"What's going to happen to me now?" asked Wymond, looking very uneasy.

"Well, for starters, I'm going to take you to the doctor so he can set that broken leg," Zachariah told him.

"And then what?" asked Wymond, petting his ferrets. "Will I really have to go to trial? I don't want to go to jail. I'm scared. Please, Sheriff, can't you pardon me?"

ZACHARIAH LOOKED over at Vivienne who stared up at him with that look on her face that she always had when she didn't want him to do something. She rocked the crying girl in her arms, her mouth set firm as she waited for his answer.

"If it weren't for Wymond, our children could be dead right now," Vivienne stated, making him wonder why she used the word *our*. He supposed it was because she had a good heart and seemed to consider herself a mother to everyone's children even though she had none of her own. "Wymond doesn't deserve to be punished. His life was threatened by the Pied Piper. What was he supposed to do? He tried to make things right, and almost lost his life doing so."

Once again, Zachariah was in a position where he'd rather not be. He stepped to the side to let the constable and Richard pass as they carried the mayor's body out to the wagon.

"Even if I let you go, Wymond, because you worked with the Pied Piper, it doesn't bode well for you. No one in town will ever accept you."

"I know," said Wymond sadly, holding up one of the ferrets and rubbing his cheek against the animal's fur. "I'm all alone now, just like Maleine."

"No one in town will ever accept me either, will they?" asked Maleine with a sniffle. "They will all hate my father for what he did and they will hate me because of it."

"Don't say that," he told her, even though he realized it was true.

"Lady Vivienne, where will I go? What will I do now? I am so scared," said Maleine.

"If you pardon me, I'll marry Maleine if she'll have me," said Wymond once again. "We can go to another town where no one knows us."

"Thank you, Wymond, but I don't want to always be on the run," Maleine told him. "I like you, but I cannot marry you when I barely know you."

"Oh. I see." Wymond frowned and looked down at the floor.

"Sheriff, if you can dismiss any charges that might occur against Wymond, I have a place for him to live at Mablethorpe Castle," said Vivienne.

"You can't be serious," he grumbled. "Vivienne, you can't keep bringing misfits and orphans back to the castle. Your uncle isn't going to allow it."

"Nay, I'm sure he won't mind. We have rats at the castle and my aunt hates rats. She's always complaining to my uncle and telling him to do something about it but he won't."

"I can catch the rats for you," said Wymond, perking up. "With the help of Snuff and Chomp, we'll have them cleared out in no time." He smiled and held up his ferrets, as they sniffed the air and wiggled their whiskers.

"And then what?" asked Zachariah. "That job won't last forever."

"Nay, but we are in need of another stableboy and I think Wymond would be good with the horses since he seems to have a love for animals." Once again, Vivienne came up with her own solution.

"Vivienne, don't do this to me," he said under his breath.

"I do love animals," said Wymond. "And as soon as my leg is healed, I'll not only brush and feed and clean up after the horses, but I'll even ride them to exercise them. When I was young, before my parents died, my father was a stable hand and he taught me everything about tending to horses."

"Really. I didn't know that," said Zachariah.

"See, Sheriff Fitch?" Vivienne looked way too smug right now. "Just like I said, Wymond would be perfect as a stableboy. He'll fit right in at the castle. Don't worry about my uncle. I'll handle him."

"Yes. I'm sure you will," said Zachariah.

"Well? What do you say then?" Vivienne's bright blue eyes were fastened on him and once again, he couldn't tell her *no*.

"I suppose Wymond was a big help to us and we have him to thank for being able to retrieve the children. And like you said, he was being threatened by the Pied Piper to do those things. He never really hurt anyone."

"Nay, he didn't. Just the opposite," said Vivienne.

"Am I free to go live at the castle then, Sheriff? Please. I promise to be a changed person from this day on."

Zachariah sighed and ran a hand through his hair. Why was his job as sheriff so hard ever since Vivienne got involved? And why did all the challenging decisions he had to make lately all have to do with what she wanted? "I suppose that would be all right, but you've got to get to the doctor first and have that broken leg looked at. You'll be doing none of these jobs until you're back on your feet again."

"Thank you, Sheriff," said Wymond, looking so relieved.

"Yes, thank you, Sheriff," added Vivienne. "And as soon as Wymond's leg is tended to, I'll take him back to the castle myself. He'll stay there while he is healing."

"What about Snuff and Chomp?" asked Wymond, holding up his ferrets. "Will they be welcome at the castle too?"

"As long as you can keep them away from Grunt and the other hounds, I don't see a problem," Vivienne told him. "The Pied Piper's horn is in the wagon, by the way. Martin got it for you. You can use that to summon them if they go astray."

"Yes. Yes, I'll do that." Wymond smiled, looking happy for the first time. "I'll even help you clean up the dead rats I put on the doorsteps, Sheriff."

"Don't bother. I'll handle it," he answered.

"Maleine, I want you to come back to the castle with me as well," Vivienne told the mayor's daughter.

"Nay," Maleine sadly answered. "I don't belong there, my lady, and you know it. Thank you, but I think I'm going to join the abbey instead."

"The abbey?" asked the sheriff in surprise. "Why there?"

"I want to atone for my father's sins and mayhap that is the way I can do it."

"We can talk about this more, later," said Vivienne. "But in the meantime, I am taking you back to the castle until after your father's funeral. The sheriff and I will help you to collect your belongings and move you from your house as well."

"Thank you, Lady Vivienne. I would like that," said Maleine, getting to her feet and drying her eyes. She walked over to Wymond. "Thank you for wanting to marry me, Wymond. I am sorry I turned you down, but I really need to atone for my father's sins."

"I understand," said Wymond. "But if you ever change your mind and decide not to be a nun after all, my offer still holds."

"I'll remember that." She leaned over and kissed Wymond on the cheek, causing him to blush.

"Sheriff, can I assist in bringing Wymond to the doctor's before I take Lady Vivienne back to the castle?" asked Richard as he and the constable made their way back into the house.

"Richard, both Wymond and Maleine will be coming back to the castle with us after Wymond sees the doctor," Vivienne told him.

"Then I'll help them both into the wagon," offered Richard with a nod, never once questioning Vivienne about it. The sheriff liked the way Vivienne commanded respect without even knowing she did so. Or did she?

"We have to go back to the sheriff's home to get Grunt and Martin as well," she told Richard.

"You can leave them by me for the night. I don't mind," said Zachariah.

"Thank you, but I mind," she told him, which didn't sit right with him.

"You don't trust me?" he asked softly.

"Of course, I do. May I speak to you privately, Sheriff?"

"We'll wait in the wagon," said Richard, helping Wymond walk.

"I'll hold Snuff and Chomp for you," offered Maleine, getting a smile from Wymond.

"Thank you. I think my ferrets like you," he told her, probably in an attempt to flirt and get Maleine to accept him more.

They left the house talking, and when they were gone, Zachariah turned back to Vivienne and crossed his arms over his chest. "All right. We're alone," he said. "Now tell me what's bothering you because I could tell something was wrong all night, ever since we were on the beach."

"Nay, Sheriff, you're wrong. However, something is very right."

"You make no sense."

"I have to talk to someone about this before I burst."

"Well? I'm here. What is it you want to say?"

She said something then that he never could have expected. It was so surreal that he wasn't sure she wasn't making it up and he had no idea how to respond.

"I found my baby today, Zachariah."

"What?"

"Martin is the baby boy I lost seven years ago."

"That makes no sense. The page boy?"

"He's my page boy. My baby. My son. Don't you see, Zachariah? I finally found my missing child. It took seven years and a lot of luck, but I can tell you without a doubt that I am Martin's mother."

"Vivienne, don't do this to yourself." Zachariah figured after all they just went through, Vivienne was only reliving her troubled past, imagining things that couldn't possibly be true.

"What do you mean?"

"I know how much you adore the page boy," he said, reaching out to touch her on the shoulder. "You were frightened today when we almost lost Martin. I understand that, really I do. I was scared too when the Pied Piper held a dagger to my daughter's throat. But Vivienne, Martin is not your son. He has parents of his own."

"I know that he has parents, but they aren't really his parents. I am."

"Nay, you're not. Now stop saying that. You need to get some sleep. I'm taking you back to the castle where you belong. I will bring Martin and your dog back in the morning."

"No, you're not!" She angrily pushed his hand from her shoulder. "I lost my son once, and I don't intend to let that happen again. I am going to keep him close to me from now on. I should be with him now, not here with you."

"Fine. Have it your way. After we stop at the coroner's office and also the doctor's, we'll pick up Martin and Grunt and take them, and you, and Maleine, and Wymond, and his weasels, all back to Mablethorpe Castle." God's eyes, this was getting out of control. Before long, Vivienne would invite the entire town to stay with her at the castle. The way she took in orphans was one thing. But now she'd gone addled, thinking she was truly Martin's mother.

"They're not weasels, they are ferrets. And I am telling you that I really am Martin's mother whether you believe it or not."

"What even makes you think that?"

"If you'd give me the chance to explain before you start shooting me down again, I'll tell you."

"I'm not shooting you down. I just asked you to explain, so please do."

"When Martin fell in the water today, his shoe came off. While he was putting it back on, I saw a brown heart-shaped birthmark on the bottom of his left foot. The exact mark and in the same spot as my newborn baby."

"Really." He was almost afraid to comment since she looked so angry at him right now. "Mayhap it is just a coincidence. Or, it was dark, so mayhap you didn't get a good look at it?"

The angry glare on her face cautioned him not to say much

more. "Did you see his eyes and hair? He looks like me, Zachariah."

"Vivienne, I'd like to believe he's the same baby you lost, but it is highly unlikely for the newborn to have survived. And it's been seven long years! I don't want you to get your hopes up. I'm sure it is just a coincidence and nothing more."

"Don't believe me if you don't want to, but I am telling you that it is true."

"Have you mentioned this to Martin yet?"

"Well ... nay."

"If you are so positive about this, then why are you keeping it from him?"

DAMN, why did the sheriff have to ask her that question? It only put the shadow of doubt back in Vivienne's head again. While her heart told her that Martin was truly the son she lost seven years earlier, her head was saying not to get her hopes up and to listen to Zachariah instead.

"I'll find out one way or another tomorrow," she told him.

"How do you plan on doing that?"

"My uncle received a missive. Martin's mother has died and his father is coming to the castle to collect him first thing in the morning."

"You can't keep the boy, Vivienne. You have no right to take him from his father."

"It is Lady Vivienne," she snapped. "And that man is not Martin's true father! He is naught but a thief who stole my son and I want him arrested."

"What? I can't believe what I'm hearing. You really want me to arrest the nobleman when he comes to collect his son, don't you?"

"He's not Martin's father! And of course I want you to arrest

271

him since you're the sheriff. That man stole my baby and he needs to pay for it."

"All right, calm down."

"I am calm!" she shouted, making Richard stop in the doorway as he entered the house.

"Is everything all right, my lady?" asked her guard.

"Yes, Richard. Thank you for asking. Now, if everyone would please hurry, I am anxious to collect Martin and Grunt and go home."

ZACHARIAH WATCHED Lady Vivienne throw him a daggered look over her shoulder as she headed out the door and Richard followed. Constable Dorson walked in, looking back over his shoulder.

"Lady Vivienne seems upset. Did something happen?" asked the constable.

"Oh, yes. A lot happened," said Zachariah, feeling frustrated and in dire need of a strong drink.

"What does that mean?"

"It means, you'd better hold things down here in town tomorrow, because I'm going to be at Mablethorpe Castle first thing in the morning."

"Is it something I can help with, Sheriff?" asked Constable Dorson, looking as confused as Zachariah felt right now.

"Nay, Constable, I don't believe so. Honestly, this time I don't think anyone can help. And to be honest, I'm not even sure what the hell I am doing."

Chapter Twenty

Vivienne awoke early the next morning, feeling nervous, excited, and about to faint, all at the same time. Still in bed, she'd allowed Martin to sleep with her and Grunt last night, which made the little boy happy. Not so much to be sleeping next to her, but to be in an actual bed instead of on the floor of the great hall, and having his favorite dog with him.

She needed to explain to Martin what was going on before his father arrived. Since he feared his father, he should be happy that she was his actual mother. Or so she hoped. Her biggest fear was that he wouldn't accept her at all. Or perhaps that he wouldn't want her as his mother, just a friend. Or mayhap Lord Collingham wouldn't let Martin stay with her. He might take Martin back home and beat him night and day. Her stomach twisted into a worried knot. By the rood, her nerves were getting the best of her and she just wanted this over with, one way or another. Nay, she wanted it finalized and accepted that she was Martin's mother and that he'd be hers and not someone else's son from this day on.

"Good morning, my lady."

Vivienne sat up to see Maleine standing at the window, looking out. She'd spent the night on the pallet at the foot of Vivienne's bed that was once where her handmaid slept.

"Good morning, Maleine. How are you feeling today?" She got out of bed and started to dress.

"Much better. Thank you." Maleine hurried over and helped Vivienne with her gown. "My, that is a very ornate ring. It's beautiful! Where did you get it?"

"Huh? Oh." Vivienne's hand slapped down upon the king's ring that she wore on a chain hidden under her clothes. She'd been so deep in thought about Martin that she was careless and now the girl saw it. "It is ... a family heirloom. Maleine, would you mind waking up Martin and helping him dress? His clothes should be dry and are by the fire." She purposely wanted to distract Maleine before she started asking more questions that Vivienne didn't want to answer. She didn't want to think about the ring or being the king's bastard right now. Today was all about getting her son back, and that is the only thing that mattered.

"Yes, my lady. Of course, I can." She hurried over to do as asked.

There was a slight knock at her door and she hurriedly laced up her bodice, heading across the room in her bare feet. She opened the door to see Zachariah standing there. Grunt jumped off the bed, coming to greet him.

"Oh. Sheriff Fitch. What are you doing here?" She was still upset with him after yesterday. She'd opened her heart to him, looking for a friend to confide in, and he'd basically pushed it back in her face. "Coming to tell me I'm addled or mayhap totally mad?"

"Now, what kind of a greeting is that, Lady Vivienne? I am here because you asked me to be."

"I didn't think you were coming." She turned her back on him and proceeded to put on her shoes. Martin stood up on the bed while Maleine pulled his tunic over his head. He already wore his breeches.

"Hello, Sheriff. I slept in a real bed last night and I liked it." Martin jumped up and down on the bed, making the bedstrings moan and creak.

"Martin, hurry and put on your shoes." Vivienne lifted him off the bed and to the floor. "Your father will be arriving any time now and I need to talk to him."

"Nay! I'm not going home with him. He hurts me. I don't like him," spat Martin.

"Come on, Martin. I'll help you," said Maleine, taking his hand and leading him over to a chair to put on his shoes.

"Did you tell him yet?" Zachariah asked in a soft voice.

"Nay," she answered, her heart about beating out of her chest. "I wanted to let my aunt and uncle know first. It was late when we arrived last night and everyone was tired so I waited."

"Well, you won't need to tell them because I already did."

"What?" Her head snapped around so quickly that it sent a pain through her neck. "How could you? That information should have come from me, not you."

"I'm sorry. I thought they already knew. So when they asked why I was here I told them."

"Told them? Told them what?" she whispered, looking over her shoulder, making sure Martin wasn't listening. He was with Maleine and playing with Grunt. "Did you tell my uncle you are going to arrest Lord Collingham for stealing my baby?"

"Nay, not exactly. But what difference does it make? That is what you want, isn't it?"

"Well ... I ... I'm not sure."

"If I can make a suggestion, I think it might be good to take

Lord Collingham aside and first ask him if Martin is his true child, born of his loins."

"Why should we do that when we know it's not true? I don't want to even give him a chance to lie."

"Look, the man doesn't even seem to like the boy. I mean, you said that he beats Martin, plus he has six other sons and doesn't seem to care about this one."

"Yes. So?"

"So, mayhap he'd be more than happy to have you take Martin off his hands."

She glared at him. "Do you have to say it like that?"

"I mean, mayhap there is a logical explanation. And with his wife now deceased, he might just give Martin to you and not have a hard time with it."

"He'd better give him to me. After all, he's my son."

"Lady Vivienne, I hear the herald announcing someone at the gate," said Maleine from the window.

"It's my father, isn't it?" asked Martin.

"I think the herald said Lord Collingham." Maleine strained her ears to listen out the window.

"It's your father, Martin," said Vivienne.

"Come, Lady Vivienne. It is time." The sheriff held out his arm. "I promise to stay by your side and to support you. No matter what happens."

"Thank you," said Vivienne, finally feeling as if her old friend had returned.

They were halfway down the stairs with Vivienne holding Martin's hand when she stopped.

"What's wrong?" asked the sheriff.

"I need to talk with Martin. We will meet you down there."

"I understand. Come, Maleine," said the sheriff, heading down to the great hall with Maleine and Grunt.

"Martin, I need to tell you something that I should have told you yesterday." She sat on the stairs to be able to look him in the eyes.

"What is it?" he asked, seeming scared and sad. He wore his wooden sword at his side.

"First, I want to ask you something. Are you afraid of ... of your father?"

"Yes. He never liked me," said Martin. "He beats me and says I'm no good and nothing like my brothers."

"How old are your brothers?"

"They're all grown up. I'm the only little one."

"Was your mother kind to you?"

"Yes."

"Did you love her?"

"I suppose."

"If you had the chance to have a mother again, would you want to live with her instead of with your father?"

"I don't understand what you mean." Martin looked more than confused.

"Seven years ago, I gave birth to a little boy. But something awful happened to my family. Bandits killed my parents. My brother as well as my baby were lost and never found when the horse pulling the wagon ran off, taking them with it."

"So you have a boy my age?"

"You are that baby I lost that night, Martin."

"I'm confused. How can that be?"

"My newborn had a birthmark that looked like a heart on the bottom of his left foot."

His eyes opened wide in excitement. "I have one like that too. Do you want to see it?"

"I already did, Martin. I saw it yesterday when you were in the water."

"What does that mean?" he asked.

"If it means what I think, you are that same little baby I lost. I think somehow you ended up with the parents you know, but they are not really your parents, after all. I am your mother."

"Then who is my father?"

"Your father worked in the stables but he died before you were born."

"Then, you're my mother? My real mother?"

"Yes, sweetheart. I believe so."

He fell into her arms and hugged her like he never wanted to let her go. "I love you, Lady Vivienne. I want to stay with you forever."

She hugged him back, kissing him atop the head. "I'd like that too. But before that can happen we need to talk to your father."

"Nay!" The fear was back in his eyes.

"We have to, sweetheart. It wouldn't be right if we didn't."

"If you're going to be my mother, is he still going to have to be my father?"

"Nay. Not if I can help it."

"Good. Because I don't want to live with him anymore."

"That's all I needed to hear." She kissed him on the cheek and took his hand, walking down the stairs and into the great hall.

"Vivienne, this is Lord Collingham," said her uncle. "He is Martin's father."

"Good Morning," she said with a nod, trying to be polite. She noticed Zachariah standing there with her aunt as well.

"Martin, get your things. We're leaving," said Lord Collingham.

"Wait," said Vivienne, not letting go of Martin's hand. "I need to ask you a question first, Lord Collingham."

"Well, what is it? Make it fast, I'm in a hurry."

"Is Martin your true son?"

"Why do you ask that?" He looked at her suspiciously which told her that her uncle had yet to tell him about all this.

"Seven years ago, my family was on the road and attacked by bandits. My parents were killed. The wagon that held my brother and newborn son was pulled away by spooked horses. My brother and son were never found."

"Is she accusing me of murdering her parents?" That didn't sit well with Lord Collingham. His hand went to the hilt of his sword.

"Nay, my lord, Lady Vivienne is saying nothing of the kind," Zachariah broke in, coming to her aid. "I think what she wants to ask you is if you and your late wife happened to find an abandoned child on the road seven years ago."

"I didn't abandon him," she said, not liking that Zachariah had even said that. The sheriff shook his head and put his finger to his mouth, warning her to keep quiet. She had to trust that he had a plan that would somehow help her.

"We didn't steal anyone's child," snapped Lord Collingham. "Our boys were grown and my wife was feeling lonely without them. She prayed for another child, but was too old to have one. She said it was a miracle sent by God the night we found a baby on the wayside."

"Then you did find a baby," said Vivienne, starting to feel very excited. Mayhap she was right after all. "Was he in a basket?" asked Vivienne. "My baby was in a basket and he had a brown heart-shaped birthmark on the bottom of his left foot."

"Why yes," said the man, looking first at Vivienne and then at Martin. "You think Martin is the baby you lost?"

"I know he is," she told him. "I am his mother—his true mother, Lord Collingham, and I want him back."

"This is just great!" Lord Collingham threw his hands in the air. "Now I'm going to be arrested for stealing a baby when I never wanted the whelp in the first place."

"So, you admit that you found this child on the road?" asked Lord Mablethorpe.

Lord Collingham let out a deep sigh. "Yes. That is true."

"Why didn't you bring the baby to the authorities right away?" asked Zachariah.

"Babies are left on the church steps and in the woods and in the alleys all the time when people cannot afford to raise them," Lord Collingham answered with a shrug. "I suppose I didn't bother since I didn't think anything of it. My wife wanted a baby and finding one shut her up and kept my head from hurting. I didn't think it was a problem at the time. However, that little whelp has been nothing but trouble for the last seven years."

"Stop calling him a whelp, I warn you," said Zachariah. "I know you beat the child and that he is afraid of you and doesn't want to leave with you. There are legal consequences at play here."

"Really? What do you mean? "Lord Collingham seemed genuinely concerned.

"As sheriff, I am at liberty to fine you, or even imprison you if I feel it warranted."

"See? The boy is causing me trouble once again." Lord Collingham threw his hands in the air. "How much of a fine are you talking about, Sheriff? Because imprisonment is out of the question. I am a nobleman and have a castle to run."

"I'll be the judge of that," said Zachariah.

"Lord Collingham, we don't want you imprisoned," said Lord Mablethorpe. "I'm sure it won't come to that, will it, Sheriff Fitch?"

"I can't say," the sheriff answered, looking over to Vivienne. "It seems to me that Lord Collingham's actions have caused a lot of physical pain for Martin and much mental turmoil for Lady Vivienne. All of this could have been avoided if when you found the baby, Lord Collingham, you would have brought it to the sheriff at once."

"So, I made a mistake. How can we solve this in a manner that won't break me or land me in jail? Honestly, now that my wife has passed, I'm in no hurry to raise the boy. I have six other sons training to be knights and this is too expensive as it is."

"Lady Vivienne?" asked Zachariah. "I'd like to hear what you have to say. As well as Martin."

"I don't want to go back with you," shouted Martin, clinging to Vivienne. "I want to stay with my mother. My real mother, Lady Vivienne."

Vivienne felt her hardened heart start to melt. All these years of longing for her lost child and hating the bandits who took her family away from her made her callused. Today, her heart softened and a little love crept in and it felt good. Damned good.

"Martin wants to stay here and live with me, and that is exactly what I want as well," she answered, scooping him up in her arms and holding him close to her.

"Lord Collingham?" asked the sheriff.

"That's fine with me," he said, waving a hand through the air. "Like I told you, it was always my wife who wanted him and now she's gone so it no longer matters to me. He's not of my loins."

"Sheriff, you're not going to arrest him are you?" asked Lord Mablethorpe. "I am looking to gain allies, not enemies."

Zachariah looked over at Vivienne again, and she slowly shook her head. She didn't like to see anyone imprisoned or punished unless they truly deserved it. Although, he hurt her son by beating him and part of her wanted him to pay for that.

But at least he agreed to give up Martin, and that was the most of her worries.

"If it were just up to me, I'd say yes to arresting you," Zachariah answered. "However, Lady Vivienne has a good, fair, and kind heart. She does not wish to see you arrested, so I will not."

"Thank goodness. Then I'm going to leave." Lord Collingham turned to go, but the sheriff stopped him.

"However ... there will be a fine, I'm afraid."

"A fine?" Lord Collingham turned around. "All right. How much?" he asked, grabbing for his coin pouch hanging from his belt.

"I'd say for all the trouble you caused Lady Vivienne, it will have to be a high amount."

"How high?" snarled the man.

"I don't want his money," Vivienne spoke up. "How can he possibly repay me for losing seven years of living with my child? I missed his first step, his first word, and his first smile. No amount of money can bring back that time together that was taken away between me and Martin. I have what I want now. Martin is safe with me and where he belongs. And you, Lord Collingham will never be able to hurt my son again."

"Well then, I suppose that's all. I'll take my leave."

"Not so fast," Zachariah warned him, making Vivienne wonder what he was going to do next. Since Lord Collingham didn't purposely steal her baby and seemed to have thought Martin had been abandoned, she didn't feel he should be imprisoned or die for it. It sounded as if his wife gave Martin love, and that was the only thing making her feel better. In her heart, she liked to believe there was goodness inside of everyone, no matter how minute it might be. Even if she couldn't see right now what the goodness was.

"What now, Sheriff?" grumbled Lord Collingham.

"Martin was here at Mablethorpe Castle training as a page and to someday be a squire and then a knight, correct?" asked Zachariah.

"Yes. So, make your point already. I want to go."

"It is expensive to become a knight, isn't it Lord Mablethorpe?" the sheriff asked her uncle.

"Yes. Very expensive," he answered.

"I'm sure Lord Mablethorpe isn't going to want to pay for this boy's training," said Zachariah.

"The sheriff is right, Collingham. Don't expect me to put out the money because he's not my son either."

"Gilbert! Really," said his wife.

"Why not?" asked Lord Collingham. "After all, he is your niece's son as we see now. He's closer to being your son than mine, so why should I pay a penny?"

"Sheriff, do something," said Lord Mablethorpe, getting red in the face realizing he was going to have to pay for the expenses with Martin's training now and obviously not liking the idea.

"I think a small split, might work." Zachariah looked over at Vivienne and winked. "Don't you, Lady Vivienne?"

She understood now that Zachariah was trying to help her out. She couldn't let Lord Collingham get away without paying something, even if she didn't want him imprisoned. After all, he beat her baby, and some kind of reprimand must be made.

"I believe the sheriff is right, Lord Collingham. My son is going to need a way to pay for all of this and I cannot expect my uncle to do it."

"I agree," chimed in Lord Mablethorpe. "You need to pay something, like the sheriff said."

"All right, what do you want?" Lord Collingham looked disgusted but also relieved that he wouldn't be imprisoned.

"Lady Vivienne. It's all yours," said Zachariah with a nod.

"My son will need a horse, Lord Collingham. I do believe you rode a horse into the castle today?"

"Well, yes, of course I did. But that's my steed."

"It's Martin's now," Vivienne said, enjoying the shocked expression on his face. "What is that ring on your finger? It looks like some kind of gemstone?"

"This?" Lord Collingham held up his hand. "This was my father's ring and his father's ring before him. It is pure gold and the stone is sapphire."

"It's worth a lot then?" she asked.

"More than you know."

"Good. We'll take it."

"What?" Lord Collingham's eyes opened wide.

"Hand it over, Collingham. My niece wants it." Lord Mablethorpe held out his open palm. "It's that or go to jail."

"This isn't fair, Mablethorpe and you know it." He yanked the ring off his finger and dropped it into Lord Mablethorpe's hand.

"It wasn't fair to Vivienne either when you found her baby and kept him for yourself," said Lady Mablethorpe, putting her opinion out there now too.

Vivienne liked the way everyone was supporting her and Martin. It felt good. It felt like a family.

"Can I leave now?" asked Lord Collingham. "Or will you be taking the clothes right off my back next?"

"Not all of them," said Vivienne. "However, that cloak you are wearing would make some fine clothes for Martin since you only sent him here with one change of clothes."

"Damn it, this isn't funny." He tore off the cloak and handed that to Vivienne's uncle as well. "Please tell me that's all. I feel as if I'm being ravished as I stand here."

"That is good," said Vivienne, feeling he'd learned his lesson.

"Not quite," said Zachariah. "Lord Collingham, do you see that wooden sword at Martin's side?"

"Yes. What about it?"

"Martin has been learning how to use a sword."

"That's right," said Vivienne, seeing where this was going. "Martin used his little wooden sword to help save me from a killer. Did you know that?"

"So the boy is brave. What of it?"

"He'll need a real sword someday," said Zachariah.

"That's right," agreed Vivienne. "Actually, I think it would be good to secure him a sword right now. That one hanging at your side should do nicely."

"God's teeth, nay! You are not going to take my sword from me too," he complained.

"Why not?" asked Vivienne.

"It is my most prized possession. A man is nothing without his sword."

"You thought nothing about taking my most prized possession from me," she said, hugging Martin even tighter. "And believe me, a woman feels more adamantly about a baby she birthed from her womb than any man can feel about a cold metal sword."

"Hand it over," said Zachariah, reaching out for it.

"Damn it," he swore, handing over his sword to the sheriff. "I will never, as long as I live, let a woman talk me into anything ever again."

"I think it's time you leave now, and please never return," said Vivienne's uncle. "Guards, escort Lord Collingham from the castle and to the road."

"Aye, Lord Mablethorpe," his guards answered, taking Lord Collingham away. The man never even said goodbye to Martin or looked back. Vivienne was more than happy to see him go.

"Is that really going to be my sword?" asked Martin with wide eyes.

"Someday, sweetheart. When you're old enough," said Vivienne, kissing him once again, just because she could. "But as your mother, I am going to insist that you are much older before you even think of using it."

"I agree, Lady Vivienne," said Martin, patting the wooden sword at his side. "I like this sword better for now anyway. It works good hitting rat-catchers over the head."

Everyone laughed at that.

"Martin, you can call me Mother if you want," she told him, feeling nervous, not sure if he'd want to do that.

"All right, Mother," said Martin, kissing her on the cheek. "But if I forget and call you Lady Vivienne, is that all right, too?"

"Of course it is, sweetheart." Vivienne's heart grew three sizes just hearing him call her Mother. But she would be fine if he called her Lady Vivienne too. "All that matters is that we are together now, and I never want us to be apart again."

"Excuse me, Lord Mablethorpe," interrupted the guard from the gate. "There is someone here looking for Sheriff Fitch and it sounds urgent."

"Oh no," said Zachariah. "Is it my constable? I hope there isn't more trouble in town."

"Nay, Sheriff," said the guard. "It is a female. She says she knows you well."

Vivienne looked up in interest. "Really? Who is it?" she asked, putting Martin down.

"Can I at least hold my new sword?" Martin looked up at the sheriff.

"I'll hold it and you can just touch it," said Lord Mablethorpe, taking the sword from the sheriff. Grunt ran up and started to sniff it.

"Careful, Grunt. You don't want to cut your nose," Martin warned him.

"The woman at the gate is a nun," said the guard.

"A nun? What's her name?" Vivienne had a feeling she knew exactly who it was and by Zachariah's sudden quietness, and by the way he stood there holding one arm. Aye, she was sure he knew who it was as well.

"My name is Sister Magdalena," said the nun, walking into the great hall with another guard at her side. "I am here to see my brother, Zachariah."

"Magdalena? What in God's name are you doing here?" grumbled the sheriff.

"Do not use the Lord's name in vain," said the nun, blessing herself and looking up to the ceiling. "Please forgive him, he knows not what he says."

Vivienne heard Zachariah groan again.

"Sister Magdalena, it's so good to see you here," Vivienne greeted her.

"Lady Vivienne, is that you? I haven't seen you in years," said Magdalena.

"Are you still at the abbey in Maltby le Marsh?" asked Vivienne, speaking of the nearby village.

"I am," Magdalena answered with a nod. Then her demeanor changed and a dark shadow washed over her face.

"Magdalena, what's wrong?" asked Zachariah.

"Something terrible has happened, Zachariah." The woman blessed herself again and Vivienne saw Zachariah flinch and shake his head.

"What is it?" asked Vivienne, putting her hand on the nun's shoulder to try to comfort her. She seemed very upset, yet the sheriff seemed as if he didn't care. Or perhaps he just didn't want to know.

"A body has been found. In the wall at the abbey," she told them.

"What?" That got Zachariah's attention.

"Are you saying someone died?" asked Vivienne.

"Nay," said Sister Magdalena. "I am saying someone has been murdered. I need my brother, the sheriff, to help us."

"Of course, you do," she heard Zachariah complain.

"Will you help us, Zachariah? Please," begged his sister. "You are known to be the best sheriff around."

"Magdalena, Maltby le Marsh has its own constables. You need to contact one there," he told her. "I am busy enough with matters right here in Mablethorpe without having to go to a neighboring village as well."

"She did come to me first, Sheriff Fitch," said a constable from the nun's village, walking in to the great hall to join them.

"Constable Erikson. How are you," said Zachariah with a nod.

"This is serious and I don't know where to turn next," Constable Erikson told him. "I am at a dead end and need your help. You are the sheriff and in charge of the East Lindsey district of Lincolnshire and I am asking for your participation. Will you come to Maltby le Marsh at my request? Your expertise is needed."

The sheriff looked the other way and shook his head, hesitating to give them an answer.

"Yes, of course he will," Vivienne answered for him. "Sheriff Fitch would be more than happy to look into this murder for you. And I will come along as well to help investigate."

"But you are a woman," gasped Sister Magdalena. "Lady Vivienne, what do you know about investigating murders?"

"More than you'd think," mumbled Zachariah from behind her.

"Is that right, Sheriff?" asked the constable. "You and the lady both will be coming to Maltby le Marsh to help us then?"

"You heard Lady Vivienne," said Zachariah, not looking very happy about it. "We'll be there." He glanced over at her with an expression on his face that told her he was going to be talking to her about this later.

Vivienne smiled at Zachariah and then, just to see him squirm a little more, she winked at him.

"Maltby le Marsh it is," she said aloud. "Sister Magdalena, your brother Zachariah, as well as I, will do all we can to make certain justice is served. I promise you, we will catch the murderer. You have my word on that."

From The Author:

I hope you enjoyed Murder on Rotten Row and will take a quick moment to leave a review for me. This is Book Two of my ***Harlowe & Fitch Historical Mystery Series***. If you for some reason read Book Two before Book One, you'll want to go back and read ***Murder at Mablethorpe Castle***, too, in order to find out what you missed.

Rotten Row was the term used in medieval times for the bad part of town. The street that had the rundown, rat-infested homes, the taverns, the stinky tanneries, the thieves, the bums and the whores.

There are many streets names Rotten Row, the most famous one being found in London which I believe still exists and is a bridleway today. My Rotten Row, however, is in Mablethorpe and different altogether.

The story of the Pied Piper of Hamelin, Germany is a well-known legend in history, and some say a myth. Supposedly in the 13th Century, a rat-catcher in multi-colored or 'pied' clothing appeared and was hired by the mayor to get rid of the town's rats. The Pied Piper played his flute and lured the rats into the sea. When the mayor reneged on the agreed upon price, the rat-catcher became angry. He used his same pipe to lure the children away and I believe into the sea as well. I am sure there is some truth, though little as it may be, in this legend.

I found the idea of a rat-catcher (which was real in medieval times) fascinating in a horrific kind of way. Since I love writing about anything odd and I push the envelope often, I incorporated it into my story.

This series is not medieval romance like I am known for writing. Instead, its focus is on the murder mysteries, solved by my characters, Sheriff Zachariah Fitch and my sleuth Lady Vivienne Harlowe. And of course, don't forget her bloodhound, Grunt. Of course, there is an attraction between Vivienne and Zachariah and there will be sexual tension.

While each book has a new mystery that is cleared up by the end of the book, there is also an ongoing murder mystery in Lady Vivienne's backstory that will very slowly unfold. That is why it is best to read the books in the series in order. Otherwise, there will be some awesome surprises ruined. Therefore, even though Lady Vivienne found her lost baby in Murder on Rotten Row, she still searches for her brother, Adrian, and for the murderer of her parents.

Something else I like to do is to incorporate characters from other series into my books. You will find characters from some of my romance novels showing up in these mysteries once in a while. For instance, Nairnie, the sheriff's nursemaid is a very beloved character of my readers. I've been asked by many readers often to bring her back, and so I have.

You will first find Nairnie in my **Seasons of Fortitude Series**, which includes **Highland Spring**; **Summer's Reign** which is a murder mystery romance; **Autumn's Touch** which holds Nairnie's interesting backstory, and **Winter's Flame**. If you want to really see Nairnie at her best, you'll want to read my **Pirate Lords Series**. She is the grandmother of three men who are pirates. She falls from a ship and is rescued by the pirates and Nairnie sails with them as their cook and ends up probably being the biggest pirate of them all. Lots of humor in this series. Believe me, you don't want to mess with Nairnie. She'll scare the living daylights out of anyone, even pirates. I've also mentioned the **Legendary Bastards of the Crown** in this story, and they will be showing up a little later on down the road.

I am leaving you with an excerpt from my murder mystery romance, *Summer's Reign*. But before I do, I want to mention the next book in the Harlowe & Fitch Historical Mystery Series which is **Murder at Maltby le Marsh**. You've already gotten a hint at the end of this story, but there is a murder at an abbey when a body is found bricked inside a wall. You'll find out more about Sheriff Fitch as well since one of the nuns, Sister Magdalena, is his sibling. Be sure to check out all the books in my **Harlowe & Fitch Historical Mystery Series** because I have some exciting episodes in store for you.

To see more of my books (over 100 and counting) please stop by and visit my **Website** at **http://elizabethrosen-ovels.com.** You can also follow me on **Amazon, Bookbub**, **Goodreads**, **Facebook** and **Bluesky** and **Twitter**. I also have a **Private Readers' Group** on Facebook that I invite you to join.

Until next time,
Elizabeth Rose

Excerpt from **Summer's Reign**, *Seasons of Fortitude*:

Lady Summer reached for the door handle of the baron's chamber. Even though they were married, Norbert didn't want her in his bed unless he was trying to plant his seed within her.

Not wanting to share a bed with the man any more than she had to, she was happy to have a chamber of her own no matter how odd it seemed.

It was still early and Norbert never liked to rise until the main meal was ready. Even if he'd said they would leave at daybreak, she knew it would be closer to noon before they actually took to the road. He'd still be in bed and probably awaiting her. If she closed her eyes and pretended to be somewhere else, perhaps she could handle the pain. She'd do whatever it took so the act of coupling with him would be over quickly.

Releasing a deep breath, she boldly pushed open the door and stepped inside. The room was dark since the nighttime candle had burned out. The window was covered with a tapestry and the hearth was cold. A shiver ran through her. Something wasn't right. She could feel it in her bones.

"Dominick?" she called out softly, fearing for her son. There was no answer. "Husband, where is our son?" She took a moment to let her eyes become accustomed to the darkened room. Still, no answer. Her heartbeat picked up. Something was wrong. Rushing to the window, she tore away the tapestry, letting in the early morning light. With it came a cool breeze, seeming much colder than it should be for the middle of summer.

When she turned back, she saw her husband lying on his back with his eyes closed. He didn't seem nearly as terrifying in this position. Usually, he wasn't such a sound sleeper and it worried her that he'd yet to stir.

"Norbert," she said, using his Christian name. She only called him by his first name when she was very upset or angry. Or angrier than usual, anyway. "Norbert, where is Dominick?" she demanded to know. Her eyes searched the room, not finding the little boy anywhere. What had he done with her son? Panic filled her senses. When he still didn't answer, she headed over to the side of the bed and bravely reached out to shake him. However, as soon as she touched his arm, she jumped back and stepped away.

His body was as cold as ice and felt much too stiff. With her heart pounding furiously in her ears, she took a step toward him again, reaching out with two fingers to feel for a pulse at the base of his neck. When she couldn't find a heartbeat, she wet her fingers and held them under his nose. Neither could she feel his breath. By the gray tinge to his skin, it was now evident. The baron was dead!

Also by Elizabeth Rose

Mystery Series:

Harlowe & Fitch Historical Mystery Series

Medieval Series:

Below the Salt

Legendary Bastards of the Crown Series

Seasons of Fortitude Series

Secrets of the Heart Series

Legacy of the Blade Series

Daughters of the Dagger Series

MadMan MacKeefe Series

Barons of the Cinque Ports Series

Holiday Knights Series

Highland Chronicles Series

Pirate Lords Series

Highland Outcasts

Medieval/Paranormal Series:

Elemental Magick Series

Greek Myth Fantasy Series

Tangled Tales Series

Portals of Destiny

Contemporary Series:

Tarnished Saints Series

Working Man Series

Western Series:

Cowboys of the Old West Series

And More!

Please visit http://elizabethrosenovels.com

About Elizabeth

Elizabeth Rose is an award-winning, bestselling author of over 100 books and counting. She writes medieval, historical, contemporary, paranormal, and western romance. Her books are available as EBooks, paperbacks, and some audiobooks as well.

Her favorite characters in her works include dark, dangerous and tortured heroes, and feisty, independent heroines who know how to wield a sword. She loves writing 14th century medieval novels, and is well-known for her many series.

Elizabeth loves the outdoors. In the summertime, you can find her in her secret garden with her laptop, swinging in her hammock working on her next book. Elizabeth is a born storyteller and passionate about sharing her works with her readers.

Please be sure to visit her website at **Elizabethrosenovels.com** to read excerpts from any of her novels and get sneak peeks at covers of upcoming books. You can follow her on **Twitter, Facebook**, **Goodreads** or **BookBub.** Join Elizabeth's **newsletter** so you don't miss out on new releases or upcoming events.

www.ingramcontent.com/pod-product-compliance
Ingram Content Group UK Ltd.
Pitfield, Milton Keynes, MK11 3LW, UK
UKHW042347090625
6312UKWH00002B/223